STEPPING DOWN

STEPPING DOWN

Bound by Oaths That Cross the Line

a novel

DANI GUEVAREZ

Dani Guevarez LLC
Marietta GA

Visit Dani Guevarez website at www.daniguevarez.com

Copyright © 2026 Dani Guevarez LLC. All rights reserved.

This is fictional work. Characters, organizations, and scenarios are either the products of the author's imagination or used in a fictitious manner. Any resemblance to events, actual persons, dead or living, is coincidental. No portion of this work may be used to train artificial intelligence without written permission from the author.

No part of this book may be reproduced or used in any manner without the prior written permission of the copyright owner, except for the use of brief quotations in a book review.

To request permissions, contact the publisher at daniguevarezLLC@daniguevarez.com

Library of Congress Cataloging-in-Publication Data
LCCN: 2025926866
Hardcover: 979-8-9942113-1-1
Paperback: 979-8-9942113-0-4
Ebook: 979-8-9942113-2-8
Audiobook: 979-8-9942113-3-5

First paperback edition February 2026.

Edited by Felice Laverene.

The cover's initial image was generated by an AI based tool with prompts provided by the author. Creative enhancement, revision, and final design were provided by Nisha. The human-authored contributions are the copyrighted works of Dani Guevarez.

Scripture used in this book quoted or paraphrased are taken from the Holy Bible, New International Version ®, NIV®. Copyright© 1973,1978,1984,2011 by Biblica, Inc. ® Public Domain.

Scripture quotations marked KJV are taken from the King James Version. Public Domian.

Printed in the United States of America

To all who are bound by oaths that cross the line and are willing to know the Truth.

"Am I now trying to win the approval of human beings, or of God? Or am I trying to please people? If I were still trying to please people, I would not be a servant of Christ."

Galatians 1:10 NIV

PART 1
UNDERGROUND

CHAPTER 1: THE MAHN'S FAMILY VALUES

In the heart of Macon, Georgia, sits a medium-sized brick church on three acres of well-trimmed autumn grass. God's House Church holds a multicultural congregation of about three hundred members. It's small enough for congregants to safely occupy one level, yet big enough to avoid church gossip. The non-denominational church prioritizes a personal relationship with God—above the exaggeratedly loud shouting, enormous hat-wearing, tambourine-pounding traditional church setting the Mahn family is used to.

The Mahns have been attending this church for a year. James, the head of the family, relocated them all to God's House after their move from Florida. In his late fifties, he was laid off from electrical engineering during Covid, and it forced him to move his family to Macon for work. He positions all 6'1" of himself every Sunday at an end seat near the back for easy exits to the fellowship hall. He makes swift departures every thirty minutes, checking the score of his favorite sports team, the Atlanta Falcons, on his phone app. Tina, his wife, begs him to attend the nine a.m. service instead of the eleven o'clock, to watch the game with no interruptions, but he argues, "I prefer to sleep in. Checking the game on my phone won't hurt anyone." Yet, every time a game goes into overtime, it's her who has to listen to his complaints.

God's House's modern-day "come as you are" vibe encourages congregants to dress how they'd like. And James loves that, a huge fan of the dress code that allows him to wear sports caps with matching sneakers, jeans and wrinkle-free button-ups. When he's finished modeling his Falcons cap—usually when the score is not in his favor—he removes the cap, showing off his dark, overly shined bald head.

As he quietly maneuvers back into the dimly lit sanctuary of praise from checking the third-quarter score of the NFL pre-season game, he removes his cap now with disappointment. Back in his pew, he places it on his seat and casually claps along to the worship music, attempting to blend into the atmosphere. He glances over to Tina, whose eyes are filled with tears. He gently grabs her hand, acknowledging her unashamed praise. She squeezes his hand with love as she waves her free hand in worship, tears streaming down her lightly contoured face.

Tina was raised Catholic and, in all her fifty years on Earth, has never felt God's presence so heavy until she visited God's House. She knew from the first powerful visit that it would be her family's church home. Tina's adjustment to Macon has been easy. Her work is remote, and she loves experiencing the four seasons Florida did not provide. She's close enough to Atlanta shopping malls, yet far enough from Atlanta's everyday traffic.

With Macon being the birthplace of Southern Rock, the worship service is full of God's Spirit, the musicians not skipping a beat. Sweaty with praise, they perform on a well-lit stage, while the audience sits in an air-conditioned environment with dim overhead lights. A youthful looking pastor in his forties, Pastor Jones, approaches the podium down stage center in a purple three-piece, tailor-made suit. He prides himself in being one of the only Black male pastors shepherding a multicultural church in Macon, Georgia.

Pastor Jones motions for the house lights to come on. They illuminate the diverse crowd of teary-eyed congregants, some with raised arms lifted in praise. The music lowers to a soft background score for the vocal worship. He loosens his pinstriped tie and addresses the audience.

"Boy, does God have a word for you today! Say Amen," he commands into the microphone.

The last members still sitting rise to their feet to join the standing congregation, welcoming the pastor with claps and shouts. "Amen," they repeat in unison, "*Amen*." The Pastor gestures the musicians to cease the low-playing music and motions the congregation to have a seat with one hand as he turns through pages of the Bible with the other. They all obey, adjusting comfortably and waiting for their next instruction.

Tameka, James and Tina's oldest daughter, sits directly behind James. The wild child of the family at twenty-one years old, she gives off a hot girl appearance with long, colorful nails, a changeup of hairstyle every other day and heavy make-up. Deep within, she really loves the Lord and will sermon you down in a heartbeat. Since dropping out of cosmetology school, she has developed a startup haircare business. It seems like every other week she's promising her parents, "Once the finances from the haircare line are stable, I'll pay you back for every lost penny and move out of the house, I promise."

Tameka's wearing a knee-length blue floral dress and six-inch heels, with hair big enough to reach Heaven. Thank God she's seated in the back row. She notices Tina's overwhelmed worship appearance, with tears resting on her cheeks and tear stains drying on her lightly tan-colored blouse. Tameka waves down a timid male usher handing tissue to congregants. The twenty-something-year-old white man approaches Tameka. She grabs the last tissue from the now-empty box and gives him a smile, searching for his name. She spots the golden name tag that reads *Usher* in black lettering. With a flirtatious giggle she says, "Thank you, Usher." Tameka extends eye contact with him, and he returns the glance.

Tameka accidentally gives her father a hard thump to the back of his bald head while reaching over his shoulder to hand her mother a tissue. Tina takes it, dabbing her tears dry, oblivious to the commotion. James, left uncomfortable, turns toward the usher, giving him a look of disapproval while rubbing the back of his head. The usher, aware of an angry James, scurries away to refill the tissue box and attend to other members. James squints over his shoulder, giving Tameka the dad glare *cut it out.*

It takes three long minutes of preparation—bringing out bottled water and pulpit adjusting—before Pastor Jones has finally found his placement in the Bible. Even the keyboardist has become anxious, filling in the uncomfortable quiet as the church awaits instruction. He clears his throat and instructs the anxious congregants to stand for the reading of the Word.

"Everyone, would you please turn your Bibles to Exodus 20, verse 1." Pastor Jones' voice carries authority, silencing the keyboard with one line. There's low chatter and "Amens" as the members rustle through the Bible pages. Some pull out their phones while others focus their attention on the scripture now projected on the screen behind the pastor.

"Now read," he commands.

The congregation recites along in unison: "*And God spake all these words, saying, I am the LORD thy God, which have brought thee out of the land of Egypt, out of the house of bondage. Thou shalt have no other gods before me. Thou shalt not make unto thee any graven image, or any likeness of anything that is in heaven above, or that is in the earth beneath, or that is in the water under the earth...*"

These words echo throughout the sanctuary, mixed with the soft shuffling of stiletto heels, oxfords, and occasional coughs. Most of the congregants are attentive, nodding along with the pastor's reading, while others are waiting for the pastor's instruction to sit down.

Pastor Jones motions for the congregation to take their seats as he begins his sermon. Adjusting his pants, securely fastened at his waist, he starts.

"You see, the Lord didn't bring you from your mess to worship other gods, like your money, your career, the man you met last night at the bar…" Laughs are heard throughout the crowd. "…and in the case of the Israelites, these wooden and golden objects. These objects were their gods. How dare we treat a God who loves us so much He rescued us from captivity, died for our raggedy sins, and put up with our nonsense… how dare we worship something or someone else? And in some cases, especially in the U.S., we put famous people above God, making them idols. But I'll save *that* for another sermon," he digresses, wiping sweat from his brow.

The sanctuary, once a comfortable temperature, has now risen in heat due to the brightened house lights. Some members pull out loose paper and church offering envelopes, waving them as fans for a cool breeze.

Pastor Jones continues, "The Bible mentions graven images, which are human-made objects worshipped as a deity. Can you believe that? *This* is what they were doing back then and *still* doing today! Worshipping symbols and objects…" he pauses for effect. Then his voice booms through the microphone again, "Now some of you here worship the cross around your neck. You can't leave the house without it… Don't worship the cross that's dangling on your chain; worship the Man who died on the *cross*! Can I get an Amen?"

The crowd repeats in unison with shouts and claps: "Amen!" The keyboardist hits a screeching high note on the keyboard that startles the last Mahn member, Megan. The eighteen-year-old rests her head in her hand with tiny chest-length braids adorning her crown, hiding the struggle to keep her heavy eyelids from closing in her ripped light blue jeans, jeweled toe-strapped sandals, and black short-sleeve laced button-up.

Megan enjoys God's House worship service, not because it's full of the Holy Spirit but because music is her life. She was excited about the move to Macon when she learned about its history as the home of Little Richard and Otis Redding, musicians before her time. She figured, if they could make it as musicians in this small town, so could she.

She plays the keyboard and practices every free moment of the day. The family tried persuading her to join the musicians at the church, but with her leaving for college in less than twenty-four hours, now the musical commitment would be pointless. "Weekend visits home would make your involvement possible, Megan," Tina always insists. But Megan always responds that it would be too much along with school and adjusting to college life. Not to mention, freshman rules say she cannot take the car she shares with Tameka, making consistent drives back and forth impossible.

"Weekly drives to Atlanta will satisfy my shopping fix," Tina responds with a wry smile. "It wouldn't be a problem at all."

Anxious to start college at Southern Atlanta South University, Megan's been having trouble sleeping lately, but for some reason Pastor Jones' sermon and the church heat are putting her to sleep like NyQuil.

Tameka catches a glimpse of Megan hunched over beside her. She waves her hand up and down in front of Megan's face to see if the wind from the motion will wake her. With no luck, she leans in, giving Megan a shoulder shove. "You might want to pay attention. These words may resonate someday, worm head," she whispers, referring to Megan's braids. She prefers Megan wear her natural hair—that way she has an available hair model for her many haircare products.

The eleven o'clock service goes into overtime, causing James to speed-race the family's black SUV through the Sunday afternoon traffic in hopes of finishing the game at home. He even managed to shave the usual thirty-minute drive down to twenty. The girls entertain themselves with headphones and loud music, maintaining a peaceful ride home, muting James' complaints and mumblings.

The Mahns enter their two-story, three-bedroom brick home. The smell of slow-cooked collard greens and turkey necks on the stove replaces the usual lavender plug-ins. Tina rushes to the kitchen to turn off the collards and remove the slightly burnt barbecued chicken wings from the refrigerator that James had grilled the night before. She places them on an aluminum pan to reheat in the oven, as James swiftly trails her into the kitchen, grabbing a cold beer from the refrigerator and nearly knocking the balanced wings out of Tina's hand.

He runs to the living room to turn on the game, plopping down on his brown leather recliner. He releases the side lever to kick up his feet. While opening his canned beer, he takes his shoes and socks off using only his feet. James is relieved the game is still on. He has the remote in one hand for volume control and an ice-cold beer in the other.

"Food will be ready in about 30 minutes," Tina yells out to the family.

The girls have made their way upstairs, tending to their after-church business. They share a room with a Jack and Jill bathroom connected to Tina's office. The extra room gives Tina enough space to keep her data analysis files organized with storage for her clothes-design hobby—which she dibbles into during the holidays and special occasions. Of course, the girls were disappointed to hear about the third-bedroom plans, but Megan going away for college and Tameka eventually moving out softened the blow.

Tameka changes into a pink dress, an exact replica of the blue floral one she wore to church. There is no such thing as house clothing with Tameka—she stays ready for a random social media post, her motto: *Any moment is the perfect moment to promote hair-preneurship*. She prides herself on entrepreneurship and branding, a skill her parents have yet to understand.

STEPPING DOWN

Meanwhile, Megan replaces her black top with a white oversized Southern Atlanta South University T-shirt with a golden roaring lion in the center. She was gifted the shirt last fall during an in-person college tour, where guests were required to wear masks because of COVID policies. And since room and board were undecided at the time of her visit, she's relieved that the dorms are open during her freshman year. She was nervous about staying away from her family, but she's ready to stay on campus, and this T-shirt has become her comfort whenever she gets anxious about SASU. She figured if she wears the shirt like she belongs, then she'll belong.

Acceptance has been a challenge for Megan, unlike her sister. Tameka walks into a room and every clique in the room welcomes her. Being three years apart allowed them to experience school together, where Tameka created some impossible shoes for Megan to fill. Six-inch heeled shoes. Tameka's previous teachers expected a fashionably outgoing Mahn to enter class when *Megan Mahn* appeared on the attendance sheet; instead they got Megan the loner—the music-focused introvert.

Megan tucks her T-shirt into her ripped jeans and walks over to her keyboard propped on a black, scratched-up metal stand covered in music notes and artist stickers. She plays a chord. "I would take you, but I'm not sure if I have room," she sings softly.

"Aaaaaw, you can't take your boyfriend?" Tameka mocks, giggling at her joke while fluffing out her hair. She poses in front of her camera phone, contemplating if she should promote her new hair gel hold on her twist-out style.

"At least I have a boyfriend," Megan responds, dragging her pointer finger from the lower note of the keyboard to a high note. "Just ask for Usher boy's name already."

"Nope, *he* needs to ask for *mine*. The man should lead. I just throw out the breadcrumbs. So, until then, I will keep waving him down for tissue." Tameka places her phone face-down beside her, deciding against the haircare post. She grimaces at how Megan has awkwardly tucked her T-shirt into her jeans. "You ready for tomorrow?" Tameka gets up and ties the front of Megan's T-shirt into a cute knot at the front of her jeans above the zipper.

"I guess." Megan unties the knot and strikes a low chord on the keyboard before walking over to her three suitcases, lined side by side covering her twin-sized bed. One suitcase is full of sneakers and slides, the other of jeans and T-shirts, and the third of night clothes, undergarments, and miscellanea. Megan prides herself on jeans and T-shirts with a little concealer under her eyes to conceal the hereditary dark circles passed down from her mother—a curse Tameka dodged.

The only things fancy about Megan are her jeweled sandals, the laced black top she wore to church, and her chest-length conveniently tiny braids. Tameka re-braids her hair every other month—an all-day event that makes them want to tear each other's head off. Tameka urges Megan to try different looks, but Megan's not a fan of change. On a good day she may put her braids up in a nice top bun, but they're usually down, hiding her cheekbones inherited from her father.

Tameka walks over and looks at the wardrobe packed. "Girl, I know this is not what you are wearing in Atlanta? You decided against an HBCU—your choice. But at least dress like the culture."

She was right—Megan had a choice to attend a "PWI" or an HBCU, but she felt a predominantly white school would provide a challenge, offering real-world competition she wouldn't find in a university where everyone came from similar backgrounds. Her high school was predominantly Black, and there were real-world challenges, but also a lot of drama. Now, she wanted something different; plus, she was always made to feel uncomfortable there and was ready to be done with it. Her proper speech and lax attire warranted stares that she wasn't Black enough. It didn't help that she stayed to herself. Her only acquaintances were those in the jazz band. On occasion she would join the musicians on Saturdays in a student's garage for jam sessions. But with their move to Macon, her jam sessions were held in the four walls of their small bedroom.

SASU's partial scholarship and small student body of only forty-five hundred were an added incentive.

Tameka pulls out a couple of dresses and nice colorful tops, along with unwalkable heels from her closet. "I was going to get rid of this stuff anyway," she says, removing some rolled-up T-shirts from Megan's suitcase. On second thought, from the shoe suitcase she also pulls out dingy black sneakers and a white pair that is now cream, replacing them with a couple pairs of four- and six-inch heels and throwing them in a pile on the floor. Megan stops her overzealous sister from throwing out her favorite black shirt. The thing had never faded, even after Tina's excessive heat-drying laundry days.

"You know I'm not going to wear any of this," Megan states as she examines the wardrobe exchange. "What are you going to do with the clothes on the floor?"

"Throw them out along with everything else of yours in this room. Can't *wait* to finally have a room to myself."

Once finished with the clothes replacement, Tameka falls back onto her bed with a huge sigh of relief, her arms spread out as if to have happily fallen into Usher boy's arms. "I have so many plans for this room," she says with a huge grin, looking up at the ceiling fan providing a cool breeze.

"Don't go crazy. I need a place to sleep when I visit," Megan states, zipping up the suitcases. She lines them up by the door, stepping over the pile of rejected clothes. Tameka points to an air mattress poking out from the closet with a grin. Megan scoffs and keeps moving.

"Seriously, worm head, I'll miss you," Tameka says, rising up on her elbows. The girls have a moment of silence as the realization of Megan's move to college sinks in. Megan playfully re-ties her T-shirt, mimicking the knot Tameka had made. Tameka laughs, giving a nod of approval.

"Food's ready!" Tina yells from downstairs, interrupting the Mahn sister bond. The girls race downstairs to the kitchen, grabbing their plates and utensils from the kitchen island. Tina has dressed the Sunday plates with collards, chicken wings, and a slice of cornbread she was able to whip up in thirty minutes. Bypassing the dinner table, they sit on the brown leather couch in the living room around James, who comfortably sits in his matching recliner. Tina brings him a wooden handheld tray with a fully stacked plate and half of a ripped paper towel. James lets the legs of the recliner down and adjusts himself, sitting the tray on his lap, finishing the last few swigs of his beer.

"Megan," Tina asks as she hands the girls each half of a whole paper towel, "you packed and ready for tomorrow?"

James hands Tina his empty beer can, requesting another.

Megan yells back into the kitchen as her mother grabs James another beer from the refrigerator. "I need a few more things like toothpaste, soap, linen, and towels! I could take the car for one more drive and get it myself before tomorrow…!"

"I can't hear the game!" James interrupts, eyes on the screen.

"James, you don't need the sound to see that your team is losing," Tina badgers, walking back from the kitchen with his new beer.

"Well, I know one thing—we need to make it back from Atlanta before the game tomorrow. I can't watch that game on an app. I need to see this one on the big screen."

Tina, with her hands on her hips, stands in front of the 65" TV mounted on the wall, blocking James' view. "I thought we *was* going shopping after we drop Megan off." James waves, motioning her away from standing in front of the screen. He places the tray on the side table beside the recliner, maneuvering his body to look around her. "We can shop before we drop her off. The game comes on at six. I need to be back by then." Wiping his beard with the half paper towel, he yells, "Touchdown! Yes, we won!" James, standing on bare feet, takes a sip of his beer, satisfied with the game outcome. He sits back down, grabs the tray from the side table, and reclines back in the chair, continuing to eat his collard greens. "Tina, I need another paper towel. Can I get a whole one, please?" Then, under his breath, "I don't know why women make clothes an idol anyway."

Megan braces herself for the tension increase these fighting words have abruptly caused. Tina lets Tameka handle this one as she walks toward the kitchen to pour juice for the girls and retrieve another half paper towel.

"What did you say?" Tameka exclaims, placing her plate on the table, leaning toward her father with both elbows on her knees in a stance ready for confrontation.

"The pastor said don't make nothing an idol. You and your mother worship clothes," he says, avoiding her fiery gaze.

Megan sits in silence, continuing her meal. It's one thing to bring up the forbidden words in front of the Mahn women, but now James has gone too far using Pastor Jones' sermon to defend his side.

Tameka is in full offense. "Like how you worship the game?"

Tina walks back into the tense air, placing the girls' juice on the table, giving Tameka a high five, proud of her comeback.

"…And worship beer," Tina adds, handing James a smaller paper towel than the previous one.

James sits in silence, unaware of his defeat in this fight. He makes promises every New Year's to stop drinking, but a nice cold beer in front of a sports game is his Achilles' heel. He takes a sip of beer, then wipes the remaining residue from his hands onto his jeans that the small paper towel couldn't collect.

"What time are we leaving tomorrow?" he asks, attempting to change the subject and refocus on the game highlights.

"We should leave around nine in the morning. That will give us time to shop for the rest of the items Megan needs, as well as help her unpack," Tina responds. "I also need to anoint the dorm room." Remembering, she walks to the hallway to get the anointing oil from a small marble table and places the little bottle in her purse that's hanging on the coat rack by the door.

"Ma, are you really going to do that?" With a mouth full of chicken, a piece falls from Megan's mouth onto her T-shirt. She waits for a response before she wipes it away.

"Yes, and I'll be anointing your roommate too."

Megan, embarrassed by the upcoming exorcism, attempts to clean her shirt with her half paper towel. "Can I get the other half of my paper towel, please?" Annoyed with it all, she wipes the chicken off her shirt, creating an even bigger stain.

CHAPTER 2: COLLEGE HOME

FALL 2021

WELCOME! FALL SEMESTER FRESHMAN LIONS is boldly posted on the Southern Atlanta South University marquee. Megan's mesmerized by the sign's illumination towering over the one-hour parking for freshmen unloading. Hundreds of cars are parked in the designated area. Families tote luggage and take pictures, giving kisses and hugs to restless soon-to-be students. James pulls into a parking space, giving the family front-door access to the five-story female dormitory.

"Somebody ugly," he jokes, as he does every time they get a good parking spot—a joke he's heard used somewhere before, and often repeats.

Megan gets out of the truck soaking in the vibrant atmosphere surrounding her. The lion mascot tumbles through the crowd while fraternities and sororities parade by in their colorful paraphernalia. The distant sound of band members practicing in the background creates a whirlwind of energy and excitement on campus. Her attention is immediately captured by a tall, confident male. He walks by in his black and green fraternity attire. Their eyes meet, and there's a moment of connection. The thought of leaving her keyboard boyfriend behind has now become a distant memory.

Tameka, noticing the exchange, teases Megan. "I see why you chose this school. If I had seen Mr. Black and Green in the SASU brochure, I would have enrolled too," she jokes, hopping out of the truck and joining the family gathering luggage. "And look, he doesn't seem to mind you wearing your overnight shirt and this awful black hoodie." She tugs at Megan's sleeve, bothered by the dingy black sneakers Megan managed to retrieve from the pile on the floor.

Megan had a good reason for her appearance. Tina was on a tight shopping schedule, and James' constant reminder of returning home before six forced Megan to get a second-day wear out of her T-shirt. With only fifteen minutes to get ready due to a failed alarm, a change of clothing was a decision she didn't have time to make. She only had enough time to wash up, brush her teeth, cover the chicken stain on her shirt with the black hoodie, and grab her black sneakers.

James struggles to release the shoe suitcase from a latch that has attached itself to a hook in the rear of the truck. "It's not too late to enroll. I'm sure the enrollment office is open," he gestured at Tameka, hastily nudging the girls forward to place the luggage wheels down for an easy roll.

"I went to college!" Tameka snaps back.

"Dropping out of hair school doesn't count," Tina tells her, separating her shopping bags from Megan's and handing Tameka a bag.

"And you stayed home while going to hair school. When are you moving out?" James throws in with a grump. He closes the trunk door and locks it, setting its alarm, scanning his environment. He spots an area assigned to the Greek organizations on campus. A wooden display cemented in the ground in front of the area reads, *The Yard.*

Mr. Black and Green is in the midst of the yard full of Greek organizations. He's seated on a bench that reads *Zeta Alpha Phi*, surrounded by a group of guys in matching attire. He gives Megan a smile as the Mahns, with suitcases and grocery bags in hand, haul toward the dormitory entrance, passing *The Yard* display. He notices the family's struggle carrying the unmanageable luggage and yells, "Need help?"

James adjusts his cap to find the college student with the overly deep voice. He spots the fraternity member—Mr. Black and Green—and responds, "No!"

Megan, embarrassed by her father's tone and the fact that she forgot to put concealer on her dark circles, avoids eye contact with Mr. Black and Green. She covers her face with her free hand, continuing toward the five-story dormitory as her father mumbles, "Devil steppers."

†††

The elevator is out of order. Five flights of stairs later, an out-of-breath family enters a compact dorm room. The layout is similar to the sisters' bedroom minus the Jack and Jill. The dorm bathrooms are down the hall, shared with a floor of eighteen freshman females. Two twin beds are placed opposite each other against the dorm room walls. One bed is occupied by April, a brown-skinned girl with loose curls. She quietly sits on her bed, watching the family bring in luggage. Posters of affirmation quotes adorn April's side of the room, showing evidence that she has been in the dorm for a while, unpacked, and already claimed her territory.

"I can't believe the elevator's not working," Tameka complains, cautiously sitting on the available unmade bed. She takes off her heels and begins to massage her feet.

"Why are you complaining? You made Dad carry the suitcase *you* were supposed to be handling," Megan points out, placing her suitcase in the empty closet; her father follows suit with the remaining luggage.

Tina places a bag of bed linen next to Tameka, hinting at the task of making up Megan's new bed. "We need to unpack those suitcases and fix up Megan's side of the room. Turn it into a home." Tina swiftly walks toward the closet to take out the luggage, following her own command.

"We don't have time, Tina. We have one-hour parking, plus the game. Fifty-dollar fine if we're ticketed—and we already spent *thirty* minutes walking up five flights of stairs. Megan can handle it," James reminds her, grabbing the luggage and placing it back into the closet.

But Tina moves on to plan B. She pulls out the anointing oil from her purse and begins anointing the space, drawing crosses on the inside and outside of the room door. "In Jesus' name," she repeats over and over, as she goes over to the windowsill and does the same. Alarmed that an observant April is in the room, she walks over to April's bed, looking her up and down. April stares back nervously, knowing only of people using holy oil and water in movies during exorcisms. They have a stare-down awaiting the next move.

"Ma, stop!" Megan yells, rescuing April from Tina's holy attack. Tina turns to Megan and anoints her forehead instead, leaving a greasy cross stretched above her eyebrows.

"Looks like that's everything. We're going to miss you," Tina states, screwing the top back onto her oil bottle. She gives Megan a goodbye kiss on the cheek with an unbearable squeeze.

James chimes in with a firm reminder, checking his phone for the time. "Stay focused on your studies, don't get distracted, don't come home unless it's for the holidays or summer break, and stay away from that boy."

Megan, embarrassed by their nonsense, slightly motions her parents toward the door. "Dad, I assure you I have no intention of returning home."

Tameka completes her foot massage, adjusts the straps of her heels, and approaches Megan. She tugs at Megan's shirt, tying it into the fitted knot, swoops Megan's braids over her shoulders, then hugs her tightly. "You better come home for the holidays and bring that boy with you. Worm head," she teases.

"What boy?" April inquires, interests piqued. Tina reaches back into her purse to pull out the anointing oil, but Megan gives her a stern look to chill out.

"I'll let Megan fill you in on Mr. Black and Green," Tameka explains.

James' eyes slightly water as he says, "Alright, enough. We must go, or they will charge us for overstaying our parking welcome, paying for everyone's tuition." Megan could hear how the joke was overcompensating for the emotion forming a lump in his throat.

"You are so cheap, James," Tina whines, pleading for more time to soak in every moment left with her now-college daughter.

"Are you going to pay the parking fine?" James asks. Tina remains silent. "Maybe we can use that money on some paper towels," he jokes, giving Megan one last hug before his exit.

With their final goodbyes and hugs, Megan watches her family rush out of the room, down five flights of stairs, leaving her to begin her college journey.

"That's my family," Megan says to April, relieved by their departure. She walks toward the bag of linen sitting on her bed. She unzips the packet that consists of the bed sheets.

"I'm lucky you missed mine," April states, pointing toward a baby-blue framed photo of her mother along with two older women, one sitting in a wheelchair, all wearing the same blue-colored shirts. Above the photo frame, an affirmation catches Megan's eye: *If one fall, we all fall.*

"Seems like your mother really cares about you." April laughs while pointing at the oil cross on Megan's forehead.

"A little too much." Embarrassed, she wipes it off with the back of her hand. Excited that her family is gone, and no longer under their supervision, she asks, "What's next on the agenda?"

April holds up a freshman itinerary with a roaring lion on its letterhead. "Freshman orientation at three." She places the itinerary next to the framed photo on her wooden nightstand and hops off her bed to give Megan a handshake. "I'm April."

Megan's surprised by April's height. She's standing at about 5'4", appearing taller when seated on the bed.

"Megan," she responds, reciprocating the handshake, standing four inches taller than her. Looking over April's shoulder, she sees her appearance in a mirror hanging on the back of the door. She rushes to the mirror, tying her hair up in a bun, and withdraws her concealer from a small bag in her miscellaneous suitcase, applying it under her eyes. With a breath of relief, she's now ready for freshman orientation—to make a first impression with SASU's student body. A chance to reinvent herself.

✝✝✝

It's 3:30 in the afternoon, and Megan and April aimlessly stroll toward the crowd of freshmen on an open field near the yard. The field is prepped with a stage and bleachers adorned with black and gold balloons. Students in SASU attire fill the bleachers. Some stand along the grass blocking the girls' entrance to a seat. Megan could tell that many of the students had also attended the campus tour because they were wearing the same T-shirt she often wore from her own tour experience—minus the chicken smudge.

"Oh shoot," Megan mumbles, remembering the stain displayed at the center of her shirt. She zips up her hoodie, concealing its embarrassment.

The two arrive at the peak of orientation, happy to have missed the long, drawn-out rules presented by Dean Jackson. He stands on the stage wearing a black suit with a green Zeta Alpha Phi tie, similar to the lettering Mr. Black and Green was wearing.

"Let's ROAR, Lions!" His words are met with cheers and excitement from the freshman crowd. He continues, booming his voice over hundreds of roars. "Let's give a warm welcome to all our freshmen here at Southern Atlanta South University." He makes a motion for the band to play. The pulsating music throbs from the drumline, and the horns join in. He begins by introducing the sports teams, followed by the different departments, including the music, drama, and engineering programs.

Then he introduces the Greek organizations. Students cheer for the ones they seemed to have interest in. But then something happens—Dean Jackson begins to introduce the sororities and fraternities of the Black Greek organizations, and the atmosphere shifts into a Black cultural experience. Students ignite in applause and shouts as these organizations begin to stroll through the crowd, doing their individual steps toward the yard. The mesmerized freshmen go wild, following the organizations to their designated areas marked by benches and trees that are painted to match their Greek symbolic colors.

Megan doesn't understand much about these organizations or what they stand for, but they have a strong presence that's gaining her attention. She remembers seeing a few ladies back home wearing the Greek letters, emblems, and shields on clothing and car tags, but she's never had the courage to ask questions about their involvement.

Megan's eyes spark with excitement as she watches them stroll, seemingly free in a mixture of colors with confidence and unity—a unity she's never experienced. Everyone seems to receive praise and respect. Each group has a distinct look. Some are dressed up with heavy makeup and heels, others dressed down or in business attire. The males have matching canes and hats, suits or clean-pressed tees. She spots Mr. Black and Green fraternizing with his group. His smile's so bright she's caught herself lost in his radiance. Shaking the feeling off, she continues scanning the scenery.

The non-Black Greek organizations are posted at tables, passing out pamphlets to freshmen who walk up to them—handing out cupcakes and other trinkets.

The band is still in an uproar, adding to Megan's thrill. It draws Megan into its rhythm as she finds herself swept in the infectious energy. Calls from the groups are heard that sound like animals in the wild. A high-pitched call that sounds like a bird chirping for its mate captures Megan's attention. She turns and notices a group of girls having a great time enjoying the music.

"That's my group right there!" Megan exclaims, pointing at the sorority strolling in an area decorated in royal and baby blue with emblems of bluejays. The girls are in unison with their steps and dance movements, their long hair flowing amongst the wind. Megan's excitement is palpable as she mimics the confident strides from afar and does their chirp call. April, being familiar with the rules of sororities, grabs Megan's arm, pulling her back from overeager enthusiasm and embarrassment.

"You might want to chill on that," April cautions her. "Showing too much interest will put a target on your back. They can smell it like sharks smell blood in water. NPHC don't play."

Confusion comes across Megan's face as she struggles to comprehend April's warning. "NPHC?"

"The National Pan-Hellenic Council. They operate a little different than them." She points toward the other Greek organizations posted at tables passing out cupcakes.

"Well, how do I join that group, if I don't show interest?" Megan asks, pointing to the group of girls strolling in blue as she tries to manage the huge grin that wants to reveal itself.

April leans in close, her words whispering against the backdrop of the Greek calls and the band. "At their interest meeting," April explains. "It's like their recruitment period. Trust me. Play it cool.

They have a way of sensing desperation," she says, eyeing Megan's wardrobe. "Plus, you need to *look* the part."

Megan takes being desperate as an offense. She tries to play it cool, but she struggles to downplay her excitement.

"You not from here, are you?" April asks.

"No, my family just moved to Macon. You?"

"Yep. Born and raised." April does a dance exemplifying her Atlanta pride.

Unbeknownst to the girls, they catch the eye of Jasmine, the dean of pledges of the royal and baby-blue girls, Theta Kappa Rho. She's dripped in blue paraphernalia with the name *Jazz* printed on the back of her jacket. She stands arms crossed in six-inch heels, observing Megan's desperation in the distance, assessing the freshman's potential.

††††

Friday has arrived, and Megan has endured a SASU school week successfully. She sits in the front row of her ten o'clock Music Theory class wearing one of Tameka's burgundy sweater dresses and black strappy four-inch heels. Now that she's in college, maybe a different look will help her fit into her new life—college life, adulthood. April has also been coaching her on how to get noticed by Theta Kappa Rho, instructing her, "You must begin by looking the part: examine what they wear and mimic their style but avoid their colors. *Do not* wear their colors," she warned sternly. So, Megan has been putting effort into her wardrobe, wearing her braids loose to mimic the sorority's long hair tresses, and practicing her walk in heels. April provided her tinted lip gloss to give her a slightly more made-up look until Megan learns how to properly apply her own makeup.

She was thrilled to be able to enroll in a music major course as a freshman, avoiding the boredom of elective classes. Her eyes are full of curiosity as she absorbs every word from Professor Hill, a seasoned man in his sixties, hair full of grey. He stands at the podium, commanding the attention of twenty-five students in a silent lecture room. He speaks with knowledge and insight, following a PowerPoint covered in notes about the Harlem Renaissance's influence on music. Meanwhile, Mr. Black and Green lounges casually in the back of the class with a relaxed demeanor, as Professor Hill expounds upon the significance of his lecture. Not resisting the urge to speak, Mr. Black and Green raises his hand in eager anticipation.

"Professor Hill, if I may interject…" His voice is filled with playful enthusiasm that draws laughter from his classmates. Amused by the familiar student's interest, Professor Hill nods in acknowledgment, inviting him to share his thoughts.

"I believe the HR was improvisational yet captivating," he proclaims, his words holding the room captive. "It's like Duke Ellington and Langston Hughes got together for a jam session, and the result was a cultural explosion that still slaps today. So, for that, you should excuse the homework and let us enjoy our weekend of a cultural explosion of our own. One time for the Renaissance!" he requests with a solo cheer.

The students join him as laughter ripples throughout the classroom; Megan is also charmed by his charisma. Professor Hill chuckles, acknowledging the comment before redirecting the class's attention to the matter at hand.

"Well, Jeff, I see being a third-year music major has certainly improved your vernacular, if not your musical aptitude," Professor Hill remarks, turning off the PowerPoint. "But this isn't the debate team. I know this is a lot of information for the first week, so homework over the weekend is…" Professor Hill has the students hanging on to his every word, allowing the suspense to linger until he states, "Homework over the weekend is… only fair to make sure you've retained all the information for your quiz Monday." He concludes, "Now, you don't have to go home, but you need to get up out of here. See you all Monday."

The class groans in disappointment at the assigned homework while gathering their belongings to leave. Jeff, aka Mr. Black and Green, makes his way down the aisle, catching sight of Megan gathering her materials. He flashes her a charming smile.

"Hey…" Jeff greets her. He extends his hand in a flirtatious gesture as he waits for her name. Megan's caught off guard by Jeff's sudden approach. She hesitates before reciprocating the handshake, mesmerized by his beautiful straight white teeth, thick dark eyebrows that offset his brown almond eyes, and immaculate presence.

"Megan," she snaps out of her trance and extends her hand.

Jeff's grin widens as he leans in closer, his playful demeanor suggesting a hint of confidence. She can smell his oak-spiced cologne enveloping her.

"Megan. I couldn't help but notice you enjoying my performance back there," he teases. "Maybe we can hang out, enjoy a real performance with drinks, now that your pop's not around."

Megan, playing hard to get, flirts back. "My pops warned me about guys like you, Jeff."

He laughs and hands her a piece of torn notebook paper with his number written in pencil.

"'90s much?" She jokes playfully, taking the paper from him.

"Your dad warned you about guys like me, yet you took notice of my name. I never introduced myself." Jeff flashes Megan a confident wink before disappearing out the door.

She's left blushing, staring at the handwritten number on the piece of paper—yet slightly embarrassed because she *did* take notice of his name. However, *he* had taken notice of *her*, the awkward introvert.

†††

Megan lounges on her fully made bed covered with music books, pencils, and her laptop. Her attention is divided between schoolwork and a phone conversation with Tameka. She cradles the phone between her shoulder and ear, flipping through pages of a music book.

"Are you going to any parties tonight?" Tameka asks with anticipation.

"Nah, I'm going to lay low," Megan replies, leaning back onto her silk pillowcase. "We've been assigned homework this weekend, so I'm focused on that. I've been sitting in the front row of my classes to stay focused. You should be proud."

"Front row? We can barely get you to sit in the front row at church, let alone stay awake," Tameka jokes. She continues the interrogation. "Do you have a boyfriend yet?"

Megan rolls her eyes. "It's only been a *week*, Meka—but I *am* kind of feeling somebody," Megan adds with excitement, sitting up to anxiously continue fluttering through her Music Theory book.

"Who?!"

"His name is Jeff," Megan responds, spotting the ripped notebook paper with his number on it which she's been using as a bookmark.

"Is Jeff short for Mr. Black and Green?"

Before Megan can respond, a text notification interrupts their conversation, drawing her attention away from her sister's eager inquiry. Her focus has now shifted to the message on her phone.

"Let me call you back."

"No. Tell me more about Jeff. Is that short for Mr. Black and Green?" Tameka protests, but Megan ends the call before giving an answer.

Megan reads the mysterious message, and a sense of intrigue washes over her.

You have 30 minutes to meet us behind the cafeteria. Wear all black and don't tell anyone where you're going. DELETE ALL MESSAGES RECEIVED FROM US. AND NO PHONES.
Theta Kappa Rho.

The cryptic instructions ignite a thrill of excitement as she contemplates the mysterious text.

How did they get my phone number? she wonders. Looking over at April's empty bed, she realizes she doesn't even have April's phone number. She walks over to April's nightstand, sifting through paperwork in hopes of finding April's contact information. With no luck, she spots the SASU itinerary and reaches for a pen to write down her whereabouts on the back of it. As she turns the itinerary over, she immediately remembers the instructions not to disclose her location.

She places the itinerary beside April's framed photo and notices that April's mother has on a Theta Kappa Rho shirt, along with the other older women in the photograph. Megan hadn't connected the dots until now.

"That's why she had so much insight into TKRho—her mother is a part of the sorority," Megan concludes.

With a surge of adrenaline, Megan springs into action. She goes to her closet and pulls out her black hoodie and her favorite black T-shirt from her unpacked suitcase. Searching through the suitcase, she manages to find black jeans without rips in them and wipes off her dingy black sneakers. She can't believe she's prepared for this moment. She has the recommended wardrobe. It must be fate.

She deletes the message from her phone and tosses it on her bed, covered in school supplies. She takes a final glance around the room for her room key and grabs it from the dresser near the door. She slips out, tiptoeing through the empty Friday night hallway as she makes her way toward the mysterious meetup.

CHAPTER 3: BEING MADE

The fall temperature has dropped cooler than the fall eighty-degree Florida weather Megan's used to. She zips up her hoodie, shielding herself from the cool breeze that's intensifying her nerves. She looks around the secluded darkness behind the cafeteria and finds herself met by whispers of unseen figures calling and waving her forward into a wooded area. Heart pounding through her ears, she steps cautiously into the mysterious space.

Megan joins four other girls in black attire, lined up shoulder to shoulder according to height, including her roommate April, who is second in line. Their eyes meet in silent acknowledgment. April motions for Megan to stand at the tail end since she is the tallest of the five.

"A smart tail she is, falls right in line," an unseen voice is heard.

The figure emerges from the shadows, revealed to be Jasmine—Jazz—the TKRho Dean of Pledges. She comes out from the darkness holding a royal blue wooden paddle, slapping it against her hand. She steps forward to the beat of the slap. TKRho Greek lettering is engraved along the paddle

Jasmine takes her position in front of the five girls, followed by the president of the Omega Zeta chapter of TKRho, Toya. She takes her place to the right of Jasmine. The rest of the members form a line behind the two, all commanding respect. They're dressed as if coming from or going to a girls' night out. Their hair is straightened and their faces covered in makeup, appearing older and more mature than college students.

"Ladies, I am the dean of pledges, and Toya is the president of the Omega Zeta chapter of Theta Kappa Rho. We have been carefully watching you for the past week and have selected you for a pre-trial—Omega Zeta's underground process," Jasmine declares with authority.

"If we are wrong about your interest, please leave. If you are not looking for a sisterhood or up for a challenge, you can leave. If you are legacy, you are free to leave."

Megan is curious if April will leave because she is legacy. Afraid to look in April's direction, she listens for footsteps of departure. No footsteps are heard except for Jasmine's, who is walking up and down the line of potential candidates.

"Your stay shows us you're committing to a process that will gain you a sisterhood for life," Toya adds, her voice slightly softer than Jasmine's. Her nervous eyes scan the five girls, hoping she's made the right decision in their selection—that these girls will vow to secrecy regarding the process and this initial meetup.

The phrase *a sisterhood for life* rings in Megan's ear. She likes the sound of that. She's surprised these girls are interested in her. They seem like they would only want the best dressed, best all-around, life-of-the-party superlative winner—girls like Tameka. Maybe that's why she's drawn to them, because they resemble her sister, whom she secretly admires. Just maybe, she thinks, going through this underground process will help groom her into that superlative winner. This process will allow her to be a part of a clique, finally accepted.

Patrice, a girl leading the line of candidates, shorter than April, voices her concern. "Is TKRho a hazing sorority? I was told we can get in by paying an initiation fee?"

"Is TKRho a hazing sorority? I thought I could join by being 'paper'!" Jasmine mocks. She walks up to Patrice, paddle in hand, addresses her face-to-face, and yells, "Do you want to be paper, or do you want to be made?"

Patrice stumbles back, glasses sliding down and landing on the tip of her nose, alarmed by how close Jasmine is to her.

Seeing how startled Patrice is, Toya responds with a softer approach. "The Omega Zeta Chapter has an underground process. If you're not willing to earn your place in this chapter, you will not earn respect in this sisterhood. Are you a legacy?"

The girls wait for a response. None is given. Patrice remains silent.

"Let me tell you ladies something. You're welcome to leave. We don't need you. We just thought you'd be fun," Jasmine states, positioning Patrice's crooked glasses into place. The ladies of TKRho chuckle at the action.

Patrice hesitates to make her next move, seeking validation from the other candidates in line. When no one comes to her defense, she ultimately chooses to leave. She pulls her hood over her bob-length hair and walks away from the line. Unable to look in Patrice's direction, Megan measures her stride. Her steps weren't heard as stomps of anger, and they weren't tiptoes of hesitation, steps of embarrassment.

Her departure is met with indifference from Jasmine and the fellow sorority sisters. Toya follows Patrice out of the secluded area to make sure there are no hard feelings and to confirm the secrecy of the meeting. The line of four looks into the darkness ahead, unable to see the interaction behind them. The wooded area is quiet; only the soft whisper of an inaudible conversation is heard. They all wait to see if the holdup will intensify into a screaming match or if the introduction into sisterhood will continue.

Megan no longer hears whispers behind her. Footsteps are heard—one departing further into the background and another approaching the area. Toya comes back to the group, giving Jasmine a nod to continue, assuring her Patrice has left with no resentment. With relief, Jasmine resumes the initiation process.

"Looks like we have a new ace, a new number one, since the former wants to be paper," referring to Patrice. "I will text number one when a message needs to be delivered to you all."

Jasmine then addresses April. "How you get their number is up to you." She looks at the new line of candidates. "Because none of you should have your phones."

"I left my phone on—"

"Is someone speaking without permission?" Jasmine's rhetorical question interrupts Megan's explanation. She begins walking down the line toward Megan, continuing with authority: "Never bring phones to set. Always answer calls and messages given from your ace. No walking on the grass. No wearing the sorority's colors. Never chirp TKRho's call. And always dress up with heels. You'll address me as 'Big Sister Jazz' and respond to all sisters as such. Do I make myself clear?" Jasmine commands.

The candidates respond with clashing answers.

"Yes, Big Sister Jazz!"

"Big Sister Jazz."

"Yes!"

"…Big Sister… Jazz?"

"I can't hear you—and in unison this time!" Jasmine yells.

"Yes, Big Sister Jazz!" they shout.

Jasmine directs her attention to April, making it known that she is aware of April being the legacy of a founding member and that she will not go easy on her. "Legacy or not, ace, you will put respect on our blood, sweat, and tears. You understand me?"

"Yes, Big Sister Jazz!" April shouts, proud of her responsibility yet scared of the pressure of being legacy.

"Good," Jasmine continues. "Church service is Sunday, where you *will* be in attendance. If you want to be a part of this sisterhood, I expect to see you all at service every Sunday. This sorority stands on Christian principles, and we will honor God as such.

"Like I've said, we've been watching you. You may look like a Theta woman, but are you emotionally a woman of Theta? So, for that, you must not wear any weave, no makeup, and no boys. If you have a problem with that, then this sorority is not for you. Confidence is built from the inside out. We don't need validation from anyone—especially the opposite sex."

Jasmine waits for objections. None are heard, and she continues. "This process is to be secret. If you so much as breathe a word about this to anyone, I'll personally make your life a living hell. Understood?" She slaps the paddle against her hand.

The startled candidates shout in unison. "Yes, Big Sister Jazz!"

"You will have set every weeknight at 9:10 unless otherwise told differently. If you are uninformed of the significance of the time, then you should evaluate your reason for being here. Now fall out!" Satisfied with her commands, Jasmine dismisses the candidates.

Megan's mind races with questions about the significance of 9:10 and the rules regarding hair weave. When she dares to speak up, Jasmine's response is sharp and dismissive.

"Did I stutter while stating the rules?" Jasmine asks.

"No, Big Sister Jazz, it's just my braids—"

Jasmine cuts her off and begins reciting a known quote amongst the Black Greek organizations as she away with the other members of TKRho: "Excuses are tools of incompetence, used to build bridges to nowhere and monuments of nothingness. Those who use them seldom amount to anything or nothing at all."

She turns to Megan before exiting the wooded area. "Don't amount to nothing at all, Number Four."

The members of TKRho laugh as they walk away in the opposite direction of the candidates. Toya joins them.

April quickly pulls Megan away as they disperse. "Girl, are you trying to get us killed?" April exclaims in frustration.

"*Us*? What are you even doing here, legacy? You don't even have to go through this process. You could have left with that girl." Why *hadn't* she left? Why would she go through this when she didn't have to, when she had an automatic place in the sisterhood?

"...And do you see how tiny my braids are?" Megan continued. "My sister took all day to do my hair... and what does 9:10 even *mean*?"

She hasn't worn her hair out in years, since being forced to go natural. Tameka applied a relaxer to her hair while testing out of a cosmetology course, and it broke her hair off—one of the many reasons Tameka dropped out of school and began creating her own products. Megan did the big chop and is now left with an unmanageable afro hidden under her braids.

"Yes, I'm legacy, but I want to be made, not paper. And 1910 is TKRho's founding date. Girl, you have so much to learn," April replies as they walk toward their dorm room.

"This is not what I signed up for," Megan says, kicking a pinecone in defeat.

"But you stayed when you had a chance to leave with 'paper,'" April states, picking on Patrice. With a softened response, she continues. "Remember that feeling you had at orientation? That sense of belonging when you saw TKRho strolling on the yard?"

Megan remains silent.

"We can now belong. Plus, being a part of this sorority opens doors. Look at Kamala Harris—she's in a sorority, and she's the Vice President."

Megan interjects with furrowed brows. "This sorority did not make her Vice President."

"True, but she's in a sorority. And to get to Vice President status, we must play the game to get ahead. So, if that means getting yelled at and wearing no makeup for a while, then so be it." April allows the moment to resonate with Megan before asking her next question. "So, are we taking out some hair this weekend, Number Four?"

Megan sighs, reluctantly giving in to the inevitable makeover. "I guess… but I don't want to be Vice President. I'm going to be President."

She playfully whispers TKRho's chirp call. April gives her a shove as they laugh at the forbidden act. Megan regains the feeling of excitement for the unknown process ahead and what her unraveled braids shall reveal.

†††

Megan scans her final appearance as the dormmates prepare to leave for the mandatory Sunday church service assigned by Jasmine. Impressed with the outcome of her freshly styled wash-and-go, Megan stands in front of the full-length mirror hanging on the inside of their dorm room door. The braid takedown took all day and night Saturday, allowing her and April a bonding moment that only a client and her hairstylist could share—a pastime Megan's beginning to miss with her sister.

During the transformation, they discussed the ladies in the framed photo. The eldest, in the wheelchair, was April's great-grandmother, and her grandmother stood beside her with her arm resting on her mother's shoulder. They were all members of TKRho. In 1910, April's great-great-grandmother Annie Williams, along with seven other African American women, founded Theta Kappa Rho Incorporated on SASU's campus. April feels great pressure from her mother and grandmother to continue the Williams women tradition.

Over the course of those hours, April taught Megan more TKRho information to prepare her for sets to come. She reminded Megan that she must do her own research as well and earn her spot, repeating the very words her mother tells her: "You must prove yourself in my organization. Once you get in, then you may utilize the connections." A confusing statement, because it's April's connection to the Williams women that's giving her an in-road into TKRho.

The girls created song melodies to remember the founders' names. They learned the sorority motto by repetition and secretly practiced the chirp call for the official moment when allowed to chirp. Megan was also able to complete Professor Hill's assignment along with the homework given by her other professors. Juggling school and TKRho pledging seems to be an easy manage so far.

Megan is engaged in conversation with her mom. She has Tina on speakerphone, careful not to divulge any information about the sorority. April, sitting on the edge of her bed, eavesdrops on the conversation while putting on her shoes, making sure no clues about Friday's set are mentioned.

"How was your first week?" Tina inquires through the speaker of the SUV as the Mahn family drives to God's House eleven o'clock service.

"It was good. I got through all the assigned homework like a pro. Feeling like a summa cum laude," Megan proudly replies.

"That's my girl. Stay on top of that, because your dad's stressing about tuition. If those grades go down, the checks will too."

Focused on the road, James gives a 'sho-you-right' nod.

"I'm on it," Megan assures the family.

"Tameka mentioned you have a boyfriend," she says, fishing to see if Megan will take the bait.

James, attentive at the mention of a boyfriend, slows the vehicle as if slowing down will help him hear better.

"Boyfriend? No…" Megan states, steering the conversation away from Jeff. "…but I am headed to church."

James, pleased with her response, accelerates back to the speed limit.

"Church? Well, praise God," Tina responds. "What's making you go?"

Megan's mention of church makes April nervous. She's worried Megan will reveal why they are going to church, exposing the secrecy of the pledge. She walks over to the full-length mirror, making her presence known as a reminder not to mention a word about TKRho. Megan gives her an assuring wave to calm down.

Tameka, from the back seat, loudly interrupts, demanding answers about Jeff. "Stop stalling—spill the tea about Jeff!"

"Jeff? Better not be that grown-man-voice boy!" James exclaims, speeding up through the church parking lot.

"Is this Jeff going to be at church?" Tina asks while clenching tightly to the door railing that's providing her safety from James's speed racing.

"No, Ma," Megan quickly reassures her.

"She's lying!" Tameka interjects.

April checks the time on her phone. With a sense of urgency—and relief from the change in conversation—she motions for Megan to get off the phone or risk being late for service. Megan, gives her a nod and hastily ends the call. "I have to go—can't be late for the Lord."

"You may be late to church, but remember God is always on time guiding your steps. Slow down, James!" Tina yells.

"Who is Jeff?" James questions, speeding over every speed bump in the church parking lot.

Megan ends the call before more questions are asked.

"Let's hope God guides our steps to church on time," April jokes as the girls rush out of the room.

CHAPTER 4: TRIAL BY SORORITY FIRE

Megan and April were hoping to have gotten away from the ladies of TKRho, avoiding consequences from the previous commotion at church. But they seem to have been found. Jasmine and a few other members are milking every moment to torture the girls, seated in a corner of the chatter-filled campus cafeteria.

Megan and April nervously sit with their lunch trays untouched, scathed from Jeff's earlier actions causing the two to run out of the church like runaway slaves. Thank God they decided to change into business-casual clothing and heels before heading to the café or another strike against TKRho pledging rules would be added to the inevitable punishment Jasmine was brewing. April reminded Megan that they were always supposed to present themselves in business casual attire, even if they weren't expecting a TKRho stare-down.

"I want to eat, but I can't with TKRho eyes watching," April says, picking at the chicken on her plate with her fork.

"Is there a TKRho way to eat too? I think I know the difference between a salad fork and a regular fork, but I don't need to be quizzed on it," Megan jokingly asks. But then she seriously begins to wonder if there is a correct TKRho way to eat. Her mother once enrolled the girls in an etiquette class. Tameka enjoyed the class, but Megan saw no point in eating with different silverware—it only created more dishes.

Out of the corner of her eye, Megan sees Jeff walk into the cafeteria alone as if on a hunt to find her. "Would he stop already!" Megan hides her face under her hand.

Unaware of her subtle cues, Jeff approaches her table anyway. "Why are you running from me," he asks, "leaving me in the church solo? Give me a call, then I wouldn't have to stalk you."

"Bug-a-boo much," April mumbles under her breath.

Megan slyly looks over at the TKRho table. She is receiving stares from them, making known their disapproval of Jeff being in her presence. Rushing the conversation, Megan replies, avoiding eye contact, "I've been meaning to call, but I've been buried in Professor Hill's assignments and other things."

Jeff leans in with a whisper. "TKRho things?"

Megan is shocked that her pledging has been so obvious. She thought she was doing well hiding her involvement. She can feel the fire blazing from the sorority's eyes a few tables away observing their interaction. Her body begins to feel hot all over. She wipes the invisible sweat from her dry forehead.

"I'll catch up with you later. Please, *leave*." She subtly pulls away from him, glancing nervously at her nearby assassins who watch her intently.

Jeff takes the hint and exchanges a knowing nod with April, confirming his awareness of Megan's sorority involvement. April gives him a look to leave too. His gaze lingers on Jasmine and her sorors at the other table before turning back to Megan.

"I'm liking this new vibe," he says, referring to her natural look.

Megan blushes, then quickly returns to her attempted inconspicuous demeanor. Jeff departs, leaving Megan slightly flustered.

April's phone buzzes with a text message, her expression shifting to alarm. "We need to go." April hastily rises from her seat. Megan follows suit as they abandon their trays of untouched food. A disgruntled cafeteria attendant passes by, yelling at the girls, "Y'all better eat this food!"

They rush from the cafeteria, sprinting back to the dormitory, heels in hand, avoiding the grass. The girls hurry into their cramped room, five stories later, with panting breaths filling the air. Like a true friend, Megan had ran and asked questions later.

Her voice trembles with anxiety as she questions their abrupt return, knowing in her gut it had something to do with TKRho and Jeff. "Why did we have to run? What did they say?"

April shoves her the phone. Megan's eyes widen in disbelief as she reads the text message from Jasmine.

"Seriously? They made us run here? We can't leave until we meet for set tonight? *And* they want us to bring food?"

She tosses April her phone.

"Yes, yes, and yes! And I made plans for tonight!" April responds angrily. "Sundays are *not* TKRho days!"

She deletes the incriminating message and creates a new message for the group chat.

Sit tonight. We must bring food.

"Jeff needs to chill," April continues, tossing her phone aside. "Now he's getting *me* caught up in this horny scavenger hunt. TKRho is going to crush us because of him," she says, pounding her hand into her fist. "He is gonna learn not to play with me when I'm hungry. I had chicken and potatoes on my lunch plate! I left a great meal on the table because of him!"

"You weren't eating it anyway," Megan points out, then offers a promise to address the situation with Jeff. "I'll speak to him."

She checks the group text notification on her phone from April.

"You spelled *set* wrong." She emphasizes the correct spelling in the group chat: **Set**. Then she places her phone on the dresser. Changing the subject, Megan asks, "When is this supposed interest meeting happening? It's only been two days, and I'm already tired of being humiliated."

"We had our interest meeting," April makes Megan aware. "Us staying Friday night showed them we were interested. I can only assume Jasmine going this hard, this soon, means the official interest meeting is coming very soon."

"I'm supposed to *like* my sisters. But I hate these girls. They make my sister Tameka look like an angel."

Megan's stomach roars like a lion full of hunger. She walks toward the small counter space in their dorm room, their makeshift kitchen. She prepares a packet of noodles in the microwave. Thank God for Tameka's suggestion on having an abundance of dorm room snacks and noodles. While shopping for miscellaneous items for Megan's college stay, Tameka kept loading snacks in the cart, so much that James had to drag her out of the store. Megan is unsure of how Tameka would know to do this—she has never stayed away from home. More and more, her sister is starting to look like an angel—but Megan wouldn't dare tell her that.

April attempts to lighten the mood. "Technically, they're not our sisters yet. Think of them as irritating older siblings you're stuck with but desperately need on your side."

Megan doesn't respond to the mood-lightening attempt. She continues preparing two bowls of noodles. "Now we're stuck in here eating these dry noodles," she mumbles.

"Your *man* is the reason we're eating these dry noodles."

They both laugh at the shared experience they hope will be funny once Theta Kappa Rho finishes tearing them down to bring them up.

Megan likes the thought of Jeff being her man. He would be her first serious boyfriend if they were to become a thing. She has always been immersed in music and her keyboard, never the idea of turning a crush into a relationship. She smiles at the thought of cheating on her keyboard with Jeff.

†††

"Sorry, Big Sister Jazz!" the four pledges yell as their breath vapors formulate in the cold.

Jasmine hovers over the girls, clearly enjoying her impromptu meetup. She surveys them as their raw, bare knuckles knock down tree bark, slapping the wooden engraved paddle against her clasped hand, humming a rhythmic chant.

The girls have quickly learned that an unsupervised Jasmine is a dangerous Jasmine. Less than half of the chapter members are in attendance, and Toya had a family emergency. Jasmine is basking in their absence, abusing her power and loving it. She threatened to hit the four candidates with the wooden paddle if they were unable to knock down a tree in five minutes. Of course, the girls were confused about how to complete the task. They were not provided with an axe or a chainsaw, and five minutes was not enough time for them to find one.

But, with fifteen seconds remaining, April had a brilliant idea. "Big Sister Jazz, we would knock down the tree like knocking on a door, Big Sister Jazz!" April proudly yelled.

The girls lit up at the brilliant idea. Exhales of relief were shared among the four.

However, verbally solving the riddle was not enough for unsupervised Jasmine. She needed them to demonstrate the solution. And boy, did she bring the punishment back around full circle—making sure the girls knew why they were being punished in the first place.

It was all Jeff's fault.

"No *boys*! Remember that rule?" she reminds them, with intense glares into Megan's soul. "Seems you ladies cannot get enough of knocking on wood's door. So, knock down this wood for thirty minutes and repeat, 'Sorry Big Sister Jazz,'" she demands while pointing to a tree with sharp, thorny bark.

Their bodies are aching—thighs sore and trembling from the up-and-down motion of pounding the tree, knocking on every piece of bark within reach. Trish has blood trickling down her arm and is holding back tears of pain. Jasmine takes a close look at her with slight compassion but then notices her dark blue shirt.

"Are you wearing blue?" she asks.

The girls stop their repetitive "Sorry Big Sister Jazz" chants, making sure they heard correctly. Is Trish wearing blue when it is forbidden?

Trish is terrified to respond. The wind escapes her, and she is unable to speak.

"Did you all know that Number Two was wearing blue?" Jasmine asks.

The girls remain quiet, confused as to why Trish would break Theta's most important pledging rule.

"Did I speak *Spanish*? Did you *know* Number Two was wearing blue!" she repeats.

The girls quickly fall in line, backing away from the tree, shouting with scattered replies.

"No, Big Sister Jazz!"

"Yes, Big Sister Jazz!"

"No, Big Sister Jazz!"

Megan does not respond. She is taken aback as to why Trish is wearing blue. She hadn't noticed it before, because the tint of blue was so dark in the night's light, but now she could see it clearly. Jasmine approaches Megan, aware of her lack of response.

"Are you just as shocked as I am?"

Megan is not sure if the question is rhetorical, so she remains silent, looking into the woods ahead.

"I asked a question, Number Four. Did you know Number Two was wearing blue?"

"No, Big Sister Jazz!" Megan yells.

"Take your tops off!" Jasmine abruptly demands.

The overshadowed members let out gasps of shock. The four look at each other, praying for a saving grace. One of the members pulls Jasmine aside to provide a better plan. The member notices Megan is wearing a black hoodie over a black shirt. She suggests Megan give her hoodie to Trish.

Megan does as commanded, suppressing her anger as she hands Trish her hoodie. Trish, ashamed, pulls it over her blue top, mouthing "thank yous."

With Megan's loss of warmth, the cold breeze causes her to shiver. Jasmine catches the tremors and makes the girls do push-ups to warm up. Set has now turned into a workout session. The girls are forced to perform bear crawls, jumping jacks, and mountain climbers through the wooded area.

Megan knows for sure her clothes will not survive another set. They are drenched with sweat. Her hoodie is covered in dirt due to Trish falling over during the strenuous workout.

"Fall out!" Jasmine finally yells.

The members gracefully walk away, leaving the candidates in the woods catching their breath.

Donna interrupts their cooldown by slapping Trish on the back of the head as they gather their belongings to exit the area. "What made you wear blue tonight, idiot?" she asks.

Megan and April wait anxiously for Trish's retaliation, but she does not. Instead, she admits her wrong. "I didn't have another clean black shirt."

"This is only our second set. You don't have any other black shirts?" Donna questions.

Megan, not having many choices of wardrobe herself, understands Trish's dilemma. She just has no shame in wearing the same clothes more than once. Maybe she will vocalize her empathy to Trish, but she is too tired to speak on it now. She just wants to make it to her dorm room, take a nice hot shower, and do whatever she needs to make it through the school week.

"We wouldn't be here if her boyfriend wasn't harassing us," Trish shyly points out, handing Megan her dirty hoodie.

Trish was right. Megan knows it is her fault. Jeff is the cause of tonight's punishment, and Trish's blue shirt added fuel to the flame.

"One fall, we all fall," April sings in her *I told you so* tone.

†††

It's a low-spirited Monday, and Professor Hill's lecture class has yet to begin. Students are slowly making their way to their seats. Jeff enters and notices Megan sitting at the back of the class, buried face-down in crossed arms on the desk. He slides into the chair beside her and whispers, "Not much rest?" When Megan looks up he smiles, "I can help, but you would have to use the number I gave you."

Megan does not respond. She is upset with him. He is the reason they had to run back to the room up five flights of stairs, eat noodles for lunch, and have a Sunday night set.

"I get it. I have been through something similar," he mentions, referring to his fraternity pledging process. "Let's hang out sometime; I'll teach you the fine art of ignoring me properly while pledging."

Megan's fatigue is evident. She turns toward Jeff, so badly wanting to shout the words, *Well, if you get it… leave. Me. Alone!* But his calm eyes melt her frustration away.

Instead, she softly asks, "How did you manage to survive it? It's only been two days for us, and I'm overwhelmed."

"Have you taken wood?" he asks.

She thinks about the paddle Jasmine slaps against her hand. *Is that the wood he's talking about?* she asks herself.

He doesn't explain but continues, "You'll make it through. You know you don't have to do it alone. Whether you need a joke or a drink, give me a call." Jeff gestures toward her phone tucked under her arm.

Megan misses the moment to tell Jeff to chill out; instead she gives him a grateful nod, imagining him being a comforting boyfriend. Their conversation is interrupted as Professor Hill enters the room. Jeff takes a seat a few rows up from Megan, giving her space. It's as if he knew his interaction would cause havoc with TKRho, and it was the only way to get her to show him attention. If this was his plan, it's working.

Professor Hill greets the class. "Good morning, class. Ready for the quiz?"

As Professor Hill passes out the quiz, Megan pulls out the ripped paper used as a bookmark with Jeff's number written on it and quickly sends him a text expressing her gratitude for his support.

Thank you. Lock me in. Megan.

Before she can fully digest her message, another buzz from her phone draws her attention to a text from April, adding another layer of responsibility to her already burdensome load.

Forward from TKRho: **Bring dinner to set. It's going to be a long night.**

Sighing heavily, Megan realizes that her obligations extend far beyond what she can handle. *What have I gotten myself into?* She slams her head back into her folded arms. Professor Hill slides the quiz underneath them.

"Quiz time. Not sleep time," he states.

†††

"Two more minutes!" the candidates hear as their backs are pressed against the brick foundation of the cafeteria. The line is painfully squatting with their knees extended out ninety degrees from their ankles and arms outstretched in front of them. Members of TKRho sit on nearby benches enjoying the food the candidates brought to set. April receives a weekly allowance from her mother, which she uses to purchase the requested meals.

Jasmine, throwing her half-eaten plate away in a nearby trash can, approaches the four in line, placing blindfolds in their hands.

"Do you trust me?" she asks, handing them the black cotton blindfolds.

They respond in unison, "Yes, Big Sister Jazz!"

"Then put these over your eyes," she commands.

The four stand at attention, blindfolding themselves.

"Lock up!" Jasmine demands.

The girls interlock their arms and are guided with firm hands to a destination unknown. They are led with careful precision into a nearby building. The girls stand in line with blindfolds blocking their vision. A sense of dread hangs heavy in the air, intensifying with each approaching footstep. Megan hears footsteps that sound too many to be the ten or so TKRho members. Someone else has joined them, but who?

Jasmine's authoritative voice cuts through the tension, commanding them to straighten their posture and hold their heads high. The girls comply. Suddenly, the silence shatters as they're bombarded with a blast of shouts and unexpected assaults. With swift hands, their blindfolds are removed, revealing the presence of Omega Zeta alumni chapter sorors and big sisters of TKRho from other schools and grad chapters standing before them.

Jasmine's voice cuts through the chaos, explaining the presence of the visiting sorors. "Those who stand before you are sorors from other chapters and grad chapters. They wanted to meet the fresh meat and see how tender you are. There may be a few new girls joining the line soon, most likely 'paper.' So, consider yourselves lucky you have somewhat earned our respect."

Megan's heart flutters with a sense of relief, realizing that the addition of new girls meant initiation was drawing near. She wonders what the process would be like then. Would Jasmine finally chill out?

The sorors waste no time unleashing their demands and critiques upon the initiates. Screams, yells, and shouts are loud yet unintelligible. The girls don't know if they're being asked questions or commanded to do things. Each girl has about five sorority members surrounding them. Spit flies everywhere as long, straight hair slaps them in the face.

"Number Four, what's TKRho's motto?" a graduate chapter member yells at Megan, breaking through the noise.

"That I use my trained intellect to strengthen the name of Theta Kappa Rho. To use wisdom, knowledge, and have a sound mind to wherever it leadeth me in the new day. Big Sister!" Megan recites to a woman who looks to be in her thirties, with straight hair down her back, wearing a TKRho sweatshirt and jeans, managing to steady herself in six-inch heels.

Megan is surprised she was able to memorize the motto under pressure. The many repetitive recites with April paid off. The atmosphere is overcome with an unexpected silence. Jasmine walks over to Megan, and Megan wonders if she said something wrong in the motto or if Jasmine is approaching to congratulate her.

Among the silence, a stomach growl is heard from Trish.

"Are you hungry, Number Two?" Jasmine yells.

Trish hides behind her afro and doesn't admit to the growl.

"So, you don't want to admit interrupting my set with your stomach talk." Jasmine motions for one of the members to bring four bowls with what appears to be bird food. They place a bowl in front of each candidate. "If you're hungry, eat!"

None of the candidates move.

"I said, eat!" Jasmine repeats.

"Yes, Big Sister Jazz!" the girls shout, getting down on all fours.

The members tie the girls' arms behind their backs with blindfolds. Struggling to keep their balance, they eat bird food while the members of the sorority laugh and chirp.

The girls' faces are buried in the bowls. Megan splits the shells of sunflower seeds with her tongue, spitting them out.

"Don't spit on my floor! Eat it!" a Big Sister yells.

Megan, surprised at the command, takes her time creating saliva that will make swallowing whole sunflower seeds easier to bear. She worries about Donna and the seeds getting caught in her braces.

Where's Toya to stop this madness? she wonders.

†††

Over the next few months, Megan struggles to maintain schoolwork. If she thought that joining the worship service at God's House would have been a burden her freshman year, pledging TKRho, avoiding grass, not wearing blue, neglecting her hair, and being blindfolded to random set locations topped that burden one hundred percent.

Jeff is bringing in a new line with his fraternity, so their time together has been limited. They sneak FaceTime calls and texts. If lucky, they steal quick smiles and winks in Professor Hill's class. They have also managed to sneak a few Saturday night dates outside of Atlanta to make sure no one spots them. They almost got caught sneaking back on campus one night. Megan ducked down in the passenger seat of Jeff's car riding back on campus passing the yard. Toya was looking in their direction, but nothing was ever mentioned.

Megan keeps the relationship secret so the girls don't think every set punishment is because of Jeff. April hasn't said anything about the quick phone hang-ups when she walks into the room or the long visits to the bathroom, but Megan suspects she knows about Jeff. April was all for "if one fall, we all fall," but after the months of torture she's tired of her responsibility as ace. She's ready for the process to be over with. Megan has noticed that the affirmation poster above the Williams women photo has been removed.

It's the last day of the semester and Professor Hill's lecture hall is filled with relieved students ready for the holiday break. Professor Hill addresses the class: "All right, everyone, that concludes today's session. I trust you're all looking forward to winter break. Just a quick reminder before you depart. I've submitted your grades, and they'll be available for viewing in the next twenty-four hours. Regardless of the outcome, I encourage you to take some well-deserved time off to unwind and embrace the holiday spirit."

A buzz of excitement fills the air as the students begin to gather their belongings. Jeff discreetly approaches Megan as the other students start to leave. "Text me if you need a ride home tomorrow." Megan remains silent, but the unspoken interaction between them is understood.

Professor Hill approaches Megan with his briefcase in hand, ready to exit the class for his holiday break. "I will be your new counselor moving forward," he tells her casually, then walks off.

That was weird, she thinks to herself. *Are my grades that bad or what?*

CHAPTER 5: HOME FOR THE HOLIDAYS

CHRISTMAS BREAK 2021
Megan texted Jeff, taking him up on his offer for a ride home for the holidays. They met at the Southern Atlanta South Bank parking lot that sits at the intersection of the school and the church she attends with TKRho.

It is Saturday evening, and because students are traveling home for the holidays, she hopes to stay clear of a TKRho member spotting her appearance. She is wearing her SASU lion T-shirt, black hoodie, and dingy black sneakers. She attempted to pull her hair back into a slick ponytail, but nothing is slick about it. She had no gel, and the water she used to slick her hair back dried up by the time she got to the intersection.

Walking with her suitcase across the crosswalk, she spots Jeff. He has gotten used to her lackluster appearance, understanding the stress of the underground process. He is waving her down from his black Dodge Charger parked in the first parking spot at the bank near the intersection.

Hearing her dad's voice—"Somebody ugly"—she laughs, because she was the ugly one.

Jeff's smile is gleaming, happy to see her.

They arrive at the Mahns' house, parallel parked on the front street. Megan unbuckles her seatbelt, searching for words to end their night.

Jeff turns off the roaring engine and lights, avoiding unwanted attention to their presence. Megan assumes him shutting down the vehicle means he wants to sit in the car for a while and talk before she exits. What could they talk about? The ride down to Macon was spotty with minimal conversation. Jeff was short of words. She sensed something was on his mind. Should she invite him in?

She sifts through her purse slowly as if looking for lost keys. She waits for him to break the silence.

"I needed this road trip," Jeff exhales like he's been holding his breath the whole ride. "The new line is killing me. I don't understand why these new guys don't understand that if you know your information we won't go hard on you," he says, rubbing his right hand.

Megan, relieved that the trip has gone into a nightcap, notices his bruised knuckles. She doesn't ask him about it; instead, she comes up with a plan to invite him in, to ice his hand.

"You want to come in?" Megan suggests. Jeff doesn't respond. His mind is elsewhere. She playfully adds, "...and officially meet my pops?" to lighten the mood.

Is it about Zeta Alpha Phi, or is there more to his distraction and quietness? she wonders.

"No, I'm good. We can wait a while before we do the family introductions. Enjoy your family," he says, turning the key to start the ignition.

"Are you sure? It's a two-hour drive back." Really, she wants to hear more about the bruised knuckles, anything, before he goes.

"Enjoy your family. You only get one."

Those words make her pause. Jeff knows about every Mahn member, but she knows nothing about Jeff's family. He doesn't talk much about them, and when Megan asks, he changes the subject.

After a moment of silence, Jeff starts back in, "I go hard for ZAPhi. They're all I got… I wish this new line coming in understood why I be hard on them like that…" There's so much passion in his voice that Megan wonders where all this is coming from. Maybe something happened last night? She hadn't sensed this heaviness in him yesterday.

After a long silence, Jeff admits, "I hit him." *Now we're getting to the cause of the bruised knuckles—but hit who?* "I had to show him tough love. You *must* show respect to those who care about you—and I care for those guys. They need to show me respect."

Megan notices a slight shift in Jeff's demeanor. He slouches back in his seat, chest caved in. She doesn't understand the passion behind ZAPhi or who he has hit. She waits a moment before gathering her things slowly, not knowing what to say.

Jeff senses her hesitation, straightens, and says, "Enjoy your family, Megan."

"You enjoy yours as well," she responds, hoping he'll go into more detail about his biological family and his plans for the holidays—or who he hit. But he does not. Instead, he wanders back into thought about what happened the night before.

~

"What's the ZAPhi motto?" Jeff yelled at a male standing in line, connecting at eye length in an intense stare-off.

The candidate stared Jeff in the eyes with no response. The room was still; all in attendance were waiting for a response. The smell of the candidate's meal could be smelled on his breath with a mixture of the stale hardwood lining the ZAPhi frat house floors.

"I asked you a question, bruh. What's the ZAPhi motto?"

The candidate stood firm-chested against Jeff's. He bumped Jeff with a hard thrust, challenging Jeff's position as a man of Zeta Alpha Phi Fraternity, Incorporated.

"We ain't family. Don't call me bruh." The candidate yelled back, pushing Jeff out of his space.

We ain't family. The phrase rang in Jeff's ear repeatedly.

Rage began to swell up in Jeff from his gut down to his right fist that connected to the daring candidate's left jaw. The candidate dropped back, headfirst onto the hardwood floor. Jeff blacked out and jumped on top of the candidate in full throttle. His swings connected to the guy's face—left hook followed by a right hook.

The members of ZAPhi made quick haste to the altercation, grabbing Jeff from the unconscious candidate. The guys stood in silence awaiting the candidate to respond by moving or opening his eyes. Instead, he lay stiff, and Jeff panted breaths of worry.

~

"Thanks for the ride," Megan says, interrupting Jeff's memory.

He opens his eyes, realizing he dozed off into last night's event. He exits his car, opening the trunk to pull out Megan's suitcase.

"Do you need help with it?" he asks, placing the luggage on its wheels.

Megan, uneasy from his previous silence, explains that if he is not ready to meet her parents, then she should handle the luggage from here. With less commotion at the door, her parents will not be as curious to know who dropped her off.

Megan leans into Jeff, offering the only comfort she can provide—a hug. The hug lasts for what seems like an eternity. Jeff looks up toward Megan's old room and sees the blinds shift. "We may have some watchers," he points toward the window.

Megan shakes her head, knowing it is her nosy sister, Tameka.

He gives her a kiss on the forehead and walks to the driver's seat. He clicks his seatbelt, and it's evident that he still has something on his mind. But Megan turns and approaches the Christmas-decorated porch. She takes another look at Jeff before inserting her key into the doorknob. He gives her a nod that he's okay and drives off. Megan hasn't figured out the many layers to Jeff in their few months of dating. She knows she'll get down to the bottom of it some day. Like her mother always says, "Only time will tell."

The living room of the Mahns' home is decorated like a Christmas-themed HGTV episode. The Christmas tree twinkles with themed lights, ornaments, and sprinkles of silver tinsel meticulously placed. Tina, carefully balanced on a ladder, places the star topping on the tree. James is sitting in his recliner, attentive to the football game, enjoying a glass of milk and cookies.

Megan enters the home with her luggage, no makeup, and hair tousled. Despite her fatigue, she manages to muster up excitement upon seeing her family gathered in the living room.

Tina turns toward the doorway, spotting Megan, "You're finally here!" Tina exclaims with a warm smile. She carefully steps down from the ladder and greets Megan with a big hug.

"Looks like the party hasn't started without me," Megan states with playful sarcasm.

"We were trying to wait for you to arrive. Had to put out the milk and cookies for Santa before Santa pleaded for a beer," Tina says, referring to James, who reluctantly turns away from the game to greet Megan. He's slowed up drinking beer due to his last doctor's visit. He sneaks one in occasionally, but it's a start. God works in mysterious ways. If science is used to get James to stop drinking, then so be it.

James rises from the recliner, bee-lining toward the window. "I heard a friend was dropping you off. Hope it wasn't that deep-voice boy."

He looks out the window to spot evidence of a driver. He sees no one and continues to give Megan a hug.

"Oh yeah, Jeff. How is he?" Tina asks.

"How are those grades?" James questions.

Megan nervously fidgets with her luggage, not sure how to answer either question.

"I haven't received my grades yet, but I'm sure everything's fine," she replies, sounding more confident than how she feels. She still can't figure out why Professor Hill has suddenly become her advisor. Her grades must have dropped tremendously. The wide-eyed front-seat student has turned into a nap-in-the-back-of-the-class student.

Tameka comes from upstairs, interjecting with a sigh, "Daddy, she literally just walked in. Let her catch a breath before the interrogation. And can we please take this tree down? It's not exactly biblical."

Megan is relieved by Tameka's timing and change of subject.

"Let's not get into the 'pagan Christmas' debate, Meka," Tina argues.

Tameka eyes Megan's disheveled appearance with concern. "Worm head, what happened to your hair? Yall don't do wash-and-go's, flexi rods, or twist-outs at SASU? I know we're outnumbered at the school, but I *did* see a sprinkle of afros. Somebody could have helped a sistah out."

Megan runs her fingers over her frizzy hair, full of embarrassment. "I… uh, haven't had time," she mumbles. She wasn't lying, but as long as TKRho didn't complain about her hair, then she was fine.

"I can braid your hair if you want—or a relaxer," Tameka jokes.

The thought of a relaxer was not a bad idea; maybe Megan would have more control over her mane.

Tina intervenes. "Make sure it's presentable for church next Sunday and the Christmas program. I picked out the costumes for the Christmas play. I cannot *wait* for you all to see."

"I've been attending church every Sunday at school. Can I just watch the livestream?"

"No," James interjects.

"I'm here for two weeks. Do I have to attend both Sundays and the Christmas program?" Megan argues.

"Yes, you do," he firmly states, attention back on the game, dipping his cookies into his milk.

As Megan pouts, her phone buzzes with a message from Jeff. She pulls her phone from her purse and reads the text:

Thanks again for the road trip. The holidays are hard for me. If you need a ride back, hit me up. I can use your presence. Next to it was a yellow heart emoji. Then, *Oh yeah, grades are in.*

†††

The girls share a nostalgic moment in the confines of Tameka's new room. Posters adorn the walls, reflecting Tameka's vibrant personality and newfound sense of ownership. Tameka is sitting on the bed while Megan is on the floor, propped up on a pillow for cushion, between her sister's legs.

"So, what do you think of the room? I've tried making it my own," Tameka asks, two-strand twisting Megan's hair with her new product.

"It looks good," Megan states, offering a tired compliment.

"Oh yeah, Usher boy's name is Marcus. We've been talking and stuff… Megan, what's wrong?" Tameka asks, noticing her sister's exhaustion and the disarray of her once immaculate hair strands. "You look exhausted, and you didn't even notice that I placed your keyboard over in the closet with the air mattress."

"Oh, that's where it went," Megan responds halfheartedly.

Tameka stops doing Megan's hair. She grabs Megan's chin, turning her around to face her, "What's going on with this hair?"

Megan avoids eye contact, wrestling with the weight of her secrets. She pulls her face away and stands up to retrieve her keyboard from the closet for comfort. She feels around in the closet for the stand as Tameka patiently waits for a response. Megan puts together the stand, plugs in the keyboard, and places it on top before she musters the courage to speak.

"I checked my grades today. I got a 'D' in Music Theory," Megan confesses, striking a D note on the keyboard.

Tameka's eyes widen with shock. "A 'D'? What happened? And what does that have to do with your hair looking a mess?"

Megan struggles telling her sister what is really going on at SASU. Her heart is getting heavier with every beat, and she gives in to the pressure.

She sits by her sister and says, "I can't really talk about it, but… I'm pledging in a sorority."

"A sorority? Are you trying to become a Devil Stepper?" Tameka yells.

"Shhh," Megan quickly places her hand over Tameka's mouth, quieting her from alarming their parents.

Tameka pushes her hand off. "You know those sororities low-key worship other gods," she explains. "They incorporate Greek gods into their rituals. At least, that's what I've heard on YouTube." Tameka wipes her mouth as if Megan gave her the cooties.

"I thought it would be worth it, but now… I'm failing school, and my hair is a mess. I just…" Megan trails off with uncertainty.

"Am I not sister 'hood' enough for you?" Tameka jokes.

Megan doesn't respond.

Tameka repeats herself with a serious tone. "Am I not sisterhood enough for you?"

"No!" Megan exclaims. Megan startles herself with the anger that came with that two-letter word. She didn't know she had that much pent-up anger—was that transferred energy from Jeff? Megan continues, "You get along with everyone. Everyone gravitates to you. I don't make friends like you. So, if finding a group that will accept me… requires me to sacrifice a little, then that's what I'm going to do. They're making me a better version of me."

Tameka has never heard Megan express herself this way. They sit in silence, allowing the last statement 'They're *making me a better version of me*'—to ring through the air.

Tameka, careful with her words, breaks the silence by saying, "Megan, your wellbeing is more important than any sorority… think about this… do you think God would want you suffering just to fit in with a secret?"

Megan takes a moment to ponder Tameka's words before speaking.

"Please don't tell Mom or Dad. No one can know about this, or they'll make my life a living hell."

"Make your life a living hell? What have you gotten yourself into?" Tameka stands over Megan, voicing her concern. She paces around the room, searching for words.

"And thou shalt love the Lord thy God with all thine heart, and with all thy soul, and…"

Megan cuts off Tameka's rant. "I got it, Meka!" she reassures her, stopping her from going into Pastor-Tameka mode.

"By the looks of this hair…" Tameka points at the half-finished mane.

"Meka!"

"Okay! But if anyone lays a hand on my baby sister, they're going to meet the Lord's stepper, Me Phi Meka."

She sits back down on the bed in position to finish Megan's hair. Megan adjusts comfortably back onto the pillow.

"And don't think I forgot about Mr. Black and Green," Tameka adds, parting Megan's hair for a twist. "I saw him drop you off… Why did he speed off? Was it because you haven't changed clothes since we dropped you off at SASU?" she jokes, tugging at the black hoodie.

"Let's just hope Marcus, usher boy doesn't speed off on you when Dad finds out you're dating a white guy."

"That would be the least of Dad's worries when he finds out you about to be devil stepping," Tameka jokes back.

†††

It's the Christmas Sunday service, and the Mahn family sit together in the packed church, waiting for the God's House Christmas Program. All eyes are attentive to a festive Pastor Jones. He stands at the pulpit wearing a red suit with a green bow tie, surrounded by musicians. The men are wearing synchronized red button-ups with forest green slacks. The women are adorned in red sequin tops and dresses. In front of the pastor sits a couple dressed as Mary and Joseph, holding a doll wrapped in a blanket as baby Jesus, patiently waiting for their cue.

The audience anticipates a Christmas sermon on the birth of Jesus. Pastor Jones takes his time getting to the birth and speaks on other messages, a sermon that seems to feed Megan and Tameka's souls in an unexpected way.

The girls are seated side by side, near the stage. There's no sports game on, so James does not need a quick exit to the door. They listen attentively as the pastor's words resonate.

"And as it says in Deuteronomy 6:5," Pastor Jones proclaims, "…and thou shalt love the Lord thy God, with all thine heart, and with all thy soul, and with all thy might."

Tameka and Megan gasp, exchanging a glance as the pastor's message sinks in. It was as if Pastor Jones eavesdropped on their conversation from the other night.

"Are you hearing this?" Megan whispers to Tameka.

"Yeah, it's like he's speaking directly to you… You need to repent," Tameka replies with a sense of urgency.

James glances over at the girls, whose conversation is breaking his concentration from the Word. He shuffles through his Bible, attempting to follow along.

"Now we all know this next scripture, and for this very reason we celebrate Christmas, the birth of Jesus. We don't know if December twenty-fifth is His actual birth date, but what I do know is what's said in John 3:16. 'For God so loved the world, that He gave His only begotten Son, that whosoever believeth in Him should not perish, but have everlasting life.'" Pastor Jones reads.

Whispers of "Amen," "I know that's right," and "Preach, preacher," are heard throughout the congregation.

"We're finally getting to the Christmas sermon," Megan says to herself. A vibration is felt from her purse. She unzips it and pulls out her phone. It's a message from April. "Look," Megan whispers to Tameka, showing her the message.

INITIATION IS COMING. Two-point-five GPA, recommendation letters, community service, and one thousand two hundred dollars. Be ready!

"One thousand two hundred dollars?!" Tameka mouths in disbelief. "The devil is busy, all up in the church. What are you going to do?"

Megan gives a look that's a cry for help.

"I'm not writing no recommendation letters," Tameka insists. "And I ain't got one thousand two hundred dollars."

Megan's no longer listening to Pastor Jones's message. She now worries about TKRho's initiation fee. Where will she get one thousand two hundred dollars, and who would write her recommendation letters? Megan wonders how April got the inside scoop. How did she know the initiation would finally happen? Another layer of pressure has been added to the upcoming semester.

"Lord, please make it happen," Megan silently prays.

"And whatsoever ye shall ask in My name, that will I do, that the Father may be glorified in the Son," Megan snaps back into reality as Pastor Jones reads from John 14:13.

"In Jesus' name," Megan adds to her prayer.

Tina interrupts, tapping her to pay attention to the wardrobe she picked out for the three boys dressed as the wise men, coming from the back of the church escorted by Marcus the usher. Tameka exchanges glances with him, hinting at an established relationship.

Marcus directs the boys down the aisle as they balance on canes toward the manger with Mary, Joseph, and baby Jesus.

"I preferred the red robes, but the sheets don't look too bad," Tina mentions, addressing the wise men's attire.

PART 2
OFFICIAL INTEREST

CHAPTER 6: WHO'S NEW AT SASU

SPRING 2022

Megan was relieved to approach the end of her Macon stay. Being home longer than two weeks with her family would have depleted her peace of mind. James constantly hogs the TV in his recliner, watching sports games on the screen—football, basketball, followed by baseball—and halfway through, when he has fallen asleep, the game ends up watching him. When the girls would attempt to change the channel, he would wake up yelling, "Give me that remote. The game's not over!" as if he had been fully awake. Five minutes later, he'd be back asleep, waking to the slightest adjustment of the remote's placement.

    When the television is available, usually when James is working, Megan would pretend to be highly invested in binge-worthy shows, avoiding Tameka and Tina. They would constantly fight for Megan's time, using her as a model for their interests. Tameka would pressure her into participating in MEKA Haircare product makeovers, applying every product to Megan's hair. She would record mini tutorials on how to use the products with Megan as the model and post the recordings and pictures on her social pages. Megan appreciated the mini lessons on how to use the products, but she didn't like the constant washing and styling of her hair every day for a new post.

Her free time away from creating MEKA Haircare business content was sneakily used by her mother. Tina would pose Megan as a dummy to fit her newest clothing designs. She promised quick wardrobe fittings that turned into hours of standing and being pricked with fitting pins. The positive to her fashion visits was returning to SASU with a suitcase full of Tina's designs, hair products, and a ton of out-of-season clothing Tameka no longer wore.

Megan wanted to quickly get away from the Mahns. She accepted Jeff's offer of a ride back to campus instead of Tina's, who wasn't happy about being snagged out of an Atlanta shopping trip.

Jeff arrives at the house at noon as discussed. She meets Jeff outside with her luggage, preventing an awkward meeting between him and her family. She made sure to say all her goodbyes before exiting the house. She figures it will happen organically when the time is right and when Jeff is ready. He notices her suitcase is heavier than before and jokingly pretends to pull a back muscle while lifting the luggage into the trunk of his car.

"You can blame your back spasms on my mom and Tameka," Megan laughs.

She waves bye to her sister, who is blowing air kisses from the upstairs bedroom window. Jeff, aware of their interaction, gives a gentle head nod of acknowledgment toward Tameka. In return, she bashfully waves, embarrassed at being caught smooching the air. Megan shakes her head at her sister's silliness.

Taking a quick break from the television screen, James also observes his daughter's interaction with her chauffeur. He glares from the window curtains, making sure there's no foul play.

"Foul on the play," the commentator announces on the living room television. The announcement snaps James out of his observation. He is now left with a dilemma: either interrogate Jeff's foul play outside or analyze the foul play announced in the living room.

Megan looks toward the front window of the house and catches a glimpse of the floral curtains swinging back into their original position. She assumes James has left his stalker post to make his way out of the front door to introduce himself. She rushes into the passenger seat, encouraging Jeff to follow her pace. Without allowing an organic introduction to take place, they speed off before her dad could exit the house.

"A foul? That's not a foul!" James yells at the screen, scooting back comfortably in his recliner and observing the replay. Tina walks out of the kitchen, handing him bottled water.

"Did you see Jeff? It was so sweet of him to help put her suitcase in the trunk," Tina says.

"Yeah, I saw him. Did he open her door?" James sarcastically asks, his eyes fixed on the explanation of the foul.

Tina stands in thought, scratching her head, replaying her daughter's departure with Jeff. Her face scrunches as she realizes he hadn't opened her door and begins wondering about their weird rush out of the neighborhood.

"You know what, I'm going to call her and tell her how foul that was. She didn't even introduce us," Tina says, grabbing her phone.

Tameka sashays down the stairs wearing her usual Saturday, ready-for-a-quick-social-media-post attire, adding her two cents. "Mom, don't call her yet. You'll embarrass her. Give her at least two hours to arrive on campus." Tina lowers her phone, placing it in the back pocket of her jeans.

Megan pulls her phone from her back pocket, checking it periodically, awaiting a call or text from her family about Jeff. She's aware of their curiosity, spying on her departure with him. She has never introduced a male friend to her family whom she has feelings for, but as far as she knows, they're just friends. So maybe there's no reason for her to introduce them.

The two ride back to Atlanta, engaging in hollow conversations with an elephant in the room. Megan wants to discuss Jeff's family. Had he visited them during the break? Or the incident of him hitting the ZAPhi candidate. He doesn't speak about either; instead, he talks about hitting up bars with his bros and apartment hunting.

Jeff jokes that he is looking for an apartment big enough for them both. He begins talking about their future, going into detail about what living together would look like. But she doesn't entertain the idea. She knows her family wouldn't approve of them shacking up before marriage. So, if marriage is not mentioned as a step before living together, the idea goes in one ear and out the other.

Although Jeff talks about moving in together like there is a rush, he's not offended by her silence on the topic. Megan appreciates that he doesn't pressure her into anything she isn't ready for. He's learned how to be patient with her sense of reserve and vice versa. He's willing to move at her pace, understanding there are some kinks that need to be worked out first.

Jeff insists on dropping Megan off in front of the dormitory. "I'm not having my girlfriend walk across an intersection with a suitcase twice the weight it once was just to hide from TKRho!" he laughs.

Megan's heart melts hearing him call her his girlfriend. She's been afraid to ask about their status because she has never had a boyfriend and is unaware of relationship protocol. She takes Tameka's advice that a man should lead, or in this case drive, so Megan stays in the passenger seat. In her rightful place, she allows space for Jeff to drive the relationship, permitting it to unfold how it may.

But being his girlfriend, what would this change? Does this mean she needs to schedule a family introduction since they have become more than friends? Does she have to give goodbye kisses with tongue, an act she's never done? Maybe if she was bolder, she would have had more boyfriends by now and this experience wouldn't be so confusing. Boldness with boys has never been her concern. She's never been eager to turn her crushes into boyfriends. However, she does like her new title—girlfriend.

Megan's stomach is full of fluttering butterflies. She's nervous about performing her first kiss, assuming that's what girlfriends do, but most of her nerves have developed from the possibility of a member of TKRho spotting her and Jeff's arrival together. Not wanting to disappoint Jeff, she gives in to her boyfriend's insistence of dropping her off in front of her dorm building. If it wasn't for the need for discretion, he would have carried her luggage up the five-story flight of stairs as well. The elevator has been out of order for the entire first semester, and she has no hope for its function this semester either. It has become her daily exercise.

They pull up to a parallel parking spot in front of the dormitory with the familiar label: one-hour freshman unloading. Unfamiliar faces of new students are being dropped off with hugs and kisses from parents full of happy tears.

"Look. Your twin," Jeff laughs, pointing to a tall, blonde-haired white girl struggling with luggage. She's wearing a black hoodie like the one Megan wore on her first day at SASU. The view reminds Jeff of when he first laid eyes on Megan and her family fighting with suitcases and shopping bags. He shakes his head at the memory of James yelling at him, rejecting his helping hand.

"What an intro to the Mahns," he reminisces. Megan is aware of the reference, yet she brushes it off. She's back in TKRho pledge mindset.

Hearing Big Sister Jazz's voice ringing in her ear—"No boys!"—Megan rushes out of the Charger, grabbing her heavy suitcase from the trunk without a second thought of a goodbye kiss.

Once the trunk slams shut, Jeff peels off like a speed racer in hopes that no one sees him drop her off. However, the loud screech from his tires startles those around, causing heads to turn and making his departure less inconspicuous.

Megan heads toward the glass double doors to open the door for the new blonde SASU straggler. "You must be new," Megan says. Spotting a newcomer at SASU wasn't hard to do given its small student body.

The girl takes the small balanced bag on top of her luggage and wraps it around her shoulder, tangling her shoulder-length hair in its straps. Overwhelmed by the motion, she smiles at Megan and replies, "I'm Alicia. A second-semester freshman transfer." She continues to struggle with the bag and lets out a light sigh when it finally falls into a comfortable position.

"Me too…" Megan pauses to correct herself. "Well, not a transfer, but a second-semester freshman." Laughing, she jokes, "I was in your position last semester," referring to Alicia's struggle with the luggage. "Welcome to SASU."

Megan takes notice of familiarity in Alicia's eyes. She feels as if she understands Alicia's unspoken experience. She's not sure how she could understand a stranger with such few words, but something about her feels familiar. If time allows—meaning if TKRho's pledge process allows—she would like to get to know Alicia. Maybe they could be friends. She's surprised at how easy it is for her to strike up a conversation with Alicia without nerves. Her fluttering butterflies have disappeared. Maybe she's not a loner after all. Or one loner has met another.

Megan's phone chimes. It's a text notification. Their introductions are interrupted by a forwarded message from April:

Welcome back, candidates! Set tonight. Bring food. TKRho.

Megan apologizes for the interruption and continues, "I'm Megan. Hope your semester is easier than mine." She forces a smile, placing her phone into her pocket. She walks toward the elevators in hopes of a God wink, but the girls approach them and a handwritten sign reads "Out of order."

"When are they going to fix these elevators?" Megan mumbles. "Stairs are this way." She motions for Alicia to follow.

Megan's excitement for the new semester begins to decrease as she carries her suitcase up five flights of stairs. Her mind twirls with images of the night's pledge shenanigans. Beads of sweat begin to trickle down her face. Each step reminds her of how close she is moving toward another night of yells from Jasmine and the other members that will be in attendance.

Megan approaches her floor. Trapped in her own horror of thought, she hadn't noticed Alicia struggling up the five flights of stairs behind her. Alicia places her small bag back on top of her luggage and continues to roll her suitcase to a room three doors down from Megan's.

Megan yells out before entering her room, "Welcome home, hall roomie." They smile at each other as they enter their dorms.

Megan hasn't been aware of, or eager to meet, any of the girls on her hall. TKRho required so much of her time that getting to meet people outside of April, Trish, and Donna was impossible. Megan usually keeps to herself and doesn't speak unless spoken to. But there's something about Alicia. Although they are different races, they seem to have a similar spirit—a spirit that's drawing Megan to her.

Upon entering Megan's room, her phone rings. She sees Mom appear on the screen and answers. Without getting a word in, she hears, "You are foul. Why didn't you let us meet him!"

CHAPTER 7: STEP SHOW HAZE

Spring semester is surprisingly flying by like a gentle breeze. Megan has applied the knowledge of SASU culture and TKRho patterns to her semester routine, lifting the burdens of a stressful college experience. With the adaptation to this new life, she has developed an unknown confidence. She pinches herself often to make sure her new reality is real. The old Megan would not have been able to handle Megan's new life. She's developed strong bonds with her soon-to-be line sisters and has a better understanding of Jasmine and what makes her tick. Thanks to April's inside scoop on an upcoming official initiation, Megan no longer sleeps in the back of lecture halls. If she has any chance of becoming a lady of Theta Kappa Rho, she must raise her GPA, and she's determined to do so.

    Megan is seated midway between the lecture podium and the back wall of an attentive public speaking class. She struggles to keep her eyes open. But the constant thought of not becoming a lady of

Theta Kappa Rho because of her grades forces her to be more attentive. The wooden clock that's barely hanging on its nail ticks behind her, emphasizing the drag of time. She unzips her purse to retrieve her phone, checking to see if she has received a text from April. With a blank screen and no notification, she places her phone back into the inside pocket of her purse, leaving it unzipped for easy retrieval.

A tall, easy-on-the-eye male stands in front of the class. He's wearing a white oversized T-shirt with jeans and a low, fresh faded haircut. The class is curious and focused on what he is about to say because he never speaks in class. Since the start of the semester, he has sat in the back row, hidden from view. A mysterious guy.

He's presenting a speech about the effects of social media on students. Everyone is all ears and eyes. With a deep breath, he begins.

"Social media… has… made a… huge… impact…"

Megan listens carefully to his hard-to-follow speech. She's deciphering what's taking place in front of her. Can he not read, or does he have a speech problem? The clock's ticks are heard between every word as a constant reminder of how slow time is moving.

Is this some kind of joke? This guy has a speech impediment in a class where students are required to stand and speak for what already feels like hours. He bobs his head up and down from his notes to the crowd. He hints with eye rolls and deep breaths of frustration that his speech impediment is a recent problem. He fights to get the words out faster so the twenty-minute assignment does not turn into forty, but his mouth is not catching up to his notes.

A patient female professor, Professor White, listens with undivided attention. She's snuggled in the corner of the class, appreciating the break from standing at the podium. With a smile and a gentle tone, she nods and encourages him to continue. She reminds him there's no need to rush as he fights with the ticks of the clock. The girls in the class are mesmerized by his physique and his ability to look good while struggling with his speech. He could stand in front of the class mute, and the girls would still salivate on their desks.

Megan, wishing he *was* mute, begins to wander off into her own thoughts…

I wonder when April's going to forward that TKRho message. I know they want food tonight. Fried chicken and mac n cheese. The usual. My spit would probably make the mac n cheese a little cheesier, hahaha. Eeeeew, that's disgusting, Megan, don't think like that!

She shakes her head with a scrunched-up face, agreeing with her conscience. She's aware of the face she's making and relaxes her facial muscles. She looks around to see if anyone's aware of her awkwardness. They aren't. The class is in a trance, hypnotized by mystery boy in front of the class. She turns to read the time on the ticking clock in the back of the room. It's one thirty-five.

No text yet. Hmmm. Are we not having a set tonight? Who am I kidding, we have set every weeknight.

She turns back to face the speaker, adjusting herself to assume her false sense of focus.

And where is Toya? She's been MIA. Trish heard that she's focusing on her upcoming graduation. Yeah right. She's probably just as tired of Jasmine as we are.

Megan chuckles at her own joke, disrupting a nearby female student's daze and entrapment by the speaker ahead. With a side eye, the disturbed student gives Megan an evil glare. Megan mouths, "I'm not laughing at him," swearing that her chuckle was not toward mystery boy. The two quickly settle their dispute, adjusting comfortably in their chairs. Megan continues in thought…

Where was I? Oh, yeah, where is Toya? When she's absent, TKRho's pettiness is at a hundred and Jasmine's pettiness is at a thousand. I can't believe Jasmine makes us recite the Greek alphabet backwards. I bet she can't even do it. She probably has us reciting it to remind her of what the Greek letters are.

Megan lets out a deep sigh. The angry female turns back around to Megan, giving another evil eye. Megan ignores her, continuing in thought…

STEPPING DOWN

...And now Jasmine has us slapping each other when we mess up. That's ridiculous! I would love to slap her. Who does she think she is, making April slap me because I didn't give Donna a full slap? Donna's face was already red and bruised from Trish's slap.

Megan strokes her tongue against the inside of her cheek, remembering the full-throttle slap received from April.

~

It's another pledge night in the secluded wooded area behind the cafeteria. The girls are performing the reverse Greek alphabet routine. Jasmine strikes her paddle on her hand to the beat of the alphabet shouts from the candidates as she walks down the line of intimidated girls. The girls recite the alphabet in its reversed order to the rhythm of Jasmine's strikes.

Trish yells, "Gamma!"

Donna stands next to Trish, exacerbated and ready to end the toilsome pledge. She doesn't wait for the rhythm of the paddle strike and prematurely yells out, "Alpha!" when her assigned letter is Beta. Groans are heard from the candidates in line. Alpha is Megan's assigned letter.

"So close. Yet so far. Start over. But not before Number Four slaps Number Three," Jasmine commands, motioning Megan to perform the given task.

Megan steps out of line. She stands face to face with Donna. Donna inhales deeply, closing her eyes tightly to accept the abuse. "Toughen up, Donna," Donna mumbles under her breath, embracing the punishment standing before her.

Megan uses the moon's light peeking through the wooded area to observe Donna's face. Donna's left cheek is red and appears swollen from previous slaps. Tired and somewhat delusional, Megan decides to take it easy on Donna. She gives her a limp noodle slap to the untouched cheek, giving Donna's bruised cheek a break.

"Did I tell you to go light on her?" Jasmine yells.

"No, Big Sister Jazz!" Megan responds, stepping back in line.

Jasmine, filled with rage, walks toward April and commands her to slap both Megan and Donna. "Can I count on Ace to get her girls back in line?"

"Yes, Big Sister Jazz!" April shouts, yet reluctant to slap the two. She steps out of line and positions herself in front of Donna. April is visibly upset at having to perform the command; however, she refuses to receive punishment for not obeying. Making sure her slaps are not mistaken for anything less than full throttle, April winds her wrist in preparation and performs the given order.

~

April slapped us so hard we were left with purple handprint bruises on our faces. Thank God we were excused from Sunday service. Our lies would have filled the building, answering questions from nosey churchgoers about our bruised cheeks. But observing the culture of that church, I'm sure they have a sense of its members that are pledging.

Megan's chin rests in her hand as she taps her free-hand fingers on the desk. The taps, mixed with the clock's tick, create an unwanted rhythm, capturing Professor White's attention. The taps abruptly stop, and Megan snaps her fingers as if to have an idea. Professor White clears her throat, demanding Megan pay attention, but Megan's unaware of the professor's warning glare.

"That makes perfect sense," Megan states out loud as a light bulb goes off, explaining her daydream.

"Th...thank...thank you," mystery guy responds to the assumed compliment from Megan.

That's why Jasmine began holding those makeup sessions during set. To cover up the bruises. She thinks she's slick, Megan concludes, continuing in thought.

~

The girls are blindfolded, attempting to sit comfortably at a small square metal table in the center of another unknown location. The table is covered with tons of makeup. Different brands of lipsticks, eyeshadows, foundations, and makeup brushes are stacked in the center of the table. The blindfolds are removed, and Donna's eyes light up like a Christmas tree. She's in makeup heaven, while Megan's in makeup hell.

They sit in front of mirrors held up on blue stands. There is a graduate chapter TKRho member in full-face glamour makeup pacing in front of a PowerPoint projected on a solid white wall. She manages the room as if she's a Mary Kay consultant, clicking her clicker to change the slide as she speaks with confidence and pride. She gives the candidates stern eye contact as she explains the application of makeup. Donna, unhappy with the techniques, rolls her eyes at the instructions given, causing the girls to do wall sits for minutes that feel like days.

~

Megan rubs her legs, remembering them feeling like she was training for a track meet. She looks back at the clock and sees that only eight minutes have gone by. Mystery guy is still stuttering with twelve minutes left. With inaudible words in Megan's background, she goes back to her thoughts about TKRho's makeup workshops, remembering how they were tested on cut creases, smokey eye, day eye, night eye, party eye. They'd learned about every eye occasion, but when they applied wrong, the makeup connoisseur would make them remove their makeup completely and start over. Megan had been the cause of plenty of start-overs. But what did they expect from her? She only wore concealer and tinted lip gloss, which she hadn't even been allowed to apply since the first week of school. But by the end of the training, they were pros and could work for the most prestigious makeup brand if they wanted.

Hey, that's not a bad idea. Then I could afford the food TKRho makes us bring to set. She reaches into her purse for some ChapStick and applies it to her chapped lips. The thought reminds Megan of the expected text. She pulls her phone out of her purse to see if a message has come through. She usually would have received the forwarded text by now, right after lunch.

The clock's ticks are becoming louder and slower with each passing second behind her. The professor is in the corner, waving a motion that catches Megan's eye. She's holding up her hands, indicating to the speaker that he has ten minutes left. Megan opens her camera on her phone to look at her reflection. She fluffs her twist-out into a more desirable shape wondering, *Have we entered Omega Zeta chapter underground process 2.0, where appearance is now the focus? Jasmine's so picky with our appearance that I'm starting to care about these superficial things myself! What has TKRho done to me?*

"And... that's why social media... has... made a... huge... impact," the mystery guy announces, finishing early. The class claps as the mysterious male ends his speech and disappears into the back of the room, to his hidden corner. A group of girls stand on their feet, giving him a standing ovation, while the guys root in support, thrusting fist pumps in the air.

"Megan, would you please present your rebuttal?" Professor White demands, providing Megan the floor.

Before Megan can exit from her camera app to rebut, the anticipated text flashes across her phone screen.

Forward from TKRho: **Set tonight! Bring food, water, and extra towels for the extended family.**

She places her phone in her purse, then zips it to secure its contents. She sets her purse on her vacant seat and brushes wrinkles from her clothing as she properly stands. Megan notices a change in the professor's demeanor. The professor is becoming impatient with Megan's unnecessary steps before approaching the podium. Grabbing her notes from her binder, she practices her runway walk up to the front of the room in her five-inch heels, crossing mystery boy. They have quick eye contact of acknowledgment.

"Great job," Megan lies. *Did I just look at him, in his eyes, and tell him great job? The only thing I heard from him was, 'why social media... has... made a... huge... impact.' Stop, Megan. That's wrong,* she scolds herself.

She shimmies as if to shake away jitters. Awkwardly standing at the podium, arranging her notes, she thinks back to the text message.

Bring towels for the extended family? What extended family? Oh yeah, TKRho is practicing for the step show," she remembers.

"We're ready when you are," a stern Professor White says, holding up a brown leather grade book that's now magically appeared, a gradebook that was not present during mystery boy's speech.

Megan, nervous, clears her throat and begins, "This is why... social media... has not... made a... huge... impact..."

✝✝✝

The crème de la crème steppers of Theta Kappa Rho rehearse their explosive performance for the Southern Atlanta South University annual step show. Twenty-five energized members fill the stage with chants and synchronized steps in the campus auditorium. They perform full out with determination, in hopes of receiving bragging rights of reclaiming their title as the Champion Steppers of Spring 2022, beating their rival, Mu Alpha Phi Alpha Sorority Incorporated.

"We're the ladies of TKRho
We are the best, and that's fa sho.
We are here to let you know
That MuAPhiA has got to go!"

The intimidating chants bounce off the walls of the empty nine-hundred-seat auditorium. Toya has excused herself from stepping with the girls, arguing that her focus needs to be on her studies, not memorizing steps. She sits in the front row coaching the steppers, critiquing their formations and energy. Her surprise presence minimizes Jasmine's power trip, which eases the four candidates' anxiety. Jasmine is focused on her steps, exuding confidence that shines through as she stomps across the stage, switching formations with a Theta member from another chapter with matched energy.

The step show committee has allowed TKRho members from other schools to participate due to the small number of members in SASU's Omega Zeta chapter, consisting of those who attend the nearby HBCUs where Black Greek life is held on a sacred platform. This makes Megan nervous. Will they think she's Black enough? Yearning for that same respect Black Greeks receive from the other Black students, she's so ready to exchange her credit builder card for her Black card. She recognizes a few members from the haze night when the candidates were made to eat bird food. This also makes Megan nervous.

The four candidates stand backstage at attention, toting water bottles, makeup, and towels. They patiently await the command to dab off sweat from the full-face makeup-covered steppers. Taking pride in their appearance, no stepper risked ruining the sorority's reputation as the prettiest Black girls on campus. Every stepper on stage sacrificed comfort by stepping in six-inch heels, running mascara, and enduring the hassle of applying minor touchups during their sweat sessions every five minutes.

Mu Alpha Phi Alpha Sorority, their rival, prides themselves on being the girl next door, treated like a little sister to the fraternities, unlike the pretty-girlfriend reputation TKRho has. Megan often wonders if she is pledging the wrong sorority. She admires MuAPhiA's plain Jane, sister-like appearance and is a fan of their sorority colors, red and blue. But the impression TKRho made on her during orientation was a lasting one, an impression that captivated her, attracting her to them. There was a connection. She believes the attraction was a sure sign from God, telling her this is the group she needs to join, that there is a bigger purpose, and He is going to use her in this sorority for that reason.

Megan and Trish stand backstage grateful for their task of being backstage makeup artists and towel girls, as opposed to their over-the-top petty haze sessions. This task gives them a sense of belonging—creating Champion Steppers—even if their role is to wipe off sweat and apply lipstick. Donna, on the other hand, could care less about the title of Champion Steppers; their role in assisting the steppers was still part of their pledge process, and she's ready for it to end. April prefers stepping and chanting on stage with TKRho, gaining the bragging right to be called a Champion Stepper herself.

April has committed every step to memory. Her eyes dance to the intricate moves the ladies on stage perform effortlessly. She's determined to perform with the girls next year, and if she's not on that stage, she threatens that no one will be on that stage. She does not disclose how she will fulfill her threat, but she protests ever so often that she will not let another year go by without stepping front and center as step master of TKRho.

April begged her mother for an increase in her allowance to provide food, water, and money to maintain clean towels for TKRho's step practice, in hopes that Jasmine sees her efforts and will miraculously ask her to join the steppers on stage. Jasmine has made it clear: they were not permitted to perform or attend the show. Their sole purpose is to assist TKRho in practicing for a performance the crowd shall never forget and defeat Mu Alpha Phi Alpha.

Jasmine took advantage of April's financial generosity, utilizing every penny of the increased allowance, providing members with car services and gas money to attend practice. One stepper claimed to only drink energy-focused drinks during practice instead of bottled water like the other members, so the increased allowance has also gone toward her special needs as well as for separate food for the vegans.

One night, while the four were having a hair prep sleepover in Megan and April's dorm room, Megan asked April if she could teach them a step or two. April eagerly taught the girls a few steps from practice, and, to Megan's surprise, she was shockingly good. This realization made Megan anxious to perform at the next annual step show alongside April, once they've become members of TKRho, of course. Trish, on the other hand, did not catch on as easily and expressed that stepping wasn't her forte nor her favorite part about being in a sorority.

"What is your favorite part? Why do you want to join TKRho?" April asks Trish.

The girls sit in a circle in the middle of the dorm room, exhausted from their secretive step practice. April grabs the pile of clean, unfolded white towels stacked in the corner of the room. She places them in the center of the girls, hinting for them to join her in folding the towels in preparation for TKRho's step practice.

Trish grabs a clean towel from the top of the pile. Lifting her afro resting on her forehead, she removes the sweat dripping toward her chin, stalling, giving herself time to carefully think about her response. She can feel their curious gaze. Her body begins to overheat. Providing the right answer proves her worthiness of being a lady of Theta Kappa Rho. After a moment of wiping her sweat and pondering her response, she tells them that she wants to join because of the good TKRho does for the community, hoping her response is acceptable.

TRISH

Trish walks the long way home from high school, fighting the blistering Chicago wind, her books clutched tight beneath her oversized bubble coat. Thanksgiving break is finally here, but its relief feels out of reach. With every step, she prays for a solution, because as the oldest of three, she's learned to fill the gaps no one asks her to fill.

It won't be like this forever.

The words replay from that morning—her parents yelling about money, her siblings crying, doors shutting to muffle the sound. Her father storming out with his brown paper lunch and hard hat. Her mother sobbing over last night's spaghetti and meatballs. Trish rubbing her back, saying, *We don't need it*, even though she didn't know what *it* was. Her mother whispering the same promise again.

It won't be like this forever.

Trish doesn't know what that means. Divorce. More bills. Another impossible adjustment. She only knows that someone has to fix it, and somehow, that someone feels like her.

Her parents won't let her work. School is her job. A full ride to college or nothing. When she earns one to SASU, the family celebrates—but celebration doesn't erase the problem. It only sharpens it. So Trish does what she's always done: she minimizes herself. Pulls her afro low over her eyes. Becomes invisible.

That's when she sees the crowd.

A block from home, outside the community rec center, bundled bodies breathing clouds into the cold November air. Blue everywhere. Families lined up. Women passing out turkeys.

"Trish! Come get your family a turkey, girl—it's free!" Mrs. King her neighbor, waves from the line, wrapped in a blanket beside her husband.

Trish hesitates, guilt flooding back—earlier that day, poking at her reduced Thanksgiving lunch, complaining when she had no right. Hospital bills. Activities. One income. How dare she complain?

What could it hurt?

She stands in line nearly an hour as the sky darkens, her parents too busy arguing to notice she's late. When she asks who the women are, Mrs. King says, "Theta Kappa Rho. They do this every year. Real wholesome women."

Trish watches them—beautiful, polished, draped in baby blue and royal blue, scarves, jackets jeweled with birds and names. When it's her turn, a woman hands her a turkey and asks if one is enough. Trish says yes. The woman gives her another anyway.

Then she smiles. "You are a delight. That afro of yours is gorgeous and bold."

Bold. No one has ever said that to her.

"I'm Sharice," the woman says. "Come back and see us. And remember—it won't be like this forever."

The words land differently this time.

At home, Trish walks into the middle of another argument, two turkeys in her arms, books balanced on her head like a pageant queen. The room freezes. Then laughter breaks out. For one moment, the tension lifts. For one moment, there is peace.

That night, lying in bed, Trish understands something new. If a turkey could bring this much relief, imagine what belonging to women like that could do. Women who show up. Women who give. Women who say *it won't be like this forever* and mean it.

That's when Trish decides: if those ladies were giving away turkeys, they weren't struggling to receive them.

Those women were rich.

And she wanted in.

~

"So that night I pledged to myself that until I could hide behind TKRho's colors, I'm going to hide behind my afro," Trish jokes to lighten the mood, with tears of joy swelling up in her eyes. She tugs at her afro, stretching its length for full coverage, ashamed of the sentiment the question has revealed.

"What was it that your family couldn't afford, when your dad stormed out?" Donna asks.

Megan, folding a towel, kicks Donna's leg that's stretched out toward the middle of the floor, hinting that her question is irrelevant to the point of Trish's story.

Prompting Trish not to answer, Megan diverts the attention over to Donna, who's still catching her breath from the intense steps they learned while rubbing her kicked leg.

"What about you, Donna?" Megan asks. "Why do you want to join TKRho?"

Donna sits up, reaching for a clean towel to wipe her sweat that has yet to dry. Her reach is interrupted by April throwing her the used towel from Trish, preventing her from dirtying a clean one. She takes the towel and wipes the sweat dripping down her bare arms.

"I wanted older sisters that would have my back and show me how to be a girl. My mother passed away when I was ten."

DONNA

Donna walked into the hair salon in downtown Atlanta like she was stepping into a test she hadn't studied for. It was peak hour—women gossiping, mirrors glowing, licenses and family photos lining the walls. She pushed through the glass door, the bell ringing beneath a sign that promised, *Come in one way, leave out another.* She clung to that.

She needed a change.

Neo soul floated through the salon, calming her racing thoughts. In a few months she'd be a freshman at SASU, and she didn't want to walk that campus as the same tomboy with split ends and braces. She wanted something low maintenance. Something healthy. Something womanly.

Her mother used to bring her here before picture day, back when the hair fairy still existed—back when cancer hadn't taken her away. Back when Donna's hair behaved. Sitting in the waiting area brought all of it back.

She thought about her brothers, all three of them who never had to worry about hair. Brush it or don't. Go. Donna skipped breakfast more times than she could count just trying to tame hers. Ponytails. Cornrows. Baby hairs she refused to spend extra minutes on. Now everyone else was growing up, and she felt stuck in between.

That's when she saw her.

A woman walked in wearing a royal blue hat with blue jays stitched across it. Taking her seat in the waiting area, she removes her hat, revealing a low, outgrown cut—bold, clean, unmistakably feminine. Gold jewelry. Red-bottom pumps. Confidence. The woman looked like something Donna didn't know she was allowed to become.

The stylist asked Donna what she wanted. She stared at her reflection, panicked.

"I need a change."

"When a woman cuts her hair, she's due for one ," the woman said from the waiting area. "Coco Chanel."

Donna didn't think. She just pointed. "How about her haircut?"

The room paused. Then the stylist smiled. "Go big or go home."

The woman smiled at Donna as she took her seat in the stylist's chair for her appointment. "You have the face for it."

Donna wasn't sure she believed that. She spent the wait scrolling makeup tutorials, wondering how to look like a woman with short hair instead of a boy. Then it was her turn.

The cape settled over her shoulders like a hug. Her mother's hug. The clippers buzzed. Hair fell. Donna cried—soft tears she didn't bother hiding. She remembered her mother shaving her own head for chemo. That was it. This wasn't just a haircut. This was a dedication.

"Give her a full-face makeover before she leaves," the stylist said.

Donna laughed through tears when she saw herself. Who knew a makeover could turn a tomboy into a woman?

~

Folding towels with the girls, Donna finished the story quietly. "My dad did the best he could," she said. "But TKRho showed me how to be a woman. When I learned there were over one hundred thousand women in that sisterhood, I knew I wanted to be one of them."

"Who was the woman?" Megan asked.

"I don't know," Donna said. "But she was wearing blue jays… and she chirped."

Trish smiled. "She was one of us."

Donna dabbed her eyes. "If I ever see her again, I'm going to tell her she changed my life."

"Toughen up," April teased, swiping her low cut.

Donna laughed and tossed a towel at her.

April caught it like a mic, already standing, reaching for the photo on her nightstand—ready to tell her own story next.

APRIL

"Don't you dare look at them!" April's mother snaps as a group of women in red and blue—Mu Alpha Phi Alpha—stroll past during the SASU homecoming parade.

April stands wedged between her mother, aunt, and grandmother, all of them dripped in TKRho apparel, waiting to cheer. She sneaks another peek anyway. The sorority across the street is stepping—sharp, intricate, electric. April mirrors their hand slaps, their stomps, mesmerized.

Then—*smack*.

"You will not disrespect this family," her mother hisses. "Do not look, talk, or acquaint yourself with those girls. You hear me? Our family built something they would never understand. My great-grandmother would roll over in her grave if she saw you showing them respect. Straighten up. Remember where you come from."

April blinks back tears in her eighth-grade eyes. From that moment on, she understands: TKRho is not just a sorority. It is family. Legacy. Obligation. She will not be the one to dishonor what her great-great-grandmother built. There is no other way.

~

"So," April says now, lowering the towel from her mouth, "I'm legacy. My mother shall have it no other way."

She waits for applause. It does not come. Instead, the room goes quiet. The girls exchange looks—not moved, but softened. Joining TKRho is not a choice for April. It is a demand. If she doesn't cross, she'll be cut off.

Sensing the shift, April adds quickly, "But I'm lucky to be online with you all. I wouldn't trade our bond for any other." She tosses the towel to Megan. "Your turn. Why do you want to be a lady of TKRho?"

Megan stands, gripping the towel like a microphone. "I've never fit into a group," she says. "So when TKRho showed interest in me, I wanted to experience the sisterhood."

Her voice cracks. "I wasn't supposed to cry, dang."

"Use the towel," Trish says gently.

Megan dabs her eye. "I believe that if a group can finally show interest in me, then why not return that interest?" She shrugs.

April steps forward. Then Trish. Then Donna. They surround Megan, pulling her into a tight, sisterly hug—laughing, crying, holding onto the thing they have all been searching for.

Belonging. Identity. Sisters.

"We sweated our hairstyles out and cried our faces off," April jokes, eyeing their reflection.

"Towels! Now!" Jasmine yells.

"Yes, Big Sister Jazz!" The girls scatter, rushing back to duty.

"Y'all need to tighten up that last formation!" Toya calls from the front row.

And just like that, the moment folds back into motion. Their bond has been sealed, their stories told, the line still moving forward.

CHAPTER 8: A STEP SHOW DISCOVERY

Two long, strenuous weeks of TKRho step practice have passed. The time has arrived for Greek organizations to show SASU step show attendees who's who amongst the Greeks. The show is full of diss chants toward rivals, acrobatics, strolls, and lots of intricate steps.

A crowd of college students bunch together in front of the locked auditorium's double steel doors, accompanied by SASU and Greek alumni, chanting playful diss chants while awaiting the highly anticipated show. Graduate members of Greek organizations wear their paraphernalia, while SASU alumni are adorned in the school's colors with lions plastered on their attire, and the general public anxiously waits for the doors to open.

Megan, April, Trish, and Donna quickly fulfill their duties as TKRho's step show assistants, stacking towels, applying makeup, and fully stocking the dressing room with water bottles and electrolyte drinks. "One hour till eight!" a male shouts outside the dressing room, announcing the cue for the candidates to leave the premises.

They exit the auditorium through a hidden door, down a narrow walkway leading to the back of the auditorium. April oversees the girls' dismissal, making sure they are not seen by anyone in attendance at the show. Jasmine made it very clear they were not to breathe air of the step show, inside or out of the building. But the girls couldn't resist.

Turning their Saturday into a girls' hangout, they rush to their rooms to change from their all-black attire into camouflage. It was Donna's idea for the girls to wear green camo to blend in with the scenery, pressuring them into hiding behind a bush that sits upon a hill overlooking the entrance of the event. With no pushback, the girls agreed to have a little fun.

It's seven thirty, and the girls squat behind a single bush, waiting for the doors to open. They observe the crowd talking amongst themselves. A loud male call is heard, imitating an ape. Eight guys, in line according to height, wearing black hoodies and green khakis, respond to the call. The men, with concealed faces, step and hop in unison through the crowd, demanding their attention. The crowd is in an uproar with surprise. It's the new line from Zeta Alpha Phi.

The guys' presence creates a huge open area, like a flash dance show. The crowd circles around them, neglecting their place in line.

Zeta Alpha Phi seamlessly hid the preparation of the new line's probate show. Megan was aware that a line was underway; however, Jeff never gave her a timeline or hint they were nearing the end of their pledge process. Megan is realizing that everything's so secretive, even to girlfriends. On the bright side, maybe now she can spend more time with him, since he's no longer pledging new members. The last couple of weeks have been busy. They've only been able to see each other for a few minutes a day through video calling and quick text responses.

Jeff steps out through the crowd with an explosive ape call of command to the Zeta Alpha Phi neophytes. He stands proud in front of the line, with his head held high, wearing his ZAPhi shirt imprinted with a line name on the back: "SMOOTH J." She's never seen him wear that shirt and has never paid much attention to his nickname. It's fitting.

Like a proud girlfriend, Megan wants so badly to run down and give him a big hug and congratulate him on crossing the new line, but she can't. They aren't supposed to be there.

The step tease amps the crowd for more. They begin chanting for an encore to see ZAPhi's official performance on stage. Megan begins to ponder how awesome it would have been to have their probate during this time as well. Then maybe she would have been able to participate in the show herself—or at least watch it. But with the delay of the interest meeting April promises, those hopes are deferred.

"This is so wack! If it wasn't for us assisting TKRho, they wouldn't even be ready for the show. We can't even watch from the stands or hand them towels backstage," Donna complains.

"We'll be there next year, and we'll be better because I will be step-master. It's going to be so dope," April exclaims. Filled with excitement, she stands, letting out a loud "CHIIIRP," overwhelmed with the thought of being next year's step master.

"Get down, stupid," Donna whispers, pulling April down and lowering her behind the bush. April, trying to keep her balance, giggles as she stoops behind Trish.

Toya, in the crowd below, turns in their direction, looking for the familiar call. She points toward Trish's afro sticking out from behind the single bush. "Why is our call coming from over there?" she asks a graduate group of TKRho members. With confused faces, they begin walking toward the afro to reveal the person who announced their call.

The four girls tighten up behind the shared bush, hoping to hide behind Trish's magical invisible afro. "We can't wait here and let them see us. Let's go," Trish concludes.

"Good idea. If they find out it was us chirping, we'll never hear the end of it," April adds.

Before the girls can run off, ZAPhi begins to recite:
"I thank whatever gods may be.
For my unconquerable soul.
I am the master of my fate:
I am the captain of my soul," followed by their call.

The crowd roars into another outburst. Toya and the graduate members are distracted by the yells of excitement and turn back toward the crowd, engulfed in the uproar. The guys do their signature moves, transitioning to another formation. Jeff, along with his bros, unveils the neophytes.

The eight men introduce themselves, removing their hoods in exhilaration. The crowd notices that the sixth guy in line has slurred speech. *It's the mystery guy.* The guy from Megan's speech class.

He stands there with confidence as Jeff pats him on the back, welcoming him into the brotherhood.

The audience couldn't make out half the words number six was saying, but they all heard him proudly say that his name was, "Tony, a man of Zeta Alpha Phi Fraternity Incorporated!"

Jeff never mentioned a guy with a speech impediment on the line. He complained about the line, but never about Number Six's speech, Megan thinks to herself.

April's phone chimes:

SET TONIGHT AFTER THE STEP SHOW! I SEE YOU. BIG DUMMIES!

April shows the girls the message.

They immediately run from the hiding spot to their rooms to change from their camo into set attire, then to the secluded area behind the cafeteria, all in thirty minutes. They weren't sure of the step show's ending, so they decided to wait at the meetup, in line, for what felt like an eternity of time.

"Don't lock your knees," they remind themselves, so no one would topple over.

The girls are terrified to move. They're not sure when Jasmine will arrive. "Did she forget?" Trish manages to whisper.

The girls do not budge or entertain the question. They're afraid that if they move from their post, punishment will be worse. Crickets loudly sing as footsteps approach the girls from behind. Jasmine stumbles into the girls' view along with two other TKRho members. Toya is not with them. The big sisters are visibly intoxicated, with the smell of alcohol on their breaths. Apparently, the girls went to the ZAPhi party held after the step show. It's midnight. Giving an exact set time would have been courteous, but given their big sisters' appearance, responsibility and courtesy left them hours ago.

Jasmine takes sips of her drink from a red Solo cup while keeping a close watch on the girls. It's clear that Jasmine is drunk. Toya not being present gives Jasmine leeway to overreact yet again—irrationally.

Megan feels her heart throbbing through her hoodie. She takes deep, slow breaths to slow her heartbeat. She's never been around an intoxicated person whom she believes is unhinged. Her dad drinks beer, but not enough to drastically alter his mindset. She's only seen movies of unhinged drunks, and Jasmine's mannerisms fit the character description. Drunk Jasmine terrifies her, and she's not sure what Jasmine is capable of at this point.

Megan begins to pray, *Lord, please help us make it through this set safely and unharmed. If You do, I will do whatever You ask of me.*

"You were at the step show after I ordered you not to be there," Jasmine slurs, walking in a zigzag down the line of terrified girls. She looks around the woods as if the trees are giving her an idea for their punishment. All the punishments they've endured flash in a sequence in Megan's memory: the exercising, eating bird food, the slaps and bruises, the Greek alphabet.

With a punishment in mind, Jasmine takes another sip of her drink and slowly turns toward the four. "Since you want to step so bad… I want you to learn the show's steps. Learn step by step every move and formation we did tonight. I want to see it performed at the next set. Fallout!"

"Yes, Big Sister Jazz!" they shout in unison.

The girls, in awe of the light punishment, quickly dismiss and rapidly walk away. When they are clear from Jasmine's sight, they let out sighs of relief. They dare not ask questions after the fallout was called. If so, their set would have included every flash memory that came to Megan's mind.

"Was that a joke?" Trish asks in disbelief.

"Let's not wait around to find out. Come back to our room to perfect these steps," April responds.

The issue wasn't learning the steps. They'd already learned most of the show from what April taught them the other night. The issue was completing this assignment along with SASU's assigned weekend homework. If an official interest meeting was approaching, they needed to focus on their schoolwork to maintain a 2.5 GPA, not Big Sister Jazz's assignments.

Scrolling online, Donna lucked up and found a recording of the full step show posted an hour after it ended. Although the girls knew the steps, they needed to watch for precision, formations, and specifics of stepping right versus left.

They took several breaks during their practice to watch the other sororities' and fraternities' performances. When Zeta Alpha Phi stomped into formation on the screen, they noticed the new line performing along with them.

April, taking notice of Tony, mentions how cute he is. "If his speech was straight, I'd holla."

"It's rumored that his speech impediment came from pledging, but no more information has been released. Everyone's so hush-hush about it," Trish says.

Megan's antennas go up. *Does Jeff have anything to do with it? He mentioned hitting someone but not causing a speech impediment.*

Donna, standing in the middle of the room, not giving the rumor much thought, reflects on the ease of the night's set. "We should start bringing alcohol to set. Maybe Jasmine will ease up."

"I would be down for that," April agrees.

Donna rewinds back to TKRho's performance, stepping along with the video. She's relieved to have a head start on the routine. Trish attempts to join in, but the speed of the performance is too fast.

"I'm having a hard time taking this all in," she states as she sits on Megan's bed, frustrated, taking a quick breather before returning to the fast-paced steps. Defeated, she asks, "April, how do you know for sure initiation is approaching?"

April joins Trish on the bed, leaving Donna alone to practice with the video. She explains that her mother attended a graduate chapter meeting, and the interest meeting was mentioned. Her mother began hounding her about her grades and accumulating community service hours.

When on break for the holidays, she also overheard her mother speaking to the TKRho advisor, planning the interest meeting. Her mom would speak softly and take the call to another room when dates were discussed. The calls were frequent, implying that an interest meeting would be this semester.

This was Megan's first time hearing about an advisor. She hadn't given thought to Jasmine and the girls having a boss. Someone over them? Advising?

Megan's phone rings. It's a FaceTime call from Jeff. She's been so caught up in TKRho that she forgot to call or send Jeff a congratulations text. She quickly grabs her phone and scurries toward the door, hiding the name appearing on the screen.

"Don't be long. We got to have this down by tomorrow," Donna yells after her.

Megan exits the room into the hallway.

"Hey, beautiful," Jeff smiles from ear to ear on the screen. He's had a few drinks, but he's handling himself well, unlike Jasmine. A party can be seen behind him, with ape calls and yells off-screen.

Three figures shuffle down Megan's dorm hall. It's Alicia, being carried down the hall by two guys in Zeta Zeta Pi T-shirts, her arms draped over their shoulders. There is yellowish vomit stained on the front of her white T-shirt. Her legs drag along the hallway carpet, and her hair is stuck together from either sweat or vomit—Megan can't tell.

The guys pull her key out of her side pocket and unlock her room door, dragging her inside. Megan looks on in worry, keeping a keen eye on the room to see when the guys exit. She plans to give the situation two minutes, assuming they will place her comfortably in her bed and exit the room.

"Hey, that's your twin," Jeff states, managing to recognize the familiar face in Megan's background. "She looks like she was at that Zeta Zeta Pi frat party. They're getting loose at that house. I walked by and saw kegs everywhere. Is she trying to pledge?"

"I don't know. Why?"

"You may want to tell her not to party too much. That may hurt her chances of getting a bid."

A bid? What's that? Megan ponders to herself.

Her thoughts are interrupted by the two frat boys running out of Alicia's room, disappearing down the hall. Noticing the quick drop-off, Megan's relieved that Alicia is in her room safely—or so she hopes.

"I didn't see you at the show. And you're not at this party," Jeff says, playfully looking around as if searching for her at his location. "We brought out the line I was telling you about. Them boys made me proud," he boasts with a huge grin.

"We weren't allowed to come to the show, but I did see the new line. They did good."

"How did you see the probate if you weren't at the show?"

"We have our ways, SMOOTH J," she teases.

"Oh, you spying on me," Jeff laughs.

"How come you never told me your nickname?"

"It's on all my jackets and shirts. You don't pay attention to nothing but TKRho, huh?" he says, laughing while taking a sip from his Solo cup.

"Well, how come you never told me about the guy with the speech impediment?" she continues her interrogation, seeing that he is more open with alcohol. "I believe he's number six?"

"That's Tony. He's the truth," Jeff states, as if a proud father.

Megan patiently waits for more, letting the silence breathe.

"Megan, they made a last-minute change to a step. Come on!" Donna whispers in exclamation, sticking her head through the room door and peeking into the hallway.

"I'll let you go," Jeff insists. "Give me a call tomorrow. Oh, wait—it *is* tomorrow," Jeff smiles. He's right. It's two a.m.

Megan closes the FaceTime call and quickly walks back to the room. What a pointless conversation. She's left with no answers about Tony, and no lead on whether Jeff had anything to do with his speech problem. She notices that Jeff seemed happier than ever before. The line crossing was a huge deal to him, and Tony looked proud in his ZAPhi paraphernalia.

Maybe it's nothing.

But a new worry comes over Megan.

Is Alicia okay?

CHAPTER 9: RUSH WEEK REALIZATIONS

RUSH WEEK is posted boldly on the SASU marquee sign. It's a warm, sunny Monday afternoon after a morning of thunderous rain. The campus is covered with laminated, rainproof Greek rush flyers posted on every available surface. Greek organizations are in attendance, with tables adorned with colorful balloons representing their groups, lined along the wet campus sidewalks. Greek members hand out brochures filled with organization information and upcoming rush events. Interested applicants crowd around their prospective organization tables while familiar songs blast through the campus speakers, adding to the campus energy.

Rush Week is where the Panhellenic Council (PHC) and the Interfraternity Council (IFC) Greek organizations begin their process to seek out new members. Potential members are encouraged to believe they're choosing the organization that best suits their interests, while the organization sizes up the potentials to see who best fits theirs.

First impressions are important. Appearance is important. Reputation is important.

April explains to Megan how the National Pan-Hellenic Council pledging process is different from the bidding and preferencing that tends to happen with Rush. Megan recognizes the word *bid*—the term Jeff mentioned on the video call during Alicia's discreet drop-off. Megan's still unclear what the word means, but more importantly, she's unclear about what happened that night with Alicia and whether she's okay. Megan hasn't seen her on campus or near the dorms. She's been meaning to check on her, but life's been lifing.

April's explanation of the Rush process leaves Megan confused. If she had to depend on bidding and preferencing, she would never join a sorority. With April's guidance, being seen by Theta Kappa Rho was a breeze. Somehow, the big sisters received her number and invited her to an underground pledge that has consumed her college experience.

The Black Greek organizations of SASU participate in Rush Week, giving them an idea of the newbies on campus who are interested by keeping a close watch, sizing up beforehand who may appear at the interest meeting.

Megan and April maneuver through the crowded sidewalk, striding in six-inch heels. Their faces are bare of makeup. Their hair is freshly styled and hydrated with moisture from Tameka's haircare products, free of extensions. Megan wears Tameka's hand-me-down business casual clothing from her holiday trip home. The new rags have given Megan a sense of confidence—a confidence she hadn't had first semester.

The girls spot TKRho's table across the dewy grass. April informs Megan not to approach the table, as they are actively involved in the pre-pledge process. Showing interest during Rush Week would put eagle eyes on them and their involvement. Instead, she tells Megan to keep a close watch for hidden flyers. Interest meeting flyers are usually hidden under other flyers or posted on tiny sections of school bulletin boards, preventing an overwhelming number of interested girls. Keeping recruitment at four would be ideal to continue the above-ground process.

Theta Kappa Rho's table is covered in royal and baby blue paraphernalia, with statues of bluejays and pamphlets. Jasmine sits at the table, staring at Patrice, the first candidate to drop line in the unofficial underground process. Patrice stands in front of the members, practically begging them to give her another chance. She's wearing a blue sundress with heels, proudly showing how well she would represent Theta Kappa Rho.

"I guess she left set early that night before hearing Jasmine's rule about wearing the colors," April jokes as they subtly walk past the table.

Jasmine stands up angrily, directing Patrice away from the table. The members of TKRho stand in solidarity with Jasmine as Patrice storms off. Megan and April quickly pass by the commotion, avoiding eye contact.

Megan's left confused as to why Patrice would be willing to give the sorority another chance, knowing there is a process to enter. She starts a conversation to deviate from the altercation.

"I'm going to talk to Professor Hill since he's my counselor now. Maybe he can provide me with some makeup work to bring up my GPA. I'll need a job to pay for that one thousand two hundred dollar initiation fee, plus recommendation letters..." She trails off, realizing that her deviation from the altercation has detoured into stress.

A new reality hits her. She doesn't have everything together for the official interest meeting April constantly speaks about. The date of the interest meeting is still in the air, but April promises it will be this semester, per her mother's pressure.

Patrice crosses between the girls, visibly upset, almost knocking them over. April loses her balance. "Excuse you!" she snaps without hesitation. Patrice keeps walking, ignoring the rage. Heels are heard aggressively slinking against the sidewalk.

"That's their advisor," April whispers, pointing toward a woman walking up to the TKRho table.

Jasmine and the girls shift their demeanors as if a commotion had not just taken place. Seeing the advisor on campus makes an official initiation a reality. It's for sure approaching, because the woman April mentioned speaking to her mother on the phone is here on campus—manifested in physical form. She stands tall among the girls with an air of confidence. Looking at the group, one could tell she has authority. Jasmine's demeanor is that of a quiet mouse next to her advisor.

After a few deep breaths and realizing they have a bigger issue at hand—an upcoming interest meeting—April continues the conversation. "Maybe you can look into getting a cash advance on a credit card. My mom says when those initiation letters go out, we have two weeks to turn everything in."

"What if you have everything and still don't get in?"

"Why wouldn't you? If you don't have everything together, then you've wasted your time pledging. They wouldn't put you through all this if they didn't want you," April responds.

She was right. If a sorority didn't see potential in you becoming a member, they wouldn't risk taking you through a process to prove your allegiance. And it's a huge risk. Chapters can be suspended, not allowed to make their presence known on campus. No more royal or baby blue bluejay paraphernalia or chirps if that happened.

"This is stressful. My parents don't know I'm pledging," Megan admits.

"…And they shouldn't."

"My sister said she's not helping with money or a recommendation."

"How and why does your sister know you need money and a recommendation?" April asks.

"Long story," Megan mumbles. She continues before April can ask further questions. "I still need fifteen hours of community service, a C-plus average, money, and I can't wear my concealer while gathering all this," she attempts a joke as they walk in silence, contemplating a plan.

April receives a notification on her phone. It's a text from TKRho: *Zeta Alpha Phi Spring Kickoff Party Saturday night. Wear sexy black. TKRho.* April forwards the message to the group chat. Megan reads the forwarded message.

"Why black?"

April shrugs.

"Anyway, I have the perfect black dress with pockets. Tameka—" She's interrupted by a light-skinned girl wearing pink and blue sorority paraphernalia. The girl could easily pass as a white female if her blonde hair texture hadn't given away her African roots. She hands them a flyer with the Greek words Gamma Alpha Alpha Phi boldly printed across its heading. Megan looks over the flyer, curious as to what their process may entail.

"Is it as hard as TKRho? Do I need a 2.5 GPA? Do they do that bidding and preferencing thing?" she wonders out loud.

April snatches the flyer from her hand, quickly throwing it in a nearby trash can. She glances over at the TKRho table to see if any of the members saw what had just transpired. They didn't. They were huddled around their advisor, focused on something else grabbing their attention.

†††

Megan sits in Professor Hill's wooden-themed office. She grips the armrest with her unpolished, low-cut nails. Blood rushes to her fingertips as she waits nervously for a solution to improve her GPA. The room is decorated with music certificates, trophies, and small golden instruments adorning the tan-colored walls. Music usually calms Megan, but Professor Hill's musical office atmosphere gives no comfort to the nerves TKRho has bestowed upon her.

Professor Hill sits across from her at an oversized desk full of loosely structured papers and folders. He flips through a grade book labeled *Music Theory Fall 2021*. Looking over his thin-framed glasses, he scans Megan's semester assignments and grades. After spotting what he's searching for, he addresses Megan. "You can redo your tonal theory essay, but the highest you can get is a 'B.' That should bring up your GPA."

He closes the grade book, placing it on top of a stack of ungraded papers, examining Megan's discomfort. "How did your first semester treat you, besides my class?"

"It was fine," she responds. She keeps her retort short, avoiding what he's really asking. Becoming self-aware of her tense finger grip, she loosens the armrest and clasps her hands in her lap.

"Not too many freshmen are capable of diving into their major studies first year," Professor Hill adds. "Was it too much for you?"

"No. I'm determined to graduate in four years. Being awarded a partial scholarship, I figured I should dive into it."

"Is that why you're requesting makeup work? You don't want to lose your scholarship?" Professor Hill rubs his white beard with gentle strokes, as if it's the trick to summoning a response.

Megan gives a quick head nod to avoid a verbal lie. She's hoping Professor Hill doesn't see through her false response, but his beard-stroking makes her more nervous. She grabs the armrest to regain her center.

Due to his knowledge of Rush and secret underground pledging, he assumes that's the real reason she's desperate for an increased GPA. Students tend to get overwhelmed during these events. He receives more student visits seeking makeup work advice for Greek organizations than during finals week. The students never reveal their pledging involvement, but he knows why they sit across his desk, gripping the armrest with looks of plea.

"You don't have that same energy as the girl who walked into my class the first week of fall semester. You were attentive, aware, and sharp. I've seen a decrease in your enthusiasm for music. Do you want to talk about anything not related to your schoolwork?" he asks with genuine concern.

She ponders his question, filling the room with silence. With TKRho occupying Megan's time, she has forgotten that music was the main reason she attends SASU. Pledging has been so time-consuming that she only has time to eat, sleep, and pledge. When she thinks of music, it's only in terms of raising her grades to become a member of TKRho. She had hopes of joining the church worship team, but instead she sits in church observing how the sororities coordinate their Sunday's best paraphernalia.

Although the room is silent, her thoughts are loud. *Should I give in and allow the counselor to counsel me on how to balance pledging while maintaining my grades? Maybe he will understand my struggle. Maybe he will feel sorry for me and write my recommendation letter.*

She breaks the silence with a mild joke. "I took my braids out after the first week of school. Maybe that was my decrease in energy. I removed a lot of weight," she states, forcing a chuckle. She playfully fluffs her braid-out hairstyle, directing attention from her changed attitude to her changed hair.

Giving in to Megan's avoidance, Professor Hill agrees. "Yes, maybe that's it."

"Thanks for allowing a redo on the tonal theory paper. I'll have it in ASAP," she responds quickly, turning toward the door to exit.

He acknowledges her deflection, giving her space to discuss the real issue when she's ready. "I know I'm just your counselor, and an old man, but I was also Greek once upon a time," he adds with a warm smile.

She takes his statement into consideration as she exits his office. *Did I say something to give my Greek involvement away?*

Megan steps into the hallway. Her phone rings with a video call notification. It's her mother. She's grateful for the timing of the call. It prevents any further conversation if Professor Hill were to follow her into the hallway to talk more about Greek life and her involvement.

"Hey, Ma," she answers with relief.

"Hey, Megan. What are you doing?"

"I just finished talking to my counselor—"

"Hey, do you know a girl named Alicia?" Tina interrupts, segueing quickly into the real reason she called.

"I believe I do. Why?"

"Small world. Her parents go to our church. We were gathered at Saturday prayer service, and we prayed over our children, you included. Her mom mentioned she had a daughter that goes to your school. A transfer freshman."

"I don't know her, but we met once."

"Oh, okay. What did you talk to your counselor about?"

Careful not to lead the conversation toward TKRho or her GPA affecting her scholarship and giving her father a heart attack, Megan searches for an outlet to avoid answering the question. "Are you working on something new?" she deflects, looking into her mother's background on the phone screen. She spots a red dress she likes.

"Yes, I am. Do you like it? I've been working on my designs more since your father got a raise. God's been so good. If you haven't gained pounds, I can measure it to your size if you'd like."

"Yes, please do. I like that one." She spots Jasmine walking toward her in the hallway. "Ma, I have to go," she whispers quickly, ending the call. Even though she isn't on set where phones are forbidden, Megan feels awkward having her phone in Jasmine's vicinity.

Jasmine struts by, hair blowing in the wind, without saying a word, avoiding eye contact. Megan lets out a sigh of relief, but a small flutter of fear appears in her stomach. *Was I supposed to speak?* she wonders.

She receives a text notification: **Hope everything's okay. Love you. Mom.**

✝✝✝

The four candidates briskly walk half a mile from campus to the Zeta Alpha Phi fraternity house. They carry their heels in hand, avoiding premature ankle aches at the highly anticipated Spring Kickoff. The girls are amazed at the house's brick structure sitting on the corner lot adjacent to SASU student apartments. It stands two stories high, with its Greek lettering engraved above its patio. The outside is clean and quiet, while the inside hosts its first spring semester party.

It's Megan's first time visiting a frat house—or any Greek house, for that matter—leaving her curious to know the location of Theta Kappa Rho's house, if there is one.

The girls enter the party in their sexy black dresses, five- and six-inch heels, and minimal makeup. Taking advantage of the option to wear foundation tonight, Donna applied hers to resemble a full-face contour, but the beats from the speakers, the humidity-filled room, and her thrusting dance moves have turned her two-toned contour into one solid shade covered with sweat stains.

Sweaty college students dance to the DJ's tunes. Everyone maneuvers through the crowd, trying not to spill red Solo cups full of Phi juice. Spirits are high as they dance and mingle among each other. The DJ booth is elevated above the crowd in the corner of the room. His voice echoes through the air, welcoming students to ZAPhi's Spring Kickoff Party and hyping up the crowd's excitement.

The Black Greek organizations stroll in their distinctive attire. Sororities move seductively, while fraternities hop around the room with synchronized steps. Some students of other races and Greek affiliations are in attendance, getting a feel for Black Greek culture.

Megan and the girls post up in front of a table covered with cups of alcohol along the wall adjacent to the DJ booth. Donna sneaks a sip of Phi juice from an unclaimed cup on the table and passes it to April. April, without question, takes a sip. She makes sure to drink only when offered, proving control of her intake while also showing she's not afraid of a little alcohol.

April passes the cup to Trish, who scrunches her face in rejection. Megan catches the expression, unsure whether the scrunch is from not wanting to drink after Donna and April from a stranger's cup or from despising the taste of alcohol. After the rejection, April passes it to Megan. Megan declines the drink as well and instead sips water from her cup—a cup she's held onto the entire time they've been there.

She protects her water as if her life depends on it—and, per her sister's advice, it does. "Never leave your cup unattended at a party," Tameka had told her.

April lectures that drinking water from a Solo cup isn't a good idea. It could be mistaken for alcohol if their big sisters were to see, but the only cups the party provides are red Solo cups. What is Megan supposed to do? Drink water from her hands and pass out from dehydration?

She doesn't drink alcohol, and no other liquid is provided except faucet water. Of all waters, she's forced to drink bathroom faucet water from a Solo cup to stay hydrated in the hot box of a frat house. She reasons that if a big sister calls her out, she'll prove it's water by keeping a small amount in her cup. She periodically refills it when the long line of bathroom users wrapped around the corner shortens, just in case a big sister challenges her.

The kitchen is blocked off with yellow caution tape for what appears to be ZAPhi's VIP section. Megan would have loved an invitation to that area. There's space to move around, a refrigerator seemingly full of bottled water, and most importantly, Jeff. However, enjoying the VIP section with him would cause suspicion of their relationship, so standing in front of the Solo-cup-filled table by the DJ booth is her best option.

"If your cup's empty, head over to the bar and refill it with that Phi juice made by the boys of Zeta Alpha Phi!" the DJ announces.

His voice is drowned out by yells from the crowd and the startup of the next song.

Donna glances at the drinks on the table, realizing she has taste-tested every empty cup. She scans the room to see if any big sisters are headed toward the alcohol. She sees none and tiptoes to the bar to grab her own Phi juice.

"This next song is for ZAPhi!" the DJ announces.

Members of ZAPhi collect from their destinations like roaches, gathering in the middle of the room. The crowd creates space for them to stroll to their signature song. The new line of neophytes strolls with the prophyte members of Zeta Alpha Phi.

The girls salivate over Tony with the speech impediment. Who knew being in a fraternity could erase your flaws? Megan watches, envying the attention Tony's getting.

Behind Tony is Jeff, shimmying his shoulders to the groove. Megan's attention immediately shifts from envy to admiration. His presence commands the dance floor as he moves with precision alongside his fraternity brothers. He intentionally directs his flirtatious movements toward Megan.

She often questions why he's so drawn to her. She feels like she's in a fairytale. The cool guy never shows interest in the loser girl. Not even the nerdy guy likes the loser girl. She wonders if it's a pledge joke and if TKRho is pranking her—using the frat boy to show her interest, only to embarrass her in front of the SASU student body.

Maybe they're pulling a *She's All That*—a bet to get the hot guy, Zack, to date the nerdy girl, Lancy, with six weeks to turn her into prom queen—and Megan is Laney. Megan and Tameka would often spend Saturday nights reciting every word of that movie.

Realizing how obnoxious and cruel that joke would be, Megan shakes the thought and reciprocates Jeff's flirtation with smiles and laughs as she sips water from her Solo cup, disguised as Phi juice.

Jasmine, standing nearby in observation of the party's vibe, observes the exchange between Megan and Jeff. She instantly sends a text message to April. April finds it easier to forward the message to the girls rather than explain three times what the incoming message from Jasmine reads. Megan separates the vibration of her phone from the vibration of the music in the room. She pulls her phone from her dress pocket to read the message.

Forward from Dean of Pledges: **SET LOCATION NOW! TKRho**

Upon receiving the text message, the girls make worried eye contact amongst each other. Donna, making it back from the bar, approaches the four.

"Let's go!" she yells over the speakers, downing her drink.

Megan places her cup of water on the table next to Donna's and follows the girls out of the house. They run half a mile back to campus with heels in hand to their set location.

"We need to address a serious breach of rules," Jasmine demands, pacing in front of her sorors. By the finger taps on their red Solo cups, it appears they're not happy with their Spring Kickoff being interrupted by this breach of rules either. They line up behind Jasmine, gripping their cups, holding their stance like bulls ready to charge, expressions full of fury as Jasmine addresses the four.

Could the sorors be angry because they had to leave the party before strolling to their theme song? Did they see Donna at the bar requesting Phi juice? Is Donna's makeup too much?

Toya stands to the right of Jasmine in attire giving hint she has been awakened from a good night's rest. Toya's attendance brings Megan comfort and hope of good news. Maybe TKRho will announce an official initiation around the corner, or a pause in the gruesome pledge process after Jasmine addresses the breach.

"I knew one of you was going to mess up a good night," Jasmine states, scolding the candidates in the secluded wooded area behind the cafeteria. "Good thing you're all wearing black. Dressed ready for set," Jasmine continues as she extends her arm holding a purse. "Phones in. Now!"

The girls quickly rush to place their phones in the royal blue purse covered with blue jays. They fall back in line, still unclear as to why they have been called to this unscheduled set. Jasmine's gaze is fixed on Megan. Nervousness comes over her.

Megan wanders into thought. *Is this about my phone conversation with my mother outside of Professor Hill's office? Is tonight's set my fault?*

"Number Four has been fraternizing with wood during your underground process, which is strictly forbidden," Jasmine reveals, her eyes fixated on Megan, whose heart is pounding in her knees.

That's the reason this meeting was called? Is Jeff the wood she's referring to? We were just smiling at each other. I can't help it if he strolls with passion, Megan admits to herself.

"And drinking alcohol, which is also forbidden," Jasmine adds.

Megan drops her head, wondering how to explain her reasoning for handling a Solo cup at the Spring Kickoff. She can feel April's *I told you so* energy bullets being shot at her from the head of the line. How could she convince the big sisters it was water? The proof was left behind on the table back at the party.

"Hold your head up!" Toya commands through tired eyes. "As ladies of TKRho, we own our wrongs with pride."

"I'm sorry, Big Sister! It won't happen again!" Megan shouts. *Agree with thine adversary quickly.* She remembers a scripture her dad recites often from Matthew 5:25. She isn't sure what it means, but it tends to get her out of trouble, and this feels like the perfect moment to practice what the scripture preaches.

Jasmine steps up to Megan, face to face, noses nearly touching. The smell of alcohol fills the space between them.

"I know it won't happen again, because after tonight you wouldn't want to be around wood or drink Phi juice again until you cross TKRho. That's if you cross TKRho. Do I make myself clear?"

"Yes, Big Sister Jazz!" Megan shouts, holding her breath to avoid inhaling the foul alcohol stench coming from the back of Jasmine's throat.

"Why are you adding new rules? We can't drink Phi juice now?" Donna boldly questions, slightly tipsy.

Megan sees Donna swaying in her peripheral, battling the effects of the cup she downed before their exit from the party. While rushing to the pop-up set, the girls decided to keep their heels off. Good thing, because Donna can barely stand up straight with bare feet. She would have toppled over like a sawed tree if she were wearing them.

"Did I grant you permission to speak, Baldy Brace?" Jasmine shouts, storming over to Donna.

Megan is relieved to breathe in fresh air.

"Since you want to drink Phi juice so bad…" Jasmine snaps at four TKRho members standing nearby to approach the candidates with their drinks. Each girl is handed a full cup of Phi juice. "Drink!" Jasmine yells.

Donna proudly takes the drink. "Finally," she mumbles. She downs it like a pro, trying to prove to Jasmine that it's a stupid rule and she can handle her alcohol.

Trish takes her cup, coughing between every sip as if smoking a cigarette. Again, Megan's not sure if Trish's coughs are due to her being a germaphobe or simply hating the taste.

April is quiet while performing the task, emptying the contents of her cup with no pushback.

Megan, unsure how to feel about the punishment, slowly takes her sips, discovering she's not a fan of the drink. However, it's not as bad as Tameka claims alcohol to be. Tameka says it tastes like cough syrup, alters your mind, and isn't worth the headache you get afterward. From the taste alone, Megan knows for sure this Phi juice isn't worth the pounding headache the candidates are experiencing right now.

Toya stands among the girls as they struggle with their drinks. "Rules are rules, and the consequences must be enforced," she says, her tone implying she's forced to be in attendance and would prefer to be somewhere else, like a warm, cozy bed.

Toya suddenly begins to gag with pulsating movements and rushes off into the woods. The candidates dare not look in her direction, or Big Sister Jazz would have something to say. Jasmine ignores Toya's behavior and adds more nonsense to the punishment. She walks down the line, collecting their empty cups.

"Each of you will hug and kiss a tree of your choice for nineteen minutes and ten seconds. Let's get all your sexual desires out, shall we. You can thank Number Four for this make-out session also."

I bet she couldn't wait for Toya to leave to come up with this one, Megan convinces herself.

"Are you serious?" April exclaims in disbelief.

Jasmine turns to April and states, "We can't let your black sexy dresses go to waste. YES, I AM SERIOUS! You can either make out with wood or take wood. Which do you prefer?"

She retorts sharply, slapping the wooden paddle that has magically appeared in her hand. The line is shushed by the slaps of the paddle, wondering where it appeared from. It's now known to Megan that *taking wood* means being hit with a wooden paddle. She made sure to research its meaning after Jeff asked about it. At the time, she wasn't sure if she had received wood, but it's clear she hasn't—and she's hoping none of them ever will.

Jasmine continues through the line's silence.

"Thanks to your ace speaking out of turn, another nineteen minutes and ten seconds has been added to your make-out session."

She adjusts the time on her phone and motions the girls to proceed. The girls reluctantly disperse to find their designated trees. Time begins ticking as they obediently press their lips against the rough bark, enduring the punishment.

"Time is ticking, keep on licking," Jasmine yells over her stopwatch. The members observe the session, pointing, laughing, and mocking the candidates' motions. "I need to see tongue!"

Unbeknownst to them, Patrice, who has been lurking nearby, captures the make-out session on her phone.

"If I can't get into TKRho, none of them will," she mutters to herself as she scurries off to deliver the incriminating evidence to Dean Jackson.

†††

Megan stands in front of the jewel-bedazzled trim mirror hanging on the girls' dorm room door. She cautiously applies ointment to her cracked lips, preparing for Sunday's church service.

"That tree did not kiss back, and my feet are angry," she moans in frustration to April. "You hear me?" she asks, realizing she's been talking to herself all morning.

April has committed her morning to giving Megan the silent treatment, blaming her for last night's punishment. She's furious that Megan was flirting with Jeff and was caught holding her cup of water mistaken for alcohol after she warned her not to.

April shuffles through her closet, looking for an outfit acceptable for church service—one that doesn't go against pledging rules.

"No blue!" Big Sister Jazz's voice rings in her ears every morning while deciding what to wear.

Breaking her silence, April lets out a heavy sigh.

"I'm so sick of these stupid games. At this point, it's humiliation."

She scans her hopeless closet. She's not in the mood to wear anything she owns. She closes her eyes, slowly inhaling and exhaling, debating whether to rip the Band-Aid off. After a long pause, she does.

"And why are you openly flirting with Jeff and drinking from that cup when I told you not to?" she asks, glaring into Megan's soul.

Feeling the heat radiating from April's eyes, Megan whines, "It was water."

She purposefully ignores the first part of April's question. Megan then cups her hands in a mock prayer and lifts her head toward the ceiling, trying to conjure a laugh. "Please, dear God, put a stop to this TKRho craziness. We just want to make connections, have sisterhood, and look good doing it." She lowers her hands and observes April's unmoved expression. The air is tense.

April's rebuttal is interrupted by a sudden knock at the door. Relieved to break the tension, Megan rushes to open it. A folded, typed letter with TKRho emblems stamped at the top right corner falls to the ground.

The girls freeze, wondering if it's the invite letter to TKRho's official initiation process. Finally. Did Toya's run into the woods delay the announcement?

They stand in silence. A feather could be heard if dropped.

Megan opens the letter. It's addressed to all female students. The contents spell out unexpected news: Theta Kappa Rho Incorporated has been suspended from campus until further notice.

"God heard my prayer!" Megan exclaims in disbelief at her newfound freedom. "We're free… I can get my braids back! I can openly date Jeff!"

She rejoices, somewhat shocked she admitted her feelings out loud. She tosses the note to April, who stands frozen in alarm.

"Is this a joke?" April asks, her voice filled with disbelief.

Suddenly, April's phone lights up with a message: ***The line has been dropped. Theta Kappa Rho has been suspended. Forward to others and DELETE.***

April forwards the message to the line.

Reviewing the confirmation, April shouts, "No church!" with relief. Suddenly energized, she pulls a blue dress from her closet—a dress her mother gave her to wear once she crossed TKRho. She holds it against her body, posing with raised eyebrows.

"I dare you to," Megan challenges.

"Bet," April replies. "Forget church. I'm wearing this to brunch. You coming?"

It's obvious the news has erased her anger toward Megan.

"No, I'm going to see if Tameka can braid my hair," Megan responds, calling her sister to set up an appointment.

April, bursting with energy, finishes getting dressed for brunch. She picks up her family photo, kisses the frame, and says, "Sorry, great-great granny."

She rushes out, slamming the door and sending the bedazzled mirror swaying.

†††

Jeff sits anxiously at a white-clothed table, centered with a flickering candle, in the softly lit ambiance of SASU's neighborhood five-star restaurant. He awaits Megan's late arrival, twiddling his fingers along the tablecloth arranged for two.

The pressure of this dinner date creates familiar nerves, similar to the close call of meeting Megan's parents. That morning, he transferred his nervous energy into lifting her suitcase, hiding discomfort behind his trunk. Megan's rush from the front of the Mahns' house brought him relief, but the pressure of their first official date as a couple—since calling Megan his girlfriend—creates unshakable nerves.

He's mustered boldness to express what this new title requires. It's time to uncover truths he's been afraid to communicate. Time to build the kind of trust that deserves a real kiss—a kiss he hasn't pressured Megan into giving.

Megan enters, sporting newly adorned braids and a red dress with heels he's watched her masterfully learn to walk in. She rushes to the table, placing her purse near the candle.

Jeff's eyes light up with genuine delight. They share a moment lost in each other's embrace. A scent of burnt leather fills the air.

"Oh shoot!" Megan exclaims, pulling her purse strap from the candle. He laughs.

"First week Megan is here. The braids are back!" Jeff acknowledges, pulling out Megan's chair. Megan could have walked into the restaurant bald, and he still would have adored her. She makes him feel safe and secure, giving him a safe space to reveal his secrets. Tonight.

"I had my sister come by and hook me up," Megan replies with confidence, pulling her braids over her shoulder, showing off her sister's handiwork.

"Is that war paint and lashes?" Jeff teases, admiring her makeup.

With all the classes TKRho provided on makeup, she thought this would be the perfect time to put the skill into practice. Tameka helped with the final touches. Her red dress measures perfectly to show off her curves. Megan is coming fully into her womanhood and acknowledges the positive influence pledging TKRho has brought to her confidence. She is dressed in a way she would never have dressed before. Being told not to wear makeup made her want to explore the magic of makeup even more. She sees how it enhances her natural beauty, and the confidence that envelops her is undeniable.

"Don't get comfortable with your jokes. I'm just happy I can enhance my natural beauty now," Megan retorts.

"If you like it, I love it!" Jeff says, settling back into his seat as the waiter approaches.

"I'll have water," Megan requests.

"Same," Jeff adds, nodding to the timid waiter, who departs to fetch their drinks.

"Nice vibe," Megan says, scanning the upscale restaurant.

They sit next to a window like the Black Ken and Barbie, on display for the many stragglers walking by. When Tameka dropped Megan off at the restaurant after their four-hour hair-braiding session, she noticed Jeff sitting at the table, fiddling with the centerpiece candle and adjusting its placement. Seeing him so nervous prompted her to give Megan a quick tutorial on how to calm his nerves—with a kiss. She gave Megan the first degree on how to be a girlfriend, offering professional tips now that her relationship with Marcus is out in the open and official.

"I do what I do. Zeta Alpha Phi style," Jeff remarks proudly, responding to Megan's restaurant compliment by flashing his fraternity hand signals with a huge grin plastered on his face.

The timid waiter comes back with water filled to the brim. He places the glasses in front of the two, motioning that he'll be back to take their orders. Megan slowly lifts her glass, cautious not to spill it, and takes a sip.

"I wonder if this water is from a faucet, Zeta Alpha Phi style?" she jokes. Kind of.

Megan notices Jeff's attention to detail in his wardrobe. His shirt under his blazer is freshly ironed, and he has placed a diamond stud in his left ear that matches the cuff links on his blazer, a bold choice for a college student. Megan has always admired his style, but tonight he must have gone to the back of his closet for his best suit. She assumes he's as excited as she is not to have to hide their relationship. Complete freedom. Why not pull out the best outfit? It was a celebration.

"How do you feel about TKRho being suspended?" he asks, shifting to a serious note.

"I really don't know, but I'm free. I don't have to worry about Jasmine watching every move I make," Megan replies with a sense of relief.

"When TKRho gets off suspension, best believe they're remembering everything they see while on suspension. Big Sister Jazz is probably somewhere watching us now," Jeff remarks, glancing around the restaurant and jokingly lifting the white tablecloth to look under the table for Jasmine. "You still haven't taken wood, have you?" he asks, his tone calming into seriousness as he releases the tablecloth.

"No. Thank God. I think TKRho being off the yard is my sign not to join."

"Why you say that?"

"My pastor's sermons back home have been talking about having no other gods and worshipping other gods," Megan confides.

"What does that have to do with TKRho?" Jeff asks in confusion.

"I'm still trying to figure that out. My sister mentioned something about Greek gods being worshipped in these organizations," Megan explains.

"Don't get into all that. Think about all the community service we do. I joined Zeta Alpha Phi because of its brotherhood. Not even Jesus can separate me from my bros."

His statement is a little off-putting to Megan, producing a furrowed brow that she quickly releases. *Is this the same Jeff who's at church clapping and praising Jesus on Sundays?* Holding her thoughts captive, she asks, "Why do you go so hard for ZAPhi?"

Jeff takes a moment and a deep breath before revealing one of the truths that initiated the invitation to this date.

"I've been in the system since I was five," he starts. "My foster parents saw me as a check. A punching bag. So I found love in the streets. A place to release anger. I sold drugs here and there. Nothing big, just dime bags to get quick cash. I got into fights and hung with the wrong crowd. Stuff like that. When I was in high school, my counselor enrolled me in a program led by Zeta Alpha Phi. I looked up to those guys. They cared about my future more than I did. They showed me not all Black men are destined for prison or getting shot. They're the reason I'm at SASU, getting college away from that lifestyle. I owe 'em everything. That's why I go so hard for 'em," he says, holding back tears.

Megan is relieved to finally hear about Jeff's background.

"That night I dropped you off in Macon," he continues. "I didn't tell you the full story of what happened when I hit that guy on line."

There's silence. Megan is careful not to break it, or he may change the subject, so she lets him continue when he's ready. Jeff takes a sip of water, wetting his dry throat, and with another deep breath, he resumes.

"I knocked him unconscious because of my anger."

Megan cups her hands over her mouth. "What happened to him?" she asks, remembering that night's conversation. Putting two and two together, she knows this has something to do with Tony.

Jeff looks around the restaurant for the waiter to take their orders, which they're not prepared for. Revealing his truth makes him uncomfortable, but her genuine concern reminds him she's his safe space.

"I found out the next day he stayed overnight in the hospital. So I went to visit him… Tony… to apologize. He said he was okay… through slurred speech. That's when I realized what I did hurt him more than the hit itself, causing cerebellum damage and temporary speech issues."

Megan's hand is still covering her widened mouth. She's in shock, forcing herself to say something.

"Can't you go to jail for something like this?" she whispers, leaning into the centerpiece.

"Yes, but that's why I love ZAPhi. We have each other's backs. We're family. After what I did, Tony still wanted to be a part of the family. No charges were pressed because we don't snitch on family. That's what he pledged for… what I pledged for."

"But he could have died."

"But he didn't die."

"Thank God," Megan praises.

"No. Thank the bruhs. They were able to drop him off at a hospital in time. That's why I was tripping that night I dropped you off. I was scared. When he told me not to call him 'family' after all I did to bring his line in, I blacked out. I get it—we weren't family then, but we're family now, and this incident has made our family bond stronger."

This gives Megan some clarity on why talking about family has been so hard for Jeff: He never had one. But his logic and definition of family don't make sense to her. Fighting for a false sense of family gave Tony brain damage and caused a speech problem, while ZAPhi acts like nothing happened.

"Zeta Alpha Phi is one of the best things that has ever happened to me... besides you," Jeff states, assuring his affection for Megan.

Megan stares at him, wondering if this is a red flag. Does Jeff have anger issues? Will he put his hands on her? Is she in his life to show him what true family values are? "Boy, please." She lets out a nervous laugh, agreeing to change the subject that's made her uncomfortable, hiding the seriousness of the issue.

"I'm serious. You see how I stroll with you in mind. I got the best of both worlds," Jeff chuckles, relieved to have revealed his secrets, yet unaware of how uncomfortable they've made Megan.

"You strolling with me in mind got my line in trouble. You know we had to tongue-kiss trees because of you?" she jokes back.

But in her mind, Megan's thoughts are racing. *Is this the end of the conversation about Tony? Is Zeta Alpha Phi okay with what happened in their pledging process? Does the Dean know?* Megan's train of thought is interrupted by the waiter, ready to take their order.

"Can we have a few more minutes? We haven't even looked at the menus," Jeff apologizes, earning a nod of understanding from the waiter.

As Megan looks at the menu, Jeff's gaze softens with sincerity. "Will you be ready when TKRho gets off suspension? Your GPA? Initiation fee?" he inquires.

"I'm working on it," Megan replies, hoping her determination shines through her uncertainty. After hearing this, she's not sure of her safety with TKRho. If Jasmine gets out of hand with her paddle, could someone end up in the hospital—or worse, dead?

"If you need me, I got you on the fee. Can't help with them grades though," Jeff offers.

Megan snaps out of her what-ifs and asks, "Why would you do that for me?"

"Because when I saw you in church with no weaves, no war paint, and funky breath, I knew you were the one," Jeff confesses with a playful grin.

"Shut up. We were allowed to brush our teeth on line," Megan says with a laugh, still uneasy about what Jeff has revealed in tonight's conversation. She signals to the waiter that they're ready to order. The sooner the date is over, the sooner she can have quiet time to reflect on everything that's been revealed—the things that give her second thoughts about Jeff's goodnight kiss.

†††

Enjoying free evenings away from TKRho and set torture, Megan is able to dive into her first love: music. She's joined the church music ministry, alternating Sundays playing the keyboard. She receives uncertain stares from Jasmine and other TKRho members as they clap along to her melodies, wearing non-Greek attire. They praise with slightly lifted hands in the pews, exposed in their identities. Their confidence is nowhere to be found among a room of Greeks proudly wearing their paraphernalia as a badge and reminder of being active on campus. They receive constant taunts and disses from Mu Alpha Phi Alpha, happily wearing their red and blue.

Megan's tightly clenched, judgmental grip on Jeff's disclosed secrets has loosened. Jeff and Tony's fight seems to have been the best thing that could have happened to their family bond. Tony enters class with his head held high, wearing his ZAPhi attire, excited and well prepared to recite his speech assignments. He's made it very clear—after receiving standing ovations—that being in Professor White's speech class has helped him tremendously regain confidence in his speech. Megan has to agree. His stutters are few, and his confidence is undeniable. It's apparent most of his confidence comes from being in a fraternity.

Megan overhears a few of his replies to interested ZAPhi potentials in class, inquiring about the fraternity process. He responds without stutter that he's happy to be a member and wouldn't change its process for the world. From his consistent stance on the secretive intake process, Megan decides to take her foot off the worry brake and allow the boys to enjoy their family, no longer questioning Jeff's moral character.

Jeff has been attending weekly anger-management sessions with a therapist. This gives Megan confidence in their relationship, slowly eliminating a red flag that once existed. However, one red flag remains. She questions his loyalty to God when she sees him worship in church. She catches glimpses of shoulder shimmies exchanged between his brothers as they sneak in stroll moves to the worship music. *Not even Jesus can separate me from my bros* replays in her head, but she hasn't found the boldness to approach Jeff about the statement. Maybe she's overreacting. He was emotional that night and proving how dedicated he was to the fraternity. *Maybe he didn't mean it*, Megan reminds herself.

However, she's excited to express herself in blue attire. She knows deep down that in the presence of Theta Kappa Rho, they're raging inside because of her wardrobe choices, but she'll cross that bridge when and if they return to campus. Spring semester is almost over, and summer will erase the memories of her rebellion.

The dorm hall is peaceful, with minimal sleepovers from April, Trish, and Donna, and Megan is loving her long, hot showers—showers she can enjoy without being exhausted from late-night pledging or rushed by cold morning showers due to overused shared water.

Before calling it a night, Megan grabs her see-through shower bag filled with items Tameka brought during her hair-braiding visit and takes a well-needed trip to the dorm showers. In the usual Wednesday night quiet hall, a suspicious commotion comes from

Alicia's room. Megan tiptoes toward the chaotic whispers, then halts, acknowledging her forgetful nature. She forgot to check on Alicia the night she was spotted intoxicated, limp and carried to her room by frat guys. Megan hasn't been able to speak to the transfer student due to differing class schedules. She's been meaning to catch up, ask how campus life is going, and discuss their parents attending the same church in Macon.

Whatever is happening on the other side of Alicia's door, Megan believes now is the time to muster boldness and ask one of those icebreaking questions. She resumes her tiptoed steps and peers through the slightly ajar door. The unusual sound comes from a small group of girls circling a subject.

Megan's eyes adjust to the darkness filling the room. She spots Gamma Alpha Alpha Phi lettering printed on the backs of white T-shirts worn by mostly blonde-haired girls. Their focus is on a subject seated with hands tied behind her back. Buckets of water are held overhead and slowly poured onto the blindfolded girl, who lets out small stutters of a chant. Water splashes onto the carpet as the sorority jumps backward to avoid getting wet, yelling angry whispers at the subject.

Megan sifts through the sorority members to get a better look and sees Alicia.

Why is Alicia blindfolded in her own room? That doesn't make any sense. Does she not know it's Gamma Alpha Alpha Phi giving her a bucket bath? Megan wonders, entranced by the scene. The haze unfolding in the building where she sleeps is a complete shock. At least TKRho meets in secluded areas and blindfolds them while escorting them elsewhere. If TKRho pledged where Megan slept, she'd have nightmares for sure.

It's evident Megan doesn't know much about white sorority culture and is learning about BGLOs, but she thought only Black sororities went through these humiliating rituals, proving allegiance to Black pledging culture. What a surprise. She's been so involved in

TKRho that she never noticed the underground hazing happening all around her—until now.

Megan flashes back to a hand offering her a flyer during Rush Week that April immediately threw away. It was from Gamma Alpha Alpha Phi. This sorority. Megan locks eyes with one of the girls, who quickly walks over with an intense stare and slams the door shut. It's the same girl from her flashback—the Black girl who could easily pass as white. With her kinky, curly blonde hair straightened, she blended in without question.

Megan continues toward the bathroom with her shower supplies in hand, seeing the world through newly opened eyes that reveal a hidden sorority culture. With this new weight, she's unsure if pursuing sorority life is something she wants to continue. If TKRho gets back on the yard, will she resume the pledge process? Will she continue the process April proudly declares has existed since TKRho's founding?

April once mentioned a few girls dying from swimming in the ocean during a pledge process, but Megan never thought it would hit so close to home. Gamma Alpha Alpha Phi was practically drowning Alicia.

Why was she trying so hard to fit in with a group like that? Why do I need to fit in so badly? Megan asks herself.

CHAPTER 10: THE BANK ENCOUNTER

SUMMER BREAK 2022

April gleams at the news of SASU student apartments offering a first-year rental sale for summer break. With minimal convincing, she entices Megan into sharing a small, quaint two-bedroom, one-bath apartment. Megan admits that sharing a bathroom with one person is far better than her previous situation, and having a room with a door she can close for privacy feels like heaven.

April's mother agrees to pay her half of the first six months' rent. Her continued interest in TKRho determines what payment plan accrues afterward—one of the many perks of maintaining their family legacy.

Jeff moves into an apartment close enough for quick commutes to his final-year elective courses, yet far from the overwhelmed campus life. Mentions of Megan moving in with him rent-free surface often. "It would be the perfect pre-graduation gift," he jokes, usually followed by a shove from Megan. Her dad would have a fit if she moved in with Jeff or even entertained the idea. She had to fight him to cough up half the deposit and half of her first and last months' rent. After arguing he won't continue paying for tuition *and* rent, Megan is forced to find work. Going from having no expenses to now covering rent and groceries, she definitely needs a job.

Megan's job hunt stays within walking distance of the apartment. Within fifteen minutes, she spots the bank where Jeff met her during her winter break visit home. Carrying a manila folder of printed résumés, she lifts her right black pant leg—matching the black blazer her mother tailored—and carefully steps over the curb, eyes drawn to the NOW HIRING sign displayed in the front window of Southern Atlanta South Bank.

Inside the professionally lit establishment, she notices a straight-laced Black woman, appearing to be in her thirties, with straight hair pulled back into a bun. Megan assumes she's the manager, the only one buried in paperwork while others assist clients. Megan approaches the back office, knocks on the open door, and clears her throat.

"Excuse me, I saw the sign outside that said you're hiring?" Megan asks politely.

"We are," the manager replies, eyes fixed on the paperwork.

Megan notices a Theta Kappa Rho bag tucked into a corner cubby. Could this be a sign from God? Though Theta Kappa Rho is suspended, the shared interest can't be ignored. Megan can't resist commenting.

"That's a nice Theta Kappa Rho Incorporated bag you have," she says, carefully pronouncing each Greek letter.

The manager looks up, studying Megan with a keen eye, assessing her like a potential sorority candidate. She scans Megan's appearance from shoes to braided topknot. Satisfied with her minimal yet professional presentation, she leans back with a smile.

"Are you a soror?" she asks.

"Not yet," Megan replies.

Not yet? Megan internally chastises herself. She sounds desperate. The manager's smile fades, and regret washes over Megan. She's broken the first rule April taught her at freshman orientation: *Showing too much interest will put a target on your back. They can smell it like sharks smell blood in water.*

Megan stands frozen, waiting for a response as the warning echoes in her mind. As her thoughts spiral, the possibility that this manager is the graduate chapter soror present during their bird-food punishment overwhelms her.

Could she be the soror who asked—

~

"Number Four, what's TKRho's motto?!" a graduate chapter member yelled, breaking through the noise.

"That I use my trained intellect to strengthen the name of Theta Kappa Rho, to use wisdom, knowledge, and have a sound mind to wherever it leadeth me in the new day. Big Sister!" Megan recited to a woman in her thirties, hair worn straight down her back, dressed in a TKRho sweatshirt and jeans.

~

If it is her, Megan's appearance is totally different. She wouldn't be able to recognize her under the light makeup she so perfectly applied and the braids Tameka has done, making sure every strand was tucked perfectly.

"What's your name?" the manager inquires.

"Megan… Megan Mahn," she answers, unsure whether the manager has recognized her as Number Four. The manager sits quietly, staring at Megan with a poker face. The seconds feel like days as Megan stands, awaiting another response from the woman who has not revealed her unreadable connection.

"What hours are you available?" the manager pleasantly asks with a smile.

With relief, Megan responds, "It's summer break at Southern Atlanta South, so I'm flexible. I'm going into my sophomore year." Her nerves shift into hope.

The manager nods, impressed. She hands Megan a card. "Call this number to set up training, and they will send you employment paperwork. Tell them Sharon sent you. Welcome to the team." Her voice drops to a whisper. "Future soror."

Megan gleams with excitement, full of appreciation. "Thank you so much, Ms. Sharon," she says, noticing the bare ring finger. She grins as she accepts the card.

Megan walks out of the bank with attempted ease, trying to control her joy. She nearly trips over the curb she had so carefully stepped over when entering the bank.

Dialing the employment training number on the last day of its two-week preparation admission deadline felt God-led. The two-week training flew by. Although handling other people's finances is not Megan's vision for a musical career, the pay is perfect to cover her added bills, and the minimal workload won't distract her from her studies when school starts back in the fall. The training consisted of learning about customer service, a subject she wishes they had explored with more depth to enhance her people skills. Wearing business casual every day during pledging with TKRho prepared her for the training discussions about the company's dress code.

Megan starts work tomorrow, and one of the bank's rules is to have tamed hair with a professional appearance. She can manage a professional appearance, but her afro gets unruly, especially after a braid take-down. Tameka has driven their shared car into town to help her prepare for her first day on the job, and she arrives full of surprises. She surprises Megan by giving her full ownership of their shared car, brings her keyboard, and shows off an immaculate engagement ring. Marcus proposed.

Tameka assists April and Megan outside their apartment with bags of groceries and hair supplies. Retrieving the last bag from Megan's car trunk, Tameka asks, "So you got the job because she's in TKRho?"

Megan closes the trunk, balancing two arms full of bags, and nods with excitement. "Yup. Connections are everything. She didn't even ask for a résumé or interview."

April rushes past the girls up one flight of stairs to open the apartment door. "Yaaaas! Vice president," April exclaims, tucking the grocery bag handles under her chin while searching for the apartment key in her purse with her free hand.

Tameka is in disbelief at the connection Megan made with her new manager, Sharon, through a sorority. "But you're not in TKRho!" Tameka says, grounding them in reality.

"I know! But Sharon was feeling my TKRho vibe. They really look out for their sorors, and I'm not even in. Can you imagine the perks if I were?" Megan says, her imagination running wild with endless possibilities.

"President!" April chimes in as she struggles to insert the key, wiggling the knob until the door opens.

"Chirp chirp," Megan sneaks in as they both laugh at the forbidden inside joke.

"I don't know what political nonsense y'all are talking about, but TKRho sounds like a cult," Tameka says skeptically as she walks into the apartment, placing the remaining bags on the kitchen counter next to the keyboard Megan has yet to move to her room.

"Meka, relax! Just celebrate your sister's new job, my move into this amazing apartment, and my car, which is no longer yours!" Megan urges, trying to diffuse the tension. "The sorority is banned from campus anyway," she adds reassuringly as she locks the car with the key fob while looking out over the balcony. "A TKRho tag on my car would look good, though." She gives Tameka an *I'm just joking* look to ease the concern shadowing her face.

"You know I saw Gamma Alpha Alpha Phi hazing on our floor in the dorm last semester. I didn't know the white sororities haze too."

Tameka plants her hands on her hips, probing for more information about a process Megan has only partially shared. April shoots Megan a look, signaling she's revealing too much. Tameka notices the exchange and stops probing, understanding it's meant to be confidential.

"How are you getting back to Macon?" Megan asks, attempting to change the subject.

Tameka drops her hands and accepts the shift. "Mom and Dad are picking me up sometime this evening after Mom finishes shopping." She walks around the apartment, admiring her sister's upgrade. "So, who's ready for a makeover?"

Megan and April both raise their hands like schoolgirls begging for candy. Tameka shuffles through the bags, pulling out supplies for full sew-ins. April had pleaded for lace-front wigs, but Tameka knew the upkeep would require her to be in Atlanta every weekend to lay their edges properly. They settled on sew-ins after Tameka told them that's what they were getting anyway.

CHAPTER 11: A NEW SISTERHOOD

FALL 2022

WELCOME BACK LIONS is posted on the SASU marquee sign. Campus is back in full swing. New freshmen wander the grounds with anticipation. Greeks occupy their designated spaces on the yard, with tables set and covered in SASU welcome pamphlets.

Among them, Megan and April—faces fully made up, hair flowing long with extensions—navigate the crowd, their steps synchronized with the heartbeat of SASU. Amid the bustle, a hush falls over the yard as returning students notice the women of Theta Kappa Rho Incorporated, draped in TKRho paraphernalia, posted on their bench beneath their signature tree. Their presence commands attention as they chirp their sorority call.

Jasmine makes eye contact with Megan and April and gives them a pleasant wave. The girls wave back, confused.

Under her breath, April murmurs, "Are they back on the yard?"

Patrice, within earshot, responds, "Yes, they are, line sisters." She wraps her arms around the girls' shoulders, positioning herself between them. "The organization and the dean—who is a ZAPhi—came to an agreement."

~

Patrice sat at a desk half the size of its office, hands clasped, posture straight, leaning forward with both elbows on Dean Jackson's desk. She watched him with a stern gaze as he reviewed the incriminating footage of the girls being hazed—making out with trees. He studied the video carefully, uncertain how to proceed, then handed the phone to TKRho's advisor, who leaned in to watch.

The advisor sat back in her chair next to Patrice, appearing calm, though her right leg shook. Her foot tapped the desk, adorned with framed photos of the dean's wife and two young sons. Small ZAPhi trinkets rattled to the rhythm of her nervous movement.

"Time is ticking, keep on licking," Jasmine's voice pierced through the phone speakers. With visible disgust and embarrassment, the advisor paused the footage.

"What needs to be done to erase this?" she asked the dean, waving the phone in the air.

"TKRho needs to go on suspension, Sharice. I will call the regional director and inform her of what has taken place in this chapter," he stated.

"Our interest meeting is next week," Sharice explains, handing Patrice her phone. Patrice perked up at the mention.

"Well, postpone it until next semester. Hazing is not tolerated on SASU's campus," the dean retorted as he began searching for the regional director's number.

Patrice cleared her throat. "Ummm… that call may not be necessary. If there's an interest meeting, I want to receive a letter. I want to be a member of TKRho. If not, this video"—she waves the phone—"goes out, and you can continue with that call, Dean." She smirked as Sharice's jaw dropped.

The dean looked to Sharice, gauging whether the bribe was acceptable. After a long pause, she reluctantly agreed.

"Fine. But you are to have an unofficial suspension. This gives you time to speak with your members," the dean concluded. He warned Sharice that any further hazing would result in an official suspension. She agreed.

"If I let you in, Patrice, you must have all materials for the initiation process," Sharice demanded.

"I already have them," Patrice replied smoothly, standing to leave.

"Why do you want to be a part of this sorority so badly?" Sharice asked, stopping her before she could exit.

"I want to be part of a group of women who care about the greater good of America—women who volunteer and serve their community." She pulls up the footage. "Almost forgot." She deleted the video.

Satisfied, they shook hands. Patrice exited with a triumphant grin.

Dean Jackson laughed. "Time is ticking, keep on licking? That's what hazing has come to?" he joked, leaning back in his chair.

"Times have changed," Sharice said, shaking her head. "Thanks for not calling regionals."

"I had to make her think I cared. Good luck with that one," the dean replied.

~

"You're welcome," Patrice says, patting Megan and April on the back before joining the TKRho group on the shaded bench. They welcome her with hugs and smiles.

April texts the candidate group chat: **TKRho is back!**

†††

Midterm finals approach, and Megan blocks off her Monday afternoon to study. She seeks a quiet, cozy corner of the library, away from distractions. April is a great roommate, but her small talk and loud television make focus difficult.

Walking along the narrow sidewalk, Megan presses her books to her chest, shielding herself from the breeze cutting through her blue-patterned scarf. Fallen leaves crunch beneath her heels. She loves how a good pair of pumps can elevate any outfit—thanks to TKRho's influence.

"Oh shoot," she murmurs, remembering TKRho's return. She removes the blue scarf and stuffs it into her oversized handbag, sighing in relief as she scans the yard. She sweeps her long tresses forward to block the chill.

As she nears the library, Megan spots a baby-blue paper peeking from beneath a white flyer stapled to a tree. She glances around, weighing whether to step onto the grass. With TKRho's presence bold once more, and no word of underground pledging resuming, she continues to behave as if still on line—avoiding grass, maintaining business attire, with the occasional blue slip.

Curiosity wins. She tiptoes across the lawn and reads the flyer: *TKRho Interest Meeting—Next Thursday at 19:10.*

She recognizes the significance of the founding time. Her eyes sparkle as she discreetly snaps a photo and sends it to the dropped-line group chat.

Is that real? Trish replies seconds later.

FINALLY! Donna texts in all caps.

Megan slyly raises her arms in the air, as if to stretch from a five-mile jog. She discreetly snatches the flyer from the tree to hold as tangible evidence. She places it into her purse and gleefully tiptoes back onto the sidewalk. The interest meeting date being solidified increases the pressure of getting her grades up quickly. Being ready for the next step once she receives her initiation letter means having a 2.5 GPA, minimum. Megan has full confidence that after the interest meeting, she will receive a letter, or they would have dropped her from the line before the sorority was put on suspension. She hoped Jasmine's awkward wave upon returning back on the yard showed they were still interested.

Megan takes rapid steps to the library. In the distance, she spots Alicia walking in her direction, struggling to tie her hair into a top-knot bun. Tameka would have stopped to talk, but the timing was inconvenient. Megan's grades are her number one priority; the small talk would have to wait. She continues her walk into the quiet library. Five students are silently utilizing the building, spread out amongst the room. She finds a table in the corner of the quiet space to prepare for her music exam. She spreads her materials on the wooden table in comfortable placement in preparation to dive into her studies.

Alicia walks into the library, approaching the front desk where a student librarian sits staring at the desktop screen. She asks a whispered question. The librarian peers over her glasses, pointing toward Megan's direction, to the row of encyclopedias in the corner. Alicia squints her eyes along the path of the pointed finger and spots Megan, responding with a "Thank you." The librarian quickly proceeds back to work. Alicia carefully approaches Megan, avoiding an abrupt interruption. "Hey Megan. It is Megan, right?" she whispers, smiling from ear to ear.

"Yeah, it is." Megan looks up from her books. "Alicia?" she asks, pretending to be unsure. Her mother always asks about her; of course she knew her name. Megan's quick rush to the library has not erased the image of Alicia's issues—being escorted to the dorm by two random guys and being hazed in the dormitory. Megan's attention is captured by the huge pink and blue lettering on Alicia's white shirt.

"I joined," Alicia announces with a huge grin, proudly pointing to the Gamma Alpha Alpha Phi symbols, responding to Megan's uncomfortable stare at her chest.

"Congratulations! I figured you was pledging," Megan blurts out in unexpected excitement, forgetting about secrecy. The librarian peeps above the computer screen, checking in on the disturbance. "I mean… I kind of saw something going on in your room one night," she whispers, making sure no one else is made aware of her outburst.

Alicia takes a moment to digest what Megan has revealed. Ensuring the librarian has exited the exchange and they are back to a conversation of two, she ponders what to do next. Alicia grabs the seat next to Megan, scooting over to an uncomfortable closeness. Megan can smell her shampoo, a flower fragrance, as she releases her top knot that she struggled to build outside. Alicia adjusts her guilty posture of being caught in an illegal activity to a confident, no-big-deal attitude. They sit in silence, waiting for the other to break the awkward room tone of page shuffles and keyboard strikes from the five students in the library. Whispering lower than library etiquette, Alicia breaks the silence. "What did you see?"

Megan, aware that it is her turn to talk, replays the night. "I saw some girls drowning you in your dorm with buckets of water. Um. You were blindfolded, and the girls were wearing Gamma AAPhi T-shirts. Um. Was that part of a hazing thingy or something?" she asks, attempting to sound illiterate to the process, avoiding assumptions about her knowledge or experience with pledging TKRho.

Megan's response confirms Alicia's worry. Ashamed to admit that Megan is correct in what she saw, she whispers, embarrassed, "Yes, it was a hazing thingy," forcing a smile. "Please do not mention it to anyone. The chapter could get into a lot of trouble." Removing her eye contact from Megan's, she switches her focus to her phone next to her clasped hands on the table. Her hands are gripped tightly, giving her comfort before she continues. "I just moved into the sorority house, and I need the girls to like me. It's hard proving myself to them." A look of loneliness comes over her. The girl who was proudly wearing the Gamma AAPhi shirt two minutes ago now expresses sadness while talking about the same sorority. The redness appearing on her hands from her tight grip proves something is off about her initiation into sisterhood. Joining a sorority was supposed to make the initiate happy. Why was she still not fitting in?

"I mean no disrespect, but why are you still proving yourself?" Megan asks with confusion. Once you were in, that was all the approval you needed. But Alicia's eyes were saying something different.

"It's still cliquey once you're in. But I guess I knew that before I transferred. I was interested in Gamma AAPhi at my other school, but because of the cliques formed within the sorority, things got so bad that my parents made me transfer here before I was initiated. They thought my attitude change and my low grades were due to me having issues with the professors. They didn't know I was pledging. They didn't go to college, so they know nothing about Greek life." After a breath of realization, she continues. "But I'm not a quitter. I had to give it another try here at SASU, and this time I got in." She boasts, announcing how her determination has paid off.

"What is the process to get in? That is, if you're allowed to say," Megan asks with curiosity.

Alicia sits up with confidence to explain the process, retying her hair. "Before rush takes place, you have to complete an online registration. Online registration includes paying a registration fee, and you must provide your grades and extracurricular information. But by looking at this table covered with your study materials, you should have no problem collecting all your information," she jokes, assuming Megan is interested in joining. Alicia pulls her phone closer to the edge of the table, giving Megan more room to spread her materials if needed, an action adding to her humor.

Megan, not catching on to Alicia's Gamma Alpha Alpha Phi pitch, begins wondering if this is what the TKRho interest meeting will entail. But then again, April said after the interest meeting, letters will go out and they have two weeks to gather all required materials, including an initiation fee, not a registration fee. *Wait... they pay a registration fee before rush?* Megan thinks to herself. *That's backwards.*

Alicia's voice continues playing in the background of Megan's thoughts. "...After registration is complete, the potential candidates attend an orientation, like an interest meeting, where they receive an overview of the process, then you're assigned a recruitment counselor."

Megan scratches her forehead as Alicia continues.

"Next is the open house. You're allowed to visit any sorority house—as many sororities' houses as you would like—to make introductions, to get acquainted with active sisters. That is when I initially fell in love with Gamma AAPhi. Although they are cliquey, I like what they stand for. Community service and sisterhood. I think you would like them too." Alicia pauses, waiting for a response. Megan ignores the invitation and lets Alicia continue. "After the open house, you rank your preferred sororities, and they rank you."

This sounds like the preference process April mentioned, Megan takes mental notes, careful not to interrupt Alicia's explanation.

"Based on mutual preferences..."

Bingo, Megan mentally confirms.

"...you will only go to events that match the sorority that showed interest in you. That also includes the events put on by the fraternity that sorority has a close relationship with. We're really close to Zeta Zeta Pi."

That explains the guys that carried you to your room, huh? Megan learns, maintaining a straight face.

"These events are so cool because you have deep conversations with the sisters, gaining a deeper understanding of the sisterhood."

Deep conversations with Jasmine would be interesting.

"Then the sororities offer bids—an invitation to join. If you receive a bid and choose to accept it, you officially become a new member!" Alicia exclaims in her outside voice.

The student librarian comes over to tell them they are disrupting the other students from their studies. They look around to see the other patrons deeply focused in activities, not giving them any awareness. Once the librarian has adjusted comfortably in front of her screen, Alicia whispers, "If interested, I can get you in," suggesting it with a huge smile.

"No, thank you. There was a Black girl... I think... a light-skinned Black girl... she handed me a flyer during rush week to join, but I don't think I would fit in. No offense, but I don't really see my skin tone in that sorority," Megan responds, trying to tactfully express her observation.

"We're trying to get more of your skin tone girls," Alicia responds uncomfortably, using the same verbiage as Megan. "I'm hearing there could be a quota." She grimaces. "Hopefully that's a rumor. I don't see white girls in the Black sororities." She shrugs.

"You have a point," Megan agrees with a head nod.

Her phone rings. She pulls it from her purse. It's April. Forgetting to put her phone on mute, she answers, quietly placing April on hold until she's able to exit the building. Grabbing Alicia's phone to place her contact information in, she says, "It's great talking to you, Alicia. We should meet more often. Here's my number. Save it." She hands Alicia her phone. "Maybe we could ride home or attend church together," she adds. From reading Alicia's confused expression, Megan realizes that she's never brought up the fact that her mother mentioned her being from Macon and her parents attending the same church. "Long story. I'll tell you how I know about all that. Call me," she suggests, exiting the library with her gathered materials in disarray.

April is already talking when Megan puts the phone to her ear. "Let's all get together next Wednesday night to prepare our wardrobe and hair for the meeting," April demands.

Megan finds a bench next to the library to organize her materials. Multitasking her conversation with April and thoughts of having other sorority options, she ponders if Gamma AAPhi needs more girls of color in their sorority. Maybe that was the purpose of her meeting with Alicia. Was God telling her that diversity is needed within the sorority?

"Hello. Megan? Did you hear me?" an annoyed April questions through the phone.

†††

Outside the conference room door, wrapped in shiny blue wrapping paper, Megan, April, Trish, and Donna inspect their interest-meeting appearances with similar actions to their first church service meetup—except this time, their appearance is enhanced with makeup and hair extensions. Trish has straightened her afro, adding light waves. Donna stands confident with a fresh haircut, while Megan and April have added curls to their long extensions that Tameka has refreshed. Their silent confidence shines bright outside the interest-meeting room. One walking by could easily mistake them for members of TKRho.

The girls walk into the crowded room of potentials who have all found the hidden interest-meeting flyer. They take their seats in the last row. Patrice, with a huge grin, sits in the front, waving as they enter.

"Anxious much?" April grumbles.

The room is full of chatter from members lining the walls, soaking in the nervous energy coming from the center of the room. The potentials nervously sit in rows of uncomfortable folding chairs, adjusting their posture into pleasant positions, hoping to impress the intimidating members. Girls with no formal knowledge about sororities are wearing the sorority's colors in hopes of gaining brownie points while asking questions that freshman Megan would have proposed.

"Is this a hazing sorority?"

"How long will it take for me to become a member?"

"When will we learn the steps and strolls?"

Megan, observing Jasmine's softer side, is surprised she doesn't respond with unpleasant remarks and rip them apart. Maybe the suspension has changed her. Meanwhile, April appears annoyed, huffing and puffing at every question asked by the potentials.

Patrice gives head nods with teacher's-pet energy in the front row, wearing an air of confidence as if she has a guaranteed spot in the sorority. She's locked in on Toya, standing at the front of the room discussing the sorority's mission and prestigious accomplishments. Donna elbows Megan, pointing toward Toya's belly under an oversized blue trench coat unsuccessfully covering a baby bump. She's pregnant. The girls share looks of surprise and remembrance of Toya's mysterious runoff at set. Toya concludes her portion of the event and takes a seat next to Patrice, who continues her teacher's-pet act with exaggerated claps.

Jasmine walks up to the front holding an itinerary and introduces herself as the Dean of Pledges. Gasps and whispers are heard from the girls in the center. She releases a nervous smile and assures the concerned girls that Theta Kappa Rho is a non-hazing sorority. She goes on to explain her role and its importance to their initiation.

"If selected to be a member, I will be your mentor, guiding you through the process until you're a fully initiated member. That's all. Paperwork... stuff like that," she assures, with mini glances toward the four ready to call her bluff in the back.

Once the tension settles, she continues discussing TKRho's community service involvement and invites all potentials to come help with the autumn reading event in partnership with the local elementary school. The potentials take out their phones and notepads to mark the event in their calendars, which will take place in two weeks. When no further questions are asked, the sorority advisor releases Jasmine from her post with a gentle tap on the shoulder.

She takes her position in the front of the room, modeling a low, feminine haircut, shining a huge, confident smile over her audience, connecting with every potential in her presence. Trish lets out a small gasp, immediately recognizing the woman. It's Sharice, the polite lady handing out turkeys on Thanksgiving during her high school senior year. Water begins to swell in Trish's eyes.

"What's wrong with you?" Donna asks, noticing the tears flowing down her cheeks.

"She's the reason I'm here. That's the Soror I was telling you all about, passing out turkeys," she declares, patting her tears dry to avoid makeup smudges.

"Shut up," Donna responds in disbelief. She gives Sharice a close examination. "Wait a minute. That's my lady too. What are the freaking odds?" she exclaims, with her hand cupped over her mouth, remembering the low-haircut woman in the salon—her TKRho hairstyle influence.

"Why y'all look like y'all seen a ghost?" April whispers, leaning past Megan.

"Tell you later," Trish says quickly, soaking in the moment.

Sharice proudly continues the meeting, announcing the sorority's purpose and reciting the familiar motto. She mentions more community service projects the sorority participates in, including a musical event that piques Megan's interest. Megan is now completely sold on TKRho—forget about diversifying Gamma Alpha Alpha Phi. Sharice goes on to add that if the sorority is interested in a potential, the girls will have two weeks to collect all required materials, which include community service hours, an acceptable GPA, and a list of other items that will be listed in the interest letter.

"A meeting place on campus will be in the letter where you will hand-deliver said items. Then your MIP membership intake process shall begin," she adds.

Hearing the mention of a meeting place and another process gives Megan PTSD. *Is this another set location? What happens in this membership process?* Her internal temperature begins to rise at the thought of going through another gruesome process.

"Again, I ask you girls not to worry. This is not a hazing sorority. But if anyone is caught divulging the process to others, everyone involved will have to deal with major consequences," Sharice declares.

Megan, regaining her calm, locks eyes with Patrice, who has turned toward the four. Over her shoulder, she mouths, "You're welcome," holding the same expression she had while explaining TKRho's return to campus several weeks ago. Megan ignores Patrice's antics and waits for the meeting's dismissal.

The girls line up to print their names and addresses—where their letters are to be mailed—on a sign-in sheet. Patrice, visibly first in line, eagerly prints her name and address in all caps, eliminating any confusion of illegible letters.

"You changed our lives…"

"I cannot believe it's you…"

Donna and Trish speak praises to the advisor as she greets the potentials in line.

"You ladies are such a delight," the advisor responds.

"Groupies much? They act like she's giving autographs," April jokes, nudging Megan as they await their turn.

CHAPTER 12: SACRED RITES

"I really enjoyed that community service—reading to the kids," Megan acknowledges, walking with April toward their apartment. "That completes my hours needed to join TKRho. How about you? How many hours do you need?"

"My mom had me doing community service since I was a baby. I probably have rollover hours," April jokes. "Speaking of babies... Toya is so cute with her baby bump. You saw how she lit up reading to those kids. She's going to be a great mom. I wonder who the dad is."

April gasps, dropping her keys on the welcome mat in front of their apartment door. Her baby craze is interrupted by the sight of cream envelopes peeking from their mailbox, securely fastened outside their door. She removes two envelopes bearing a familiar shield at the fold. The royal and baby blue emblem catches the girls' eyes. April, with shaky hands, gives Megan the envelope addressed to her.

They nervously lock eyes, understanding the importance of this moment. TKRho either wants them to move forward with the official process or they have been denied. On April's count—"One. Two. Three."—they eagerly tear open their letters.

"Two weeks!" April exclaims, jumping for joy, crushing her keys underfoot.

Megan is relieved to have received the same great news. The words of her pastor and sister are no longer relevant in this moment. It's the sign she was waiting for. God approves of TKRho.

Both girls share a moment of uncontainable excitement, with hugs and cheers ringing through the apartment hallway. A nearby neighbor peers through his blinds to observe the commotion.

"Sorry," Megan apologizes.

The girls lower their joyful squeals as they scramble to open the door, realizing April never unlocked it due to the interruption. Searching for the dropped keys, April spots them jumbled on the welcome mat. Struggling to contain her composure, she inserts the key. Once inside safe quarters, they continue their excitement with jumps, cartwheels, and runs around the living room. Megan begins to reveal tears of relief, blessed to know that she has been chosen to officially become a member of Theta Kappa Rho.

"Two weeks!" April yells, waving her phone in the air.

Screams are heard from Trish and Donna on the other end. Megan's tears stream down her face uncontrollably as the four bask in this unforgettable moment of joy.

†††

At work, Megan musters the courage to step away from her station while the bank is low on customers. The two adjacent tellers occupy their low-traffic time at Southern Atlanta South Bank by organizing their stations before peak hour. Megan flips her workstation sign from open to closed and approaches Ms. Sharon with a request that weighs heavy on her heart.

She leans against the office doorframe with a hesitant yet determined tone and clears her throat. "Excuse me, Ms. Sharon? Can I have a moment of your time?" she asks, repeating exactly what she and April practiced the night before.

"Of course, Megan. What's going on?" Sharon looks up from a neatly stacked pile, offering her full attention with a gesture to pick a seat out of the two across from her.

Megan takes the seat closest to the door, in case the predicted scenario goes awry. She hesitates briefly before revealing her predicament. "I was wondering if it's possible to get an advance on my paycheck?"

"Yes, you may. How much?" was April's response in the role play. However, Sharon slowly stands to close the door for privacy. She leisurely walks back to her seat as anticipation fills the space. Sitting upright against her black ergonomic chair, she inquires further with concern.

"Is everything alright?"

The claustrophobic tension wraps around Megan, tightly squeezing out the words. "It's the sorority. The initiation fee. I'm short." She caves, releasing a huge sigh of relief.

Worry follows. Could Sharon think she's not ready to be a member of TKRho because she's asking for an advance? In last night's role play, Megan asked for an advance and play Sharon excitedly said, *Of course—anything for my favorite soror. How about I give you a blank check and you fill it out?* That was the best scenario; anything would be better than the silence currently filling the office.

After a moment of contemplation, "How much do you need?" the real Sharon responds.

With another sigh of relief, Megan admits, "I am about five hundred dollars short."

"I will arrange the advance for you right away," Sharon responds without hesitation.

Megan's gratitude spills forth. "Really? Thank you! I promise I will pay it back as soon as possible." Emboldened, she gathers the courage to ask another question—one not practiced the night before. "Also, Ms. Sharon, could you—"

"Write a recommendation letter?" Sharon finishes.

"How did you know I was going to ask?"

"I was waiting for you to ask. God sees your dedication and commitment to this sorority, and so do I. If you're fighting this hard to join, then I believe it's for a good reason. I would love to have you as a soror and write you a recommendation letter," Sharon assures.

Megan's eyes widen. "Thank you so much!"

"Absolutely," Ms. Sharon says. "Sometimes, the path to our dreams is not always easy, but it's clear that you're determined. Consider this initiation advance and my recommendation letter a sign that you're on the right track."

"Thank you so much, Ms. Sharon. I'll make sure to make the most of this opportunity."

Sharon offers a warm smile of encouragement. "You're welcome. Now go, soror." She gestures for Megan to leave her office without worry.

Back at her workstation, confident with newfound hope, Megan retrieves her phone from her purse to send April a text: *It went way better than how we practiced!*

Looking up from her phone, she sees the bank line quickly fill with customers. The adjacent tellers are assisting clients, and more customers are walking through the glass doors. Turning her workstation sign from closed to open, she waves with a confident smile to the couple patiently waiting their turn.

"Next in line."

†††

Eleven potentials receiving interest letters scramble to gather all required documents to hand-deliver to the assigned meeting place. Nine were equipped and ready with all required materials to proceed toward the above-ground membership intake process and become the resurrection line, the line to cross after TKRho's terminated suspension.

The resurrection line meets for study sessions to learn about Theta Kappa Rho's history before their initiation into the sorority. Jasmine sent out a text to the original four, urging them to get the new line ready for crossing without it seeming like a haze or pledge. The girls found sly ways of correcting the new candidates' revealing attire, grooming them into TKRho women. Their outward appearance, for the most part, was getting there. It was their personalities and attitudes that needed work. Their drive was different. They wanted TKRho privileges to be handed to them on a silver platter. They were spoiled brats, especially Patrice. On many occasions, April reminded them, "We're not sisters until we're initiated into the sorority," but in her mind, they would never be her sisters without going through an underground process as she had.

Megan's apartment has been appointed as the best location for the full-face makeup, assortment of colorful attire, and extension-wearing candidates to meet, study the founders of TKRho, and learn the hymn and pledge. Amid the study, chatter rises above the rest, expressing frustration with the commitment. However, the original line is grateful that memorizing the names of their founders and TKRho information are all they need to concern themselves with before tomorrow's big day. Initiation.

Megan projects among the criticisms, "Stop complaining about the work and study!"

April, in agreement, adds, "For real. You all aren't taking this seriously. We only have eight founders. Dang!"

Patrice questions the necessity of their rigorous study. "Why do we need to know all of this? They've already taken our money. We should be practicing our performance for the probate show." She looks around the room to see if the other girls agree with her complaint. Some heads nod in agreement.

"You're fully embracing the role of 'paper,' aren't you? You haven't even been initiated into the sorority yet. Know your founders first, then maybe you'll gain some respect wearing TKRho's letters!" April exclaims, storming out of the living room and slamming her bedroom door.

In agreement about needing to be more deserving of wearing TKRho's letters, Donna and Trish sit with quiet confidence in the corner, rolling their eyes at the carelessness of the girls on the matter. A hush falls over the room as reality sinks in. Megan redirects the focus back to their purpose, urging the girls to concentrate. "Everyone, please study." She directs her attention to the new ace, Lyndsey, the shortest of the girls. "Number One, who are the founders of TKRho?" She is not sure if calling the girls by numbers is appropriate, but memorizing their names is impossible given the short amount of time spent with them before initiation.

Lyndsey boldly recites the names of the founders. Her dedication brings the girls' attention back to the seriousness of the matter.

Megan receives a notification text on her phone.

Forward from Dean of Pledges: **Ready for Hell Night? OG line ONLY. Set in thirty minutes!**

April, wearing a slicked-back ponytail, comes out to the living room in all black in search of her keys on the kitchen counter. "Y'all have to go. Something has come up. Have your wardrobe ready for initiation tomorrow," she states, ready to take on the secret mission that awaits her. She gives a knowing look to the other three. They return the glance with concerned awareness.

At set, Jasmine walks down the line of the original four dressed in all black, hair styled into ponytails except Donna. "I could say I'm proud of you, but it would be too soon," Jasmine says. "I didn't think it would be fair for you ladies to experience all that you have without finishing the process properly. You don't have the luxury of going through a Hell Week, but I'll give you one hell of a night. If you don't make it through this, you'll never amount to anything. And if you don't want to be considered 'paper,'" she states in air quotes, "then you need to be 'made.' Do you want to be made?!"

What is Hell Week? Megan wonders as she responds with the line, "Yes, Big Sister Jazz!" The girls yell in unison in the middle of the heavily wooded area.

"Why do you want to be a lady of TKRho, OG Ace?" Jasmine yells, standing face to face with April.

April, with her chest out and head held high, responds. "I want to be a lady of Theta Kappa Rho because the legacy shall never die!"

"Number Two?" Jasmine continues on to Trish.

"I want to be a lady of Theta Kappa Rho to give back to the community with the best women to ever do it!"

"Number Three?" Jasmine yells.

"I want to be a lady of Theta Kappa Rho because I want to show tomboys how to be women!"

Jasmine turns her back toward the line, facing the wooded area. She cups her mouth to sneak in a slight chuckle. Jasmine's break from drill sergeant to a human with emotions is a pleasant surprise, a surprise that doesn't last long enough for the girls to enjoy. After gathering herself, she stands in front of Megan and yells, "OG Tail?" demanding an answer to the question at hand.

"I want to be a lady of Theta Kappa Rho because… because…"

"Spit it out, Tail!"

"…Because I want to be a part of the best sisterhood there is!"

Jasmine gives Megan a long stare, observing the water film coating Megan's eyes. Megan exhales heavily, looking over Jasmine's hairline into the deep woods behind her. Seconds of silence pass as the insects' sounds take over with their presence.

"Now prove it!" Jasmine demands. She pulls an egg from the front pocket of her hoodie and cracks it against a nearby rock. "Open up," she demands, standing in front of April, draining the egg white from the yolk. April opens her mouth. Jasmine slides the yolk into her mouth, oozing from its shell. "Pass it. Bind your line. Become equally yolked!" She points to Trish's mouth. "No hands," she instructs them. "Into her mouth. Now!"

April does as commanded. Trish, with hesitation, slightly turns in April's direction to accept the yolk.

"Pass it!" Jasmine yells again, demanding the pass to Donna.

Donna accepts it. Trish convulses with small gags, managing to keep it all together.

"Pass the yolk. Now!" Jasmine yells again, standing in Donna's face, demanding the pass to Megan.

Megan quickly accepts it to get this Hell Night over with. How the yolk was to be transferred didn't cross Megan's mind until her lips met Donna's in the process.

"Bind. Swallow."

Megan's eyes widen. She thought she would accept the egg and spit it out.

"I said swallow it. You are the tail. Close the bond. Now! This yolk is easy. This burden is light."

Megan stands with a dilemma. What are her choices? Swallow the egg, allow the saliva to continue formulating in her mouth, or deal with the consequences that could be much worse if she spits it out.

"If you don't swallow the yolk, give it to Ace. I'm sure she'll do it. Us Aces always come through."

"Permission to address my Tail, Big Sister Jazz?" April asks.

Jasmine motions for her to do so.

April quickly runs down to stand in front of Megan. "Give it," she demands.

Megan shakes her head no.

"Give it!" April demands.

Megan submits. April takes it and gulps it down, rushing back into her position at the head of the line. Holding her head up high, she sticks her tongue out, showing proof of a disappeared egg.

"Good work, Ace." Jasmine slow claps. "Now line up against the cafeteria wall, and I better not hear a sound."

With the unusual request, the girls tiptoe to the nearby cafeteria brick wall, minimizing the sound of leaves crunching under their sneakers.

"Turn around. Squat and place your hands on the wall."

The girls attempt to follow the random request with no demonstration to follow.

"Lower!" Jasmine demands, and the girls follow suit. "Stick your butts out."

Smack!

"What was that?" Megan questions, refraining from looking toward the sound.

Smack. Smack. Two more smacks and a slight moan from Trish are heard, inching closer.

"I said don't make a sound," Jasmine whispers.

Smack. Smack. Smack.

The sound is beside Megan. Fear comes over her.

What is happening? She wonders, afraid to look. Pressing her hands against the wall, she closes her eyes and prays.

Smack. Smack. Smack. Smack.

"Ouch!" Megan yells. "What the...?"

"I said be quiet. You want more?" Jasmine whispers.

"No... Big... Sister Jazz," Megan whispers through a quivering voice, resisting the urge to rub her butt that is burning from the connection to the wooden paddle.

"Then be quiet. Now I have to start all over," Jasmine states, adjusting her paddle like a batter waiting on a pitcher's throw.

Megan, becoming numb to what is taking place, realizes that she is taking wood. Her pledging nightmare has come true. She has entered a Hell Night.

Smack.

†††

Megan's unimpressed with TKRho sorority house's curb appeal upon arriving at the initiation ceremony, yet grateful to finally see its exterior. The outdated, chipped white-painted building, used for graduate chapter meetings, initiation processes, and small gatherings of one hundred or less, sat in a not-so-good area of Atlanta about five miles from campus. Jasmine, in all white, met the girls dressed in black outside before entering the building's front doors. She now hands each girl a black blindfold with clear instruction to securely tie them around their eyes and wait in line at the side door of the building until she calls them in to enter. They do as they're told, anxiously waiting in line with luggage packed with white dresses and shoes for a wardrobe change.

"Do you think they're going to haze us?" Patrice asks, loud enough from her position of second in line to Megan's position of second to last.

"Shhh," Megan responds as footsteps are heard approaching the girls. Slight tugs are felt as their luggage is taken inside.

"You may enter," Jasmine states calmly, guiding the girls into a warm atmosphere with a scent of jasmine covering an old wooden musk.

The resurrection line gathers in a tightly felt, dark meeting room, blindfolded in a semicircle, shoulder to shoulder. More presences are felt among the line, scattered throughout the room. A voice is heard from the front of the room announcing that all in attendance must bow their heads for prayer. Megan recognizes the voice belonging to Toya. She calmly recites the opening prayer that echoes over the gentle music filling the space.

Megan, positioned eighth in the semicircle, fidgets, adjusting to a comfortable stance, easing the soreness caused by Jasmine's Hell Night. The blindfolds make it impossible to know their current whereabouts in the sorority house. Minor light flashes peer through the darkness of her blindfold, hinting at candle flickers in the room, and slight movements create creaking sounds from the wooden floors, indicating the space's hollowness. Great. Her first time in the house and she's blindfolded, being stolen of the full experience, unable to take in every moment, especially this moment, using all her senses to revel in every detail. Megan's hearing ability is wasted on everything surrounding her: where they were in the house, who else is in attendance, could her boss Sharon be there? All of these thoughts overshadow Toya's prayer, which has ended. She has no idea what was prayed over them.

"Now join me in song," Toya commands. Assuming it's the hymn the girls learned in their meet-ups, Megan waits for the others in the room to begin before joining in harmony.

"Hail Theta Kappa Rho, we greet thee tonight,
For this noble sisterhood be always our delight.
We love our motto and the power from it flows,
When cares of life overtake us with life's given woes.
We'll always reverence TKRho forever and a day.
With lifted hearts, we praise thee.
TKRho, we give you praise."

Distinguishing the singers from non-singers, Patrice's voice pierces the room with a soprano shrill, causing small snickers throughout the room. Once the room tone returns to its soft music soundtrack and the chuckles dissipate, the girls are commanded to repeat after Toya. In unison, they repeat, "Don't urge me to leave you, Theta Kappa Rho, or to turn back from you, Theta Kappa Rho. Where you go, I will go, and where you stay, I will stay. Your people will be my people and your god my god. Where you die, I will die, and there I will be buried. May the Theta Kappa Rho deal with me, be it ever so severely, if even death separates you and me."

"Hold hands," Toya prompts. The girls blindly grab their partners' hands. "Be led," she adds.

Megan feels a tug from Donna's sweaty palms. She's pleased to have Donna by her side through this process, given the new candidates that have joined. She follows suit, slightly tugging the new tail to follow the line's lead. They are guided through the house, hands interlocked in solidarity. The music continues playing in the background while the sorority chants, "Life is a maze, which we must wander all our days." With each creak of the wood underneath Megan's feet, a sense of darkness and confusion chills through her body. She feels the tight grips from the hands she clasps, sensing they are in the same state of confusion and fear. With constant direction to turn left, she feels circles being made in their route, as if they are walking around the wall of Jericho. She feels a slight breeze and a shift of light peek through her blindfold.

"You have completed the first degree of the crossing ritual process. You may take off your blindfolds and change into your white for the second degree. You have fifteen minutes," Jasmine announces as she exits the room.

Megan pulls off her blindfold, and a brightly lit, wooden-paneled room is revealed. Their white dresses are pressed and hung on clothing racks lined with their luggage. Paintings of blue jays hang on the walls. The sorority shield and plaques of service cover the wooden panels. "Hurry up. Get dressed," Trish whispers, shoving Megan out of her wonderment. She adheres to the instruction, spotting her bag lined up in order of their line numbers. The room is filled with anxious energy as the girls rummage through their bags to retrieve their white pearls and white shoes. They exchange their black dresses for white. Some throw their black wardrobe into their luggage in regard to time, while others neatly hang their dresses on the clothing racks provided. A knock is heard at the door. The girls push into line according to height, ready for the next phase.

"Are candidates dressed and ready?" Jasmine voices through the door.

They all respond in unison, "Yes, Dean of Pledges."

She enters the room. "Put on your blindfolds." The girls swiftly rustle through their bags to retrieve their blindfolds and place them over their eyes, falling back in line. "Interlock arms." They follow suit.

"Candidates are entering," Jasmine yells out. The resurrection line enters blind, arms interlocked. The girls stand in a semicircle around the altar. "You may remove your blindfolds and hand them to the Dean of Pledges," Toya states.

Each girl takes off her blindfold as Jasmine collects them one by one. "Where are your pearls?" Jasmine asks, standing in front of Megan. In awe, Megan is speechless. *Oh no. I forgot my pearls.* The thought of the heinous consequence of this action overcomes her. Jasmine reveals a smirk and continues on, collecting Number Nine's blindfold.

Taking in the room to see if anyone else notices her missing pearls, she sees alumni members of their Omega Zeta chapter of Theta Kappa Rho standing in rows behind them, wearing white dresses also accessorized with pearls. Among the women, she sees the advisor standing next to a familiar face hidden behind a white face mask that she recognizes from April's Williams family photo. It's April's mother, standing proudly among the women. Also standing as a proud mother is Megan's boss Sharon, who, with a pleasant smile, gives Megan a wave. Megan smiles, returning the welcome with slight embarrassment due to her missing pearls.

"Tonight, we gather in the name of our sacred sisterhood, pledging ourselves to the values and spirit of Theta Kappa Rho. Thou shalt love Theta Kappa Rho, with all thine heart, with all thy soul, and with all thy might," Toya states, wearing an all-white knee-length dress, white gloves, and a white blazer fastened above her overgrown belly. She looks as if she's ready to go into labor at any moment.

"Theta has been written upon your hearts and minds. You're now ready to receive the light of Theta. Remember our motto as you light your candles before you on this altar."

The line receives white wax candles to light from an arc of candles lit on the altar, their guided light, the founders in the sorority. They hold their unlit candles until further instruction is given. Observing the altar's adornment, covered with a white cotton cloth, Megan sees an arc of eight blue-lit candles, pictures of TKRho founders, miniature blue jay figurines, and a huge white pledge book in the center next to a small brown KJV Bible.

"Recite the motto with me as you light your candles, your new life," Toya reads from the ritual book.

The girls light their candles from the arc of founders and recite the motto in unison. "That I use my trained intellect to strengthen the name of Theta Kappa Rho, to use wisdom, knowledge, and have a sound mind to wherever it leadeth me in the new day."

"To our founders we bow," Toya reads, then motions the girls to bow their heads before they are commanded to blow out their candles. Sniffles are heard coming from the front of the line. It's April, with tears streaming down her face. Sharice approaches with a folded tissue. Toya pauses to allow April to gather herself before continuing.

"Blow out your light, now that you have entered the new. This light is to now shine within you," Toya reads as Jasmine collects the unlit candles. The girls fall back into position. "These candles signify the light that burns whenever Theta Kappa Rho are assembled. It guides your footsteps as you work in the name of our sorority." There's a slight pause as she flips the page in the ritual book. She continues, "You've come to the most serious part of the intake process, the second degree of initiation. Taking the Oath. I caution you to take heed of the words that you will repeat after me. This oath must be your constant guide because, once a Theta, always a Theta."

A member pulls out a blue pillow from underneath the altar. The candidates are prompted to kneel on it, placing their right hand on their heart and left hand on the Bible, which Toya holds in hand. "You kneel before thee. Repeat the Theta Kappa Rho oath. Then sign your name in the book of knowledge, leading to enlightenment and sisterhood," she instructs.

Toya signals Lyndsey, the new ace, to kneel on the pillow. "Repeat after me." Each initiate kneels one by one, repeating the oaths recited by Toya, followed by a signature in the white book of knowledge.

Donna, expressing a huge grin, gives her signature and quickly takes her position in the member circle. Toya motions for Megan to proceed with the process. Megan kneels on the blue pillow in front of the altar. "Where are your pearls?" Toya asks, staring at her bare neck.

"I…I…" Megan stutters. Cold beads drape over her as a whisper is heard, clasping the necklace on her neckline. "Sisters come through for each other," Jasmine whispers in her ear. An exhale of relief comes over Megan. Who would have thought Jasmine would be the one to save her from ultimate humiliation? She mouths, "Thank you." Jasmine accepts with a head nod.

"Repeat after me," Toya commands. "I…"

"I, Megan Mahn,"

"Do solemnly promise to keep hidden the manner of induction and obligations of Theta Kappa Rho Sorority."

"Do solemnly promise to keep hidden the manner of induction and obligations of Theta Kappa Rho Sorority," Megan repeats.

"I…" Toya waits.

"I, Megan Mahn,"

"I shall set a guard over my mouth and keep watch over the door of my lips," Toya states.

"I shall set a guard over my mouth and keep watch over the door of my lips," Megan repeats.

"I…"

"I, Megan Mahn,"

"Pledge myself to the spirit of sisterhood, embracing the legacy of Theta Kappa Rho Sorority with unwavering devotion."

Megan repeats, "Pledge myself to the spirit of sisterhood, embracing the legacy of Theta Kappa Rho Sorority with unwavering devotion."

"Now you, Megan Mahn, may sign your name in the book of knowledge and be born again," Toya commands.

Before becoming the new Theta Kappa Rho Megan, she takes a moment to rest in the old Megan, the Megan before crossing into sisterhood. She observes the women happily waiting for each individual to join the circle. She sees the OG line waiting to welcome her to the circle, April's mom, the advisor Sharice, Sharon, alumni and graduate members, as well as the new initiates that have signed their names in the book. She locks eyes with Jasmine, who gives her a nod to continue, then looks up at Toya, who assures her that after she signs, she is a part of the sisterhood.

Ready to let go of the old Megan, she reaches for the pen held in Toya's hand. Adjusting her position, loosening the grip of her dress tightly tucked under her knelt knee, she lifts her knee, giving slack to reach for the pen. Her left elbow bumps the altar, causing a lit candle to topple over, creating a domino effect that causes the altar to ignite in flames. The women stand in awe as the pictures of the founders, the book of knowledge, and all other items embellishing the altar slowly burn. With quick reflexes, Megan grabs the Bible, preventing it from catching flame, as the advisor enters the room with a fire extinguisher. The residue from the extinguisher fills the room as the solemn music continues playing.

"Megan, you may sign your name in the book of knowledge," Toya repeats. Megan snaps out of the vision back into reality and, with shaking hands, signs her name to join the rest of the initiated members in the circle. Holding her place in the circle, taken aback by the vision, Jasmine hands her a white jacket with the name 'Blue' printed above the number eight in big, bold royal blue letters. Toya then joins the new initiates and passes each of them a pin. She proclaims, "This pin is to be worn at the apex of the heart. It holds the letters Theta for Life, Kappa for Truth and Loyalty, and Rho for Fluidity. The principles of our Sorority." The girls take their pins, and with the help of a graduate member, they pin them at the apex of their hearts. They learn the secret handshake; chirps are practiced, and the emblem symbols and their meanings are revealed. The members welcome the neophytes with hugs and tests of handshakes. The new ladies of Theta Kappa Rho, with tears flowing down their cheeks, raise their voices to sing the sorority hymn, followed by a prayer to close off their initiation.

PART 3
NEOPHYTE

CHAPTER 13: BOUND BY SISTERHOOD

The two-hour meticulously performed ceremony has ended. The ladies of Theta Kappa Rho pose stacked on the front stairs of the sorority house with huge grins, cheesing the word "Theta" under a white banner with blue Greek lettering. The last picture snaps, cellphones are handed back to their owners, and the ladies disperse. Sharon gives Megan a warm, welcoming hug into the sisterhood. Her sweet perfume scent of lavender fills Megan's nostrils as she welcomes the long embrace, the perfect substitute for her family's absence. She hasn't given much thought to when or how she would break the news to the Mahns. She dreads hearing her dad call her a devil stepper, Tameka lecturing her about god worship, and her mom... actually, she doesn't know how her mom feels about sororities.

"I appreciate you coming to my initiation," Megan thanks Sharon as they release their embrace.

"I'm happy I was able to help. I've never had the pleasure to recommend a lovely lady into my sorority."

A thud is heard as April exits the front doors of the house wearing the blue dress her mother gifted her for this special day, jumping off the last step with outstretched arms and her new white jacket in hand. "I got my letters!"

Sharon places her fingers in her ears, hinting at the loudness of April's excitement. "You got your letters!" she repeats with a smile as April approaches them.

"April, this is my boss, Sharon."

"Nice to meet you," Sharon states, releasing her fingers from her ears and extending her hand to test April with the secret handshake. April is caught off guard but takes the challenge seriously and successfully reciprocates the handshake as it comes back to her remembrance. Sharon is pleasantly surprised. "Congratulations, Sorors," she states with a nod of approval, pivoting toward her blue BMW parallel parked along the street. "I'll see you Monday, Megan."

"Close one," April whispers. "Almost caught me slippin'," referring to the surprise handshake.

"Speaking of slippin', does your mother know you already wore that dress to brunch?" Megan asks, noticing April's swift wardrobe change.

"What she doesn't know won't hurt her." April layers her jacket over her dress, pulling the sleeves over her bare arms.

"Won't hurt who?" Ms. Williams approaches the girls, still wearing her COVID protection face mask. April is startled by her abrupt entry. She continues from her rhetorical question, "I'm so proud of you." She finishes adjusting April's jacket with pats above her bold-font printed line name. "My Legacy," she reads. "I wish you could've been Ace," she states, standing the same height as April. It's clear where April gets her height from.

Ms. Williams thoroughly examines Megan's appearance and height. She walks a circle around her, discovering the name printed on her jacket. "Blue. I like it." Holding her hand out, she says, "I'm

April's mom. You must be Megan. Heard a lot about you." She sneaks in a quick secret handshake. Megan, aware of the challenge, completes her required action: right pinky pressure, pointer pressure twice, thumb circle.

"Keep her in line," Ms. Williams finishes.

"I'll try," Megan responds, assuming she completed the handshake correctly.

If Ms. Williams gives a smile of approval, Megan doesn't notice it hidden under the COVID mask. "Nice meeting you," Megan adds. She hasn't heard mention of April's father and doesn't see a wedding ring on Ms. Williams's hand.

"Is it Ms. Williams?" she asks.

"Yes, it is. We keep our maiden names in honor of the TKRho legacy." Megan controls the confused expression threatening to reveal itself. She can't tell if Ms. Williams is joking or serious due to her concealed facial expressions. However, there's no denying where her eyes are focused—on April. The maiden name innuendo is directed at April, hinting toward a demanded marriage next on her timeline. "Call me later, April," she demands, making her departure toward her car.

"Chirp!"

Assuming the muffled chirp came from Ms. Williams, April responds with a low chirp while chirps from other members fill the air.

"I told you the women in my family are die-hard Theta women and crazy," April adds, embarrassed.

"I would prefer being called crazy over Blue. I deserve a name with meaning. Like yours. Legacy. That has meaning. No explanation needed. What's a Blue?" Megan complains.

"It's the sorority color," Donna joins, wearing her jacket with the name *Brace Boldly* printed on the back. The girls laugh, understanding the pun. She smiles as the sun reflects boldly off her braces.

"Look at these cute little shields." Trish runs over, pointing to the small details on their jackets. "I wish I paid attention to what each section of the shield meant. I was so excited to finally cross; it was going in one ear and out the other."

Megan looks around to make sure what she's about to say stays between the four. "The whole process gave me anxiety. The blindfolds. I forgot my pearls. And…" She pauses before mentioning her random fire vision.

April questions, "And what?"

"None of that felt off to you?" Megan asks instead.

"Kind of, but we're in now," Trish assures them, then leans into the four. "No more pledging." She smiles.

"Thank God!" Donna exclaims.

"I don't think the pledging will stop. We've been challenged with handshakes. Hope y'all know it," Megan warns.

Donna and Trish mentally practice the secret shake.

"When did you get challenged?" April asks.

"Just now. Your mom," Megan reveals.

"Oh goodness!" April shakes her head, embarrassed. "I guess you passed. If not, I'll hear about it later. Look, everything's good now. We got through it and have these jackets to prove it." With full confidence, she cups her hands around her mouth, tilts her head back, and chirps as loud as she legally can, leading the chorus of the sorority call.

"Once an Ace, always an Ace," Donna laughs, joining the echoes of chirps fading into the atmosphere.

"Chirp, chirp, chirp!"

†††

The nightlife of SASU's campus is interrupted by anticipation and excitement for TKRho's Probate Show. The crowd erupts into cheers, capturing the moment on their cellphones with livestreams and photos. The resurrection line makes their grand entrance on the yard with bedazzled masks covering their eyes, matching long-extension hairstyles, white V-neck tops, and baby blue poodle skirts with their line names printed on the back. And, of course, their six-inch heels. Lyndsey, their new Ace, leads their synchronized, seductive slow walk onto the open area designated for revealing the new members. They halt in front of TKRho's engraved tree emblem, hands on hips, chins up, waiting for their cue to begin.

"*Ladies?*" Lyndsey yells confidently from the head of their nonagon formation.

"*Yeah,*" they respond in unison.

"*They've been waiting for us.*
We are what they need.
They've been bored without us.
The boys have been waiting.
The girls have been hating.
Say it with your chest!"

"*TKRho is the best!*" the girls shout in unison.

Lyndsey waits for the applause and a few diss remarks from the crowd to die down. She commands, "So, let's give it to 'em."

The girls perform a synchronized step, transitioning from their nonagon formation to a reversed V, with Trish at the point. Trish's hair flows in the breeze, revealing every expression as she sings a melodic song in reverence of TKRho from her diaphragm. The girls are surprised that Trish offered to sing—and even more surprised by the powerful voice that explodes from her frame.

"You better sing, girl!" "She can sang!" and "That's so beautiful!" echo through the crowd as the song ends. "She's alright," a heckler adds.

Trish rolls her eyes and begins the next step. "*We. Are. The…*" The line shifts into a straight line, meeting Trish at the point.

"*Ladies of TKRho,*" they join in unison.

"We're the best, and that's fa sho.
We are here to let you know.
If not TKRho, then it must go!"

The girls hold up Mu Alpha Phi Alpha's hand signal and smash it against their right thigh. Pretending its remains have fallen to the ground, they stomp on it with their royal blue heels. This stomping diss, added by April, is designed to trigger Mu APhiA. They take the bait. "Oohs" and "aahs" erupt from the crowd while "boos" taunt from the rival sorority standing directly in front of the line.

As the show reaches its climax, Jasmine dripped in her royal and baby blue paraphernalia with *Jazz* boldly printed on the back—takes her position in front of Lyndsey, letting out a loud chirp. This is the cue for the line to remove their bedazzled masks. The new members are revealed. The girls begin to introduce their new selves to the audience. Thunderous applause explodes from friends while teeth-sucking hisses rise from their foes.

Megan removes her mask. She can now clearly see familiar faces from class. Alicia stands amazed with her sorority sisters nearby, and ZAPhi gathers under their tree next to TKRho. Jeff's absence was expected, but she hoped somehow he'd find a way to stand beside Tony, clapping and shouting as she removed her mask. His new job wouldn't allow it. With only a day's notice, his boss said it was impossible to leave the night shift at the studio. To reschedule an artist's studio time is unprofessional, his boss says and prohibited especially if deposits have been exchanged for an engineer. "I wish I could be there, but no one would switch shifts with me," Jeff sulked with puppy eyes and a shrug. She hoped it was a lie—a cruel trick—and that he'd surprise her with blue roses.

"I'm Pressure P, a lady of Theta Kappa Rho!" Patrice announces, swinging her hair. What a fitting name.

April once told the OG line she overheard a conversation between her mother and Sharice. Sharice spilled the beans about the girls pre-pledging, and Patrice recorded the evidence to pressure her way in. April's never liked Patrice, and this revelation only adds icing to the bitter cake.

"I'm Legacy, a lady of Theta Kappa Rho!" April yells boldly, directing every syllable to her rivals standing in front of her. It's apparent she's inherited her mother's hate for the rival sorority. She refuses to wear red or a shade of blue that resembles Mu APhiA's blue.

"I'm Soul Glow, a lady of Theta Kappa Rho!" Trish sings. "Just let your soul glow," running her fingers through her waist-length silk press. *Coming to America* chants ripple through the crowd.

"I'm Brace Boldly, a lady of Theta Kappa Rho!" Donna shouts, snatching off her wig, making known the reason for her name. And boy did Donna make the girls live up to her name. They had to brace themselves with the bold curse words she shouted at them when they told her she had to wear a wig— so they could look like one at the probate show. Up until the very last minute she stood her ground not giving in until she had the great idea of making everyone brace themselves for her bold move of snatching the wig off at the show. "For you, Mama!" Donna adds tearfully.

Megan's next. She allows Donna's moment to simmer hoping that at any moment Jeff will appear carrying blue roses. She gives one more glance in ZAPhi's direction. No Jeff. Instead, she sees Tony and the bruhs waiting for her turn. She skims the audience. Everyone is waiting for her to announce herself. Jasmine chirps hinting to go. The members use the moment as a call and response. Megan's grateful for the delay and wishes for a way to stretch the interruption. Aware of the awkward silence, she shouts, "I'm Blue, a lady of Theta Kappa Rho!" She does a side-dip hip swing April taught her. The crowd cheers. Alicia and her sister's cheer. Ape shouts are heard from ZAPhi. Chirps sing and a deep ape call followed by "That's my baby Blue," projects over the noise. Megan looks in its direction. Jeff! *"It's Jeff, he made it and he's carrying a dozen blue roses."* She struggles to keep her soul from jumping out of her body. She maintains by playing it cool. The rest of the show blurs—until a voice cuts through the celebration.

"How does it feel to be a line of 'paper'?!" a Mu APhiA member taunts. April rushes towards the rival member, ready to defend her newfound identity.

"I'm not paper! Yo mama's paper!" she retorts in the rival's face.

Chaos erupts. Phones rise. Megan steps in. "Not in your letters, April. Cameras are on you."

They pull her away.

With help from Donna and Trish they manage to pull April away from the circle that quickly formed around the altercation. They tussle with her, pushing her towards the TKRho bench in front of their tree. With resistance to sit, she finally gives in to the demand as the three hover over her blocking her view of their rivals.

"We know you're not paper," Trish whispers, mindful of the onlookers. More TKRho members join around them in support, including Jasmine and Patrice.

"I knew crossing with these girls was going to be a problem. Now everyone thinks we're paper because we're on a line full of it." April vents her frustration, not minding who hears.

But Megan reassures her, "I know what we went through. *We did earn this, but this is not the place to express that,*" she emphasizes, making eye contact with Jasmine hoping to receive validation. Jasmine doesn't confirm. She walks away to join the other prophytes calming the uproar before campus security arrives.

Patrice catches the slick hidden message and addresses the girls. "You don't think I deserve to be a part of this sorority because I joined without hazing?"

"No, you don't deserve to be here, *Pressure P*," April challenges rising from the bench with balled fist.

"I was smart enough not to let anyone punk me into sisterhood. You're the stupid one kissing trees. Dummy!" Patrice shouts back.

April pushes Patrice. Patrice stumbles, struggling to regain her balance.

"They about to fight!" a voice yells. A crowd rushes towards the new altercation with raised camera phones.

Before Patrice can retaliate Megan quickly steps in once more, advocating for unity despite their differing paths into TKRho. "Everyone, chill out! We are sisters. Who cares how you got in. We just did a great show; we're wearing our letters. We are now sisters. So, chill!"

"Blue, is everything cool?" Jasmine yells out from across the yard talking to campus security that has arrived.

Megan signals that everything's under control. April dismisses herself from the kumbaya moment. "She'll never be my sister. I'm out. I'll see you at home." She walks away, leaving behind a tension that overshadows the celebration of a newfound overdue sisterhood.

"There's nothing to see here," Megan assures the crowd, shooing them from the yard. Phones are lowered and whispers are heard engaging in new gossip as they disperse.

"What's y'all line's name, the Gang Bangers?" Jeff approaches. "Is the coast clear? Is killa Legacy gone?" he laughs, handing Megan the roses.

"I didn't think you was going to show up."

"You know I wouldn't miss this for the world. You did it babe." He smiles. "Do you even know what blue roses mean?"

Megan's never seen blue roses. She was joking when she asked for them. Impressed he made them a reality; she shakes her head no.

"Mystery. Uniqueness. Admiration... love."

"Love, huh?"

"Yep. Love." He responds. Jeff pulls Megan in close. "I'm so proud of..."

"Blue, let's take a group picture!" Jasmine calls, interrupting.

"Coming!" Megan yells, handing Jeff the roses. She runs to take her place in line. The girls gather in front of their tree on the yard.

Megan finds Jeff holding the roses and mouths to Jeff, *I love—*

"On the count of three say Theta. One. Two. Three," Tony calls.

"Theta!"

CHAPTER 14: STILL A NEO

Interruptions of stomach grumbles in calculus class communicate that it's lunchtime. Megan rushes to meet up with the sorors on the yard, gathered under the assigned tree, wearing her white jacket over a blue TKRho-printed T-shirt. All SASU undergraduate members are at the meet-up for lunch except for Toya who just delivered her healthy baby girl who's now her number one priority.

"Hey, Blue," they greet Megan as she occupies the edge of the bench, squeezing between April and the metal armrest. She places her calculus materials on the grass in front of her, and a scent of alcohol passes by with the autumn wind. "What's in your cup?" she asks, sniffing the contents of what April's holding.

"Water," April responds, pulling her cup close to her chest and adjusting her sunglasses.

Megan was sound asleep before April's late arrival home last night. Leaving for calculus class this morning, she discovered April sprawled out on the couch, snoring through her phone's repetitive alarm. Next to her was an empty wine bottle with no evidence of a wine glass. Megan gave April a slight shove to wake her, and April jumped up spewing expletives, rushing to gather her morning class belongings. Megan's keeping track of April's alcohol intake. She's drinking "water," hiding behind sunglasses, and wearing the same shirt she woke up in. This gives Megan enough to press down her worry brakes.

"You did so good at your probate," a girl appears, looking down at Megan with an innocent smile. Shielding Megan from the sun's rays, she timidly waits for a response.

"Thank you," Megan states, getting a good look at the girl, who doesn't look a day over sixteen, with false eyelashes and tinted lip gloss.

The young girl standing on their post at their bench under their tree on their yard makes Megan nervous for both of them. The only non-Greek to have been seen in this area prohibited of GDIs (God expletive independent)—that's what Jasmine calls them—was Patrice, after scheming her way in. *This poor girl needs an April*, Megan thinks, someone to guide her on how to get TKRho's attention without looking like she was trying to get their attention. And now Megan needs April to guide this awkward encounter. Instead, April sits silently in LaLa Land, hidden under dark sunglasses, not coming to the rescue.

"Do you have a question?" Jasmine abruptly walks over and interrupts, handing Megan a plate of food.

Startled by Jasmine's tone, the girl grips her books as if they're a comfort blanky. "Um, I just wanted to tell you all that I enjoyed your probate show. I couldn't join the sorority this semester because of…" She lifts her books, showing that schoolwork was the reason. "…But I'll be ready next semester." Continuing through the silence, she asks, "How do I prepare to join?"

Jasmine turns away, resuming her seat on the other side of the bench.

Embarrassed by Jasmine's actions, Megan answers, "You can't join until your sophomore year, but come to our events and—"

"That's enough," Jasmine interjects. "Bye," waving the girl away.

The girl scurries off, rushing away from the embarrassment.

"Who do you think you are?" Jasmine questions Megan, peering past a silent April.

"I was giving her information on how to join."

"I know what you were doing. Why are you doing it? You're a neo. Why are you already recruiting? Stay in your place. Just because you're sitting under my tree and wearing my colors doesn't mean you can start calling shots."

April finally comes to Megan's defense. "She didn't know."

"Drunky says what? It's not even twelve thirty and you're wasted."

"Tipsy," April corrects.

"I apologize," Jasmine states sarcastically. "Y'all are neos. Leave the recruiting up to me. I'm the Dean of Pledges."

April goes back to LaLa Land, hidden behind her shades, and Megan sits eating her food in silence, afraid to speak, realizing they are still walking on eggshells with Jasmine.

"I'm a real Theta. I do what I wanta," April whispers a rap behind slurred speech in Megan's ear. "She won't be Dean of Pledges for long."

†††

"Meg, I'm so glad you called," Tina exclaims through Megan's speakerphone. Megan sits in her car, scarfing down her meal before returning to work from a thirty-minute break.

"What have you been up to? Thought I was going to have to drive to Atlanta to check on a missing daughter," Tina mentions with concern.

"I'm sorry. I should do more wellness checks. I've been busy with work and school. I've been meaning to call."

"Call on God to help with that busy schedule," Tina jokingly slides in, sitting on the sofa next to James, reclined in his chair, invested in the game.

"I call on God more than you know. I've been going to church and playing the keyboard there," she boasts, making Tina aware of her service in the church.

"What denomination is that church again?"

"I'm not sure. Why?"

"Checking to see how and who they have you worshipping."

James gives Tina a high five in agreement with her statement, believing a church's denomination can influence a believer's practice, whether good or bad. "Ask her about Alicia," James suggests while simultaneously eavesdropping, eyes still glued on the television, sipping from a steamed cup of coffee.

Tina repeats, "Have you spoken to—"

"I heard him," Megan assures Tina, keeping a close watch on the time. "We exchanged numbers in the library a while ago, and she messaged—"

"What did she message you? What did you talk about?" Tina anxiously interrupts. She waits on Megan's response in hopes that Megan will reveal a God encounter they may have had in their chats. Tina and Alicia's mom have been praying earnestly for the girls in their Saturday prayer group and send each other consistent prayer request texts.

"We talk about the semester, how it's going, and maybe riding to Macon over the holiday break." While spewing her list of lies, she realizes every Alicia encounter has been sorority-related. She changes the subject to avoid oversharing. "I was invited to a wedding next month. I need something to wear. Can you put something together for me?"

"Sure. Whose wedding?" Tina asks.

~

Southern Atlanta South Bank's entrance door swung open, letting in a swift, cool breeze. Entering with a massive smile, Sharon sashayed in with a glow of afternoon delight. She commanded her position in the middle of the bank and cleared her throat, swinging her ring finger covered by a huge diamond over the deposit slips and withdrawal station.

"I'm getting married!" she shouted. She collapsed on the table as if to have revealed a secret she could no longer hold in. Her words bounced off the walls, echoing into the ears of those in the open space. The bank tellers and the few customers congratulated her with smiles and claps. A shock came over Megan, who was finishing up with a client. She wasn't shocked because Sharon wasn't deserving; she's shocked because Megan has never seen a married Theta.

April's mother hadn't mentioned being currently married, their advisor Sharice was single, and she'd never known Sharon to date—just work and sorority and back again. But this undeniable glow Sharon now wore was beautiful. Engagement looked great on her.

~

"She must really like you if she's inviting you to the wedding," Tina states. "I have the perfect dress pattern in mind. What color would you like to wear?"

It's Megan's first time attending a wedding—a soror's wedding at that. Calling her mother for wardrobe advice was obvious, but she hadn't thought of a color. She blurts out the first color that comes to mind. "Baby blue."

"That's a good color." Tina's wheels begin to turn. "Oh, I see why you called. This isn't a wellness check. You're using me for my skills."

Tina receives an incoming call from Tameka. "That's Tameka. Let me conference her in."

"I only have ten minutes before I go back to work," Megan whines, trying to exit the call.

"No, hang on. It'll be quick. I'll—"

"Hello," Tameka joins the call.

"Hello?" Tina questions. "Hello? Are you there?"

"Ma, I'm here," Tameka responds.

Tina is frustrated and unsure of the three-way call's connection. "Tameka?"

"Ma, we're both on the phone!" the girls yell.

"Good. Megan, continue with how you're using me for this wedding."

"Wedding? What wedding?" Tameka questions.

"My boss Sharon is getting married, and I'm invited to her wedding."

"Can you bring a plus one?" Tameka asks.

"Good question, Meka. Can you?" Tina perks up with the thought of being invited.

"I can. I've already invited Jeff. So—"

"Jeff?!" Tina and Tameka both exclaim before Megan could deny their request to be her plus one.

"Jeff!" James yells, lifting up from his reclined position, spilling his coffee in response to the name. "What he do?"

"Girls, I got to go. Your father spilled his coffee. James—" She hangs up the phone, disconnecting the call.

With six minutes remaining for break, Megan gathers her belongings and exits the car. Her phone immediately rings. She scrambles to pull her phone from her purse, placing an earbud in her ear.

"I see you planting that seed," Tameka laughs, referring to Jeff being Megan's plus one.

Megan walks toward the entrance of the bank, observing the customer line formed through the glass doors. She's greeted with pleading expressions for help from her coworkers. Rushing to the break room to put her belongings in her locker, she continues the conversation with her sister. "Is it weird to have Jeff as my plus one, or should I take April?"

"April…? Never mind." Tameka decides against an argument. "Take Jeff. Isn't he your boyfriend?"

"Yes," Megan confirms, walking toward the bathroom to wash her hands from lunch residue.

"Can you see yourself being Mrs.... what's his last name?"

"Spencer. Jeff Spencer. And yes, I actually can." Stunned with her response, a heat rush comes over her. She studies her reflection in the mirror, envisioning herself as Mrs. Megan Spencer.

"Wow, my baby sister has a serious adult relationship," Tameka jokes. "Did y'all kiss yet? With tongue?"

"Meka!" Embarrassment comes over Megan. They've only had a peck here and there—nothing more—but she wasn't going to tell her sister that. She grabs a paper towel to dry her hands and turns the faucet off, then uses the paper towel to open the door, throws it in the trash, and exits the bathroom.

Off of Megan's delayed response, Tameka continues, "Well, if you do, make sure it's public, because once tongues are added, so are other things."

"Eew!"

"It's true. I had to slow Marcus down. He was—"

"Bye, Meka. I have to go." Megan cuts her off, shielding her ears from TMI her sister is excited to reveal. She hangs up, placing her phone in her pocket. She walks to her station as thoughts of tongue-kissing Jeff cloud her mind.

"Come on, girl. We need you," a fellow teller waves Megan's cloud away.

✝✝✝

"Come on, Megan. I need you. Join us." Sharon waves, pressuring Megan to join the other sorors circled around her. Sharon's wearing a gorgeous white lace dress adorned with sparkles. Her train flows through the reception hall dance floor.

"Go ahead." Jeff encourages from his seat in the back of the reception hall. Megan rises from the table with timid steps toward the circle. She's relieved she asked her mother to style her in blue.

The fitted dress blends well with the others, who are staring at her entry to join them.

"Beautiful dress," one of the sorors compliments as they grasp hands.

Megan's received many compliments on her dress and its perfect shade of blue, but the compliment she cherished the most was Jeff's nonverbals. His eyes lit up when she walked from her apartment stairs to the passenger seat of his car, and throughout the wedding ceremony he would glance in her direction in admiration of her beauty.

She waits nervously in the circle, holding hands with a soror on each side, praying no secret handshake is given. She looks over her shoulder to Jeff. He comforts her by giving two thumbs up. The sorors begin to walk around the bride, simultaneously singing their sorority hymn. An exhale of relief leaves Megan as she's grateful to know the familiar hymn, earning her spot in this Theta wedding tradition.

"Hail Theta Kappa Rho, we greet thee tonight,
For this noble sisterhood be always our delight.
We love our motto and the power from it flows,
When cares of life overtake us with life's given woes.
We'll always reverence TKRho forever and a day.
With lifted hearts, we praise thee.
TKRho, we give you praise."

"The Thetas came out to bless this wedding. Now show the crowd how a Theta bride and her sorors get down!" the DJ shouts into the microphone, blasting the Theta theme song through the speakers. Startled by the beat's bass, Megan jolts into the line of sorors performing their universal stroll. Sharon leads the line, guiding the girls through the reception hall. When the line passes by Jeff, Megan takes the opportunity to perform her seductive moves, hypnotizing him into a trance.

After a late night of Sharon's union celebration, Megan invites Jeff up to her room to finish their conversation about the wedding with a cup of coffee. Megan expresses how lovely the couple looked together on their special day, imagining her and Jeff in the same sentiment. Jeff voices his enjoyment of the food and the dance Megan gave him.

"That dance wasn't for you." Megan innocently smiles, sitting close with Jeff on her bed in privacy—a privacy SASU's dorm room could never give. A little embarrassed by her flirtatious dance act, she sits nervous, not sure where to steer the conversation.

"Whatever it was, I enjoyed it." Jeff responds, placing his hand behind her neck and leaning in for a kiss on the lips. Megan reciprocates the act. After a few pecks, she feels a slight slip of the tongue. *Once tongues are added, so are other things*, Tameka's comment reminds her. She immediately stops the action from moving forward, holding her hand against Jeff's chest, slightly pushing him back into an upright position.

"I want to wait until marriage." Megan blurts out. Afraid of Jeff's reaction to her demand, she deflects. "More coffee?" pointing to his empty mug on her nightstand.

Pondering the suggestion to wait until marriage, Jeff sits in silence, ignoring the request for more coffee. He assumed she was saving herself for something real—something they undeniably had—but waiting for marriage was a stretch. Debating the load of the situation and his feelings for Megan, he says, "It will be a struggle, but I don't want to pressure you into anything you aren't ready for. So, I have to respect your wishes." They sit in silence, and after long deliberation he asks, "Can I ask you a question?"

"Sure," she responds, taking in the seriousness of his tone. She adjusts her posture, giving him her undivided attention.

"When pledging, did you take wood?"

That's his question? He totally changed the subject, she thinks to herself, yet relieved not to talk about sex. Embarrassment comes over her at being put in a position to disclose being hit with a paddle. She takes a deep breath, exhales, and reveals, "Yes, during hell night."

"You did?" Concern comes over Jeff. He had a roundabout way of asking about this act, but he never thought she would admit to it, especially after saying she wanted to wait until marriage. Megan's innocence is what attracted him to her. He could spot a promiscuous girl easily, and from the first day of seeing Megan on campus, he knew she wasn't one of them.

"Jasmine and her stupid paddle. I received eight licks."

Jeff's eyes widen, followed by uncontrollable laughter.

"What's so funny?" Megan asks, getting upset that he would laugh about her pain, which has evolved into embarrassment now that she's vocalized it.

"I'm sorry. I didn't mean to laugh," he says, standing and stretching his legs from the tension caused by the intense conversation. "I knew that kind of taking wood was a possibility. I guess I wasn't clear when I asked if they made you sleep with other guys while you pledged—taking *that* wood."

"What? No!" she yells. "Is that a thing? I would never do that. That would have been the last straw for me." Observing Jeff's lack of mutual outrage, she repeats, "Is that a thing?"

"Yes, it is," he confesses. "When I was on line, the big brothers blindfolded me and had me sleep with some girl. To this day, I still don't know who she was. It was during hell week. It's usually a Theta. Any Theta who volunteers. It's an act to bind us."

"That's sick. No, I didn't do anything like that, and I haven't heard of any of my sisters participating in that mess," Megan assures, with disgust.

"I was hoping you didn't. I wasn't sure how else to bring it up, but it is something done in my fraternity and your sorority."

Off of Megan's disappointment, he continues, "Megan, I'm telling you this because I care about you and don't want anything to come out later that could hurt us in the future." He sits next to her, placing his hand on her trembling knee. "That girl knows who I am, but because I was blindfolded, I don't know who she is. I don't want you experiencing any unwanted surprises."

Like now? she thinks. "More coffee?" she asks instead.

She doesn't wait for his response. She reaches for his cup and exits the room. Entering the kitchen with the empty coffee mug, she exhales, releasing a tear, angry that her hopeful future husband has slept with someone else. The thought of the forbidden conversation about previous partners never crossed her mind. She understands that it was before her enrollment at SASU and she's sure he's committed to their relationship, but this mysterious sexual encounter still hurts just the same.

CHAPTER 15: MAKE THE GUILT GO AWAY

Megan invited April, Donna, and Jeff to Macon for Thanksgiving, but they declined, having other plans. April is required to attend her mother's dinner, accompanied by line sisters and graduate chapter sorors. Donna is spending time with her family, and Jeff insists he's still not ready to meet the Mahn family. He mentions that he'll be fine entertaining himself with the football game and a bucket of wings. Megan's not mad at his decision. She needs the time to process his revealed sexcapade without him questioning her comfort about it.

"Thank you for offering me a ride home," Alicia states from Megan's passenger seat, observing the autumn foliage of Georgia trees down I-75. The lie told to Tina of travel plans with Alicia to Macon has now become a reality. Megan figured that maybe Alicia's company could turn into a therapy session where they could discuss Jeff, and she'll convince her that his past unknown partner is no big deal. But the topic never comes up. Alicia seems to be in more need of a therapist than Megan is. She has a lot to get off her chest.

"I'm so happy to get away from those girls. That house is crazy. So much scandal. So much jealousy. We're around each other twenty-four-seven," Alicia explains, taking a bite of her French fry smothered in ketchup. Craving McDonald's fries, she'd begged Megan to stop at the first exit sign that displayed the golden arches.

Alicia explains that Gamma Alpha Alpha Phi are on strict diets. No fried foods or sodas are allowed in the house. The girls must sneak their forbidden foods and burn off the calories so the scale doesn't reveal their disloyalty. Alicia, savoring the taste between her rants, continues, "The sneaking of boys in the house is annoying. I try studying and a boy is looking over my shoulder. I wake up and a guy is staring at me from my roommate's bed. I thought moving in the house my sophomore year would be fun, but this is too much. It's worse than the dorms."

Alicia goes on to mention how her sisters are constantly trying to hook her up with guys from Zeta Zeta Pi. One night, the girls in the house had set up a speed date just for her. She sat at the kitchen table while about twenty guys entered one by one, having two minutes to plead why they were her best match. Against her will, she was made to choose the one with the most relationship potential. Nothing came from it. Her pick was only in it for the fraternity's image. It's ideal for Gamma AAPhi and Zeta Zeta Pi to form relationships, maintaining the perfect "relationship goals" duo.

Alicia's two-hour sorority spill-the-beans podcast brought them to Alicia's front door, leaving Megan no therapy time to discuss her relationship goals about Jeff. "That's my house," Alicia points to a ranch-style home. "Thanks again for the ride," she said, grabbing her luggage and fried food evidence.

†††

Pastor Jones stands before the congregation, revving up his sermon, mustering up "Amens" from the crowd. Megan, sitting in the Mahns' usual back pew of God's House Church, spots Alicia with her parents a few rows in front of them. They weirdly fit the description her mother thoroughly described: a small family with a wholesome, quiet demeanor. Her mother has long blonde hair with streaks of gray, and her father's black beard has silver strands. He's neatly dressed for church, wearing a solid brown suit, unlike James, who enjoys a good pair of jeans and a ball cap.

The keyboardist strikes a string of notes as Pastor Jones intensifies the message, loosening his collar. Megan revels in her mini vacation away from the Atlanta church and her music ministry duties. That church has become the Olympic competition of churches—a fashion show, a who's who of riffs and runs in the choir, a who-can-perform-the-most-intricate clap sequence to worship songs, and what Greek organization can praise the hardest. She never leaves the Atlanta church with peace, like the peace she currently feels at God's House.

Megan's TKRho pin, tucked beneath her blue blazer, begins to disturb her peace with an irritation on her chest. Relieving the constant scratch of her skin, Tameka observes the motion, catching a glimpse of the pendant. "When did you join? And I know you're not wearing that up in here?" she forcibly whispers.

Megan, irritated and defensive, responds, "What's the big deal? I'm still listening to the word."

"The big deal is you've joined a cult and brought its god in here that you made an oath to," Tameka vents.

"Shhh," Tina expresses, quickly controlling the situation before James inserts himself.

"What god?" Megan questions. She doesn't remember making an oath to a god during her initiation or any other time. She made sure of it. Candles and blindfolds, yes, but no other gods were in attendance. Assessing Tameka's words, Megan rolls her eyes in frustration, reluctantly removing the pendant and tucking it away into her purse, agreeing with her adversary quickly.

"God still knows," Tameka reminds her with conviction, referring to the concealed pendant and her new oath.

"Only God can judge me," Megan retorts, using the famous line when someone is demanding the last word.

"But those that are spiritual can evaluate all things. First Corinthians 2:15." Tameka rolls her neck, waiting for a comeback. None is given. Instead, her neck roll is met with the glare of an angry dad—James demanding silence.

Three hours later, the congregation is let out from service. Some congregants are energized, while others, like Megan, are tired and starving for Thanksgiving leftovers. Megan, waving her goodbyes to Alicia and other familiar faces, settles into the back passenger seat of the family SUV, remembering her pendant tucked away in her purse. She goes to reach for it, and her gaze drifts out the window to a distant car passing by. Its exterior is decorated with a simple yet profound message: "Stepping Down" on a bumper sticker. *See, Tameka doesn't know what she's talking about. I'm supposed to be stepping with TKRho; that's how we get down. Stepping Down—maybe that could be the title of our next party,* Megan ponders to herself.

The words "Stepping Down" continue to ring in her ear, overpowering the after-church soundtrack echoing from the Mahns' truck speakers as they ride the Macon roads home. The words on the sticker continue to stir up deeper revelation within Megan. She begins deciphering between two revelations. One is stepping down from a position. Two, her initial thought, stepping down being slang for stepping how the sororities do. Hoping it's not the former, she finds herself caught in a moment of reflection, struggling with the weight of her sister's beliefs. *Did we give an oath to a god at our initiation? Nah, we didn't. God gave me permission to join. He selected me to be a part of the sorority, hence the interest letter, or He would have stopped the whole process.*

Right? He's telling me that 'Stepping Down' needs to be the title of our upcoming spring party. Thank you, God, for that title. The girls will love it. Megan persuades herself as she pins her pendant back in position under her blazer at the apex of her heart.

†††

"Welcome to the Spring 2023 Stepping Down Blast Off, hosted by the ladies of TKRho," the DJ shouts through the speakers in the crowded room of SASU students. With permission to host their spring rush party in one of the SASU conference rooms, they expanded the space to a capacity of two hundred fifty by removing the dividing partitions of three rooms.

The space is completely filled with rowdy partygoers that somehow found a way to disobey the "alcohol is not permitted on campus" rule. Empty Solo cups overflow the trash cans, line the window sills, and alcohol and sweat aromas fill the atmosphere. Attempting to clean up after the unruly crowd, Megan spots a drunk April trying to connect rhythmic claps and steps to the TKRho stroll anthem that's blasting through the speakers. With a lack of balance, April mimics the less obvious intoxicated sorors with slight stumbles. Megan quickly grabs her from the moving line, avoiding further embarrassment. She pulls her aside, leading her to a seat in a row of chairs lined up against the wall. She hands her a bottle of water to sober up. April follows the instructions, gulping the water like it's her last lifeline for survival.

Jasmine stumbles upon the girls, wearing a "Class of '23" graduation party cap, celebrating months in advance. With consistent blunt reminders, she demands everyone to miss her presence on campus and that it would be impossible for the next line coming in to be "made" if she's not Dean of Pledges. Already having claimed the position for the upcoming fall semester, April takes this demand as a threat. Megan roots for April to fill the position—or anyone else, for that matter—then maybe the chapter events and intake process would run smoothly without hazing. Bringing in a line of paper would be ideal. Less risk. Pledging has brought division amongst the neos and the big sisters. There's also growing division amongst the original four versus the girls that joined after the interest meeting. If possible, Megan wants to avoid that tension in future lines coming in. She must find a way to become president; then maybe she'll have more of a say in the intake process.

Jasmine forcefully scooches into the seat on the other side of Megan. Leaning in, she drunkenly states, "You're a good tail. Always coming to the rescue. The probate show, now this," referring to April, who's bent over with her head rested on her knees. "You have heart and determination. Nothing seems to stop you. Not even a little last-minute haze on initiation day."

Last-minute haze? Megan's confused. She doesn't remember being hazed on initiation day. Megan doesn't respond. She waits for Jasmine's truth serum to kick in, the effects of the alcohol to reveal her inner thoughts.

"Your pearls," Jasmine reminds her. "You thought you forgot them. I hid them, making you squirm till the very last minute. I had to test you one last time. I couldn't let you into my sorority that easy," she reveals with a sinister grin. Megan gets angry that Jasmine would play games during initiation but keeps her cool. Observing Jasmine's drunken demeanor, the wrong response could turn this party into a brawl. Instead of responding in a way that would bring campus security and shut the party down, she tends to a groaning April. She hands April more water to sober up.

Jasmine leans further into Megan's ear, making sure her next words are clear. She struggles to manage her slurs as she speaks. "You think we call you Blue because it's a great color? Although it is." Jasmine laughs, proudly posing her blue outfit in her seat with hands on her hips. "We call you Blue because I saw you wearing it while we were on suspension. Remember that?"

Megan pauses her assistance with April and nervously turns to lock eyes with Jasmine.

"I figured that since you love the color so much, why not give you the name. Hazing doesn't stop because you wear blue, Blue. You're. still. A. Neo." Punching her last words, she struggles to get up, attempting to leave on a mic-drop moment.

WWJD? What would Jesus do? Megan's initial reaction is to push the tipsy Jasmine to the floor, but taking an oath to maintain their sisterly bond and act accordingly while wearing their letters, Megan chooses the sisterly route. As much as she wanted to embarrass Jasmine how Jasmine embarrassed her, she knew she would have to save it for another time. Instead, she extends her hand, aiding Jasmine's stand. *That's what Jesus would do.*

Jasmine dismisses Megan's help, struggling to accomplish the task on her own.

"Megan, I'm about to throw up." April squeamish, pulling on Megan's shirt urgently, trying to find something to relieve herself in. Leaving Jasmine to stand upright on her own, Megan tends to April, permitting Jasmine to stumble off into the party atmosphere as someone else's problem for the night.

†††

FALL 2023

Thank God the Omega Zeta chapter of TKRho has started fresh. No prophytes. No big sisters. No Jasmine demanding officer positions and praise. Toya barely completed her studies, but she has successfully found a way to balance class and mommy duties, graduating alongside Jasmine. They've all graduated; none have crossed into the fall 2023 school year. No more hazing the neos. What a relief.

Megan can now infiltrate positive energy into TKRho's membership recruiting process. She's proven leadership and acceleration in her GPA, granting her the promotion of being president of the chapter, with Trish by her side as vice president. April's fight for Dean of Pledges has paid off. Megan pleaded and begged April not to give the girls an underground process. She didn't want her senior year to be full of sneaking around hazing candidates; instead, she wanted them to have a bond that wasn't manipulated with physical and psychological humiliation. Donna chose not to hold an officer position. Boldly declaring her opinions on TKRho issues was her safe place.

The remaining members on campus—the left-behind nine—have collectively decided to postpone a Fall 2023 membership intake process. The neos are taking the time to learn and maintain the sorority's culture. It's proven to be hard work without the prophytes; however, they've agreed not to worry about new members, focus on the sorority's mission, and get a handle on their sorority events. Megan has yet to experience the musical event that piqued her interest in the interest meeting; however, the other events have been a success. Surprisingly, the sisters of other chapters attending hid their discrimination toward the neos of Omega Zeta, probably because the advisors watched closely with a keen eye for any hint of hazing behavior within or outside of the sorority.

With only nine Theta women on campus, the pressure is heavy to represent the sorority well. They fulfill the mission by wearing their paraphernalia and blasting the campus with chirp calls every chance they get. Although they are small in number, their boldness is present and relevant, a competitive reminder to their rivals, Mu Alpha Phi Alpha. The original four have no problem displaying their bold demeanor in group settings; however, the others, apart from Patrice, aren't as comfortable. April emotes a disdain that they aren't worthy of wearing the letters around her. But not Patrice. She continues to stand her ground. She declares, "I'm not paper! I'm the mastermind behind hazing. How can you call me 'paper' when I hazed Sharice into accepting me into the sorority?" April burns with fury every time she hears this argument because it stems from them being caught kissing trees, the underground haze that, if dug into deeper, could cause another absence of the sorority's presence on campus. So, April allows Patrice's sly comments while maintaining her stance on the others not being worthy.

The girls sit on the yard, scattered under their TKRho-engraved tree. With their usual banter back and forth, Trish states, "Before we go on break for the holidays, we should decide on our events for rush week in spring. I don't want to graduate a neo."

"Save this conversation for a chapter meeting." Patrice groans.

"But when we talk about a step show or a probate, you're all in? Make it make sense, Patrice," Donna interjects, annoyed with Patrice's lack of sorority dedication.

"Well, I don't want to talk about it right now," Patrice demands, stuffing her face with a handful of potato chips.

"How about you not talk, then," Trish snaps.

They're unaware of April's departure due to their quarrel. She abruptly rises from the bench, approaching a nervous girl standing on the sidewalk at the edge of the yard. The girl hands April a black plastic bag and swiftly walks away. Observing the exchange between the two, Megan recognizes her familiar rush off. It's the girl who introduced herself to the sorority last semester, with an exchange of embarrassment from Jasmine that led to a similar rush off. April returns to the bench, releasing a to-go Styrofoam container from the bag. Megan observes the fully stacked contents of turkey, mac and cheese, collard greens, and cornbread. The works.

"Wow, what's that?" Megan asks, mouth watering, observing the plate.

"Mine," April responds, taking a big, healthy bite.

Megan decides against going into full interrogation. However, the girl's avoidance of the grass, her black attire, no makeup, and suspicious soul food delivery make Megan's spidey-sense antennas erect.

✝✝✝

Before leaving for holiday break, Megan and April enjoy some relaxing roommate time on the couch with a bucket of popcorn and Skittles. They fulfill the Mahn sister tradition, a night of "She's All That." Megan throws kernels of popcorn into her mouth while mouthing the character's lines on the TV screen. It's April's first time seeing the rom-com. Enjoying the plot, she shuffles Skittles in her hand before throwing them into her mouth.

Above the television, Megan notices a new poster framed on the wall. She gets up to read it with no care of missing any part of the movie. She's seen it a hundred times. She reads, "Let the spirit of TKRho hover over you so that your works and good deeds may give peace to all mankind. — Annie Williams." Returning to her seat on the couch she asks, "Where'd you get that poster from?"

"My mom sent it. A vendor was selling my great-great-grandmother's quotes on those paintings," she replies, slightly annoyed with the movie interruption.

"That's nice," Megan responds, sensing the annoyance.

April's phone rings as Zack, played by Freddie Prinze Jr., streaks across the graduation stage after losing a bet—the bet to turn Laney into prom queen.

April rolls her eyes, irritated with the phone call interruption. "No, you may not!" She hangs up, bringing her attention back to the screen. The phone rings again. She answers after its first ring with increased annoyance. "Yes, this is her. Go on." With a poker face, she sits quietly, listening to the voice on the other end of the line. Megan pretends to immerse herself in the end credits scrolling on the screen while eavesdropping on the weird phone interaction. She attempts to turn up the volume of her invisible hearing aids to hear the caller's voice. The voice is unclear. From Megan's peripheral, she sees April waving at her to pass the popcorn.

"When did I cross?" April asks the caller, grabbing the almost empty bowl. Giving a second for a response, she hangs up. April takes a handful of leftover popcorn and reaches for the remote to turn up the volume. She studies the credits of familiar names on the screen.

"Kimberly 'Lil Kim' Jones? Hold up, that was Lil' Kim?" April yells, spotting the rapper's name. "I have to watch this again. I didn't see her."

Before Megan could respond to who Lil' Kim was in the movie or ask why the person on the phone should know when she crossed TKRho, her phone rings. It's Jeff. "Hello… What!" Megan abruptly gets up from the couch and rushes to her room to grab her belongings. "I'm on my way." She hangs up the phone, searching for her car keys in her purse.

"I'm headed to Jeff's. Tony *died*." She rushes out of the house, saving yet another April interrogation for another day.

At his apartment, Jeff swings the door open, collapsing into Megan's arms. They make their way to his rustic brown leather couch. His eyes are red, filled with tears, cheeks flushed, and crumbled tissue squares cover his glass table.

"I didn't know who else to call when I heard the news. It's my fault." He sobs in Megan's arms on the couch.

"How is this your fault? What happened?"

"A seizure. They took him to the hospital, and he died. It's my fault."

"It's not your fault." Megan holds him tightly in her arms as his head is buried in her chest. "It's not your fault." She repeats it, not knowing what else to say. She's never experienced a death before nor learned the proper response to console someone who has.

"I caused the brain injury. I caused his speech impediment. I caused his seizure. I caused his death. It's my fault!" Megan, clueless about what to do, holds him tighter as his sobs get heavier, louder, and drench her shirt with tears.

"I killed him, Megan," he whispers. Megan feels the vibrato on her chest. The weight of the situation sits heavy on her heart, leaving her speechless. She doesn't have any words to take away his guilt.

"I don't know what to do. I can't go to jail. What should I do?" He looks up into Megan's eyes with an intense plea for a savior.

Megan's only thoughts are, *WWJD? He could turn himself in. But is he really the cause of Tony's death? For all we know, Tony could have a history of seizures, an underlying disease no one knew about. It couldn't possibly be Jeff's fault.*

Filling the silence, Megan responds into Jeff's hopeless eyes, "Whatever you decide, I'm here for you, Jeff. I love you, and I will be here for as long as you need to make the guilt go away." That's what Jesus would say. She was sure of it.

Jeff is secured in Megan's eyes yet overwhelmed with emotion. He embraces her with a kiss on the lips. "Thank you." He releases intense breaths and continues to kiss her until she reciprocates. She feels tongue. But with the heightened situation, she couldn't stop him to discuss waiting for marriage. It wouldn't be fair. He needed her, and this is how he needed her at this moment. He unbuttons his shirt, revealing an engraved Zeta Alpha Phi brand on his chest that Megan's never seen. It's a healed burn from a metal rod that caused his flesh to rise.

"Are you sure?" he asks. She nods her head, giving consent.

This isn't the time to say no. I can't reject him when he's hurting the most.

†††

Megan's usual Saturday morning alarm goes off for work. She reaches for her phone in its normal spot to turn it off—only to realize it's not there. She's awakened to a room not her own. It's Jeff's room. He must have moved her from the couch once she had fallen asleep. The room is covered in Zeta Alpha Phi symbols and music posters of his favorite albums. A rush comes over her to gather her belongings, quickly adjusting to the added trip back home to maintain an on-time work arrival. She kisses Jeff goodbye. "I have to go to work. Call me if you need to talk. Love you." He gives her a head nod with swollen eyes from last night's heavy tears. Her run of shame to her car intensifies as she ponders how their first overnight together as boyfriend and girlfriend was not PG as she'd envisioned.

†††

WINTER 2023
Sharon has graciously approved Megan's meticulously dispersed paid time off request—the perfect work schedule ensuring stress-free Mahn visitations scattered throughout the holiday break. Plus, Megan's due for a hairstyle change—a style that's easy to manage, allowing for more rest in the morning. Tameka has agreed to the hair upgrade, as long as Megan models a new product she's testing: a salon chair. A potential social media sponsor has gifted Tameka a salon chair in exchange for promotional content. All she has to do is participate in a thirty-day trial where she highlights the chair in her posts. And if they're pleased, they will undergo a paid partnership program. Making the most of the opportunity, Tameka has placed the chair in the corner of their once-shared bedroom, creating a nice salon studio setup.

Megan sits in the swivel chair surrounded by ring lights, cameras, and a boom mic overhead. She's focused on her back-and-forth text conversation with Jeff. He expresses how, although he appreciates her wanting to be by his side at Tony's funeral, he prefers to attend the service with his fraternity. That maybe their brotherly camaraderie would bring him peace and assurance that Tony's death wasn't his fault. She agrees. She actually prefers having *this* conversation over a conversation about the action that took place between them. Avoiding the conversation about their night together gives her time to process her emotions. She's disappointed that she hadn't waited until marriage while questioning her emotions of not feeling guilty. Creating a deeper bond with Jeff—that, she doesn't regret.

"Put your phone down for a second. I need clear shots of a happy customer."

Bye. Love you, Megan quickly texts Jeff before Tameka can successfully grab it, placing it on the vanity that matches the aesthetic of the salon space.

"How's everything with school?" Tameka asks, tilting Megan's head toward the camera, showing off her braid extension application.

Megan puts on a fake smile for the camera. "Everything with school is good. Less stress since we have decided against bringing in a new line. We plan to bring one in next fall." She addresses the camera with a genuine smile. "I'm a member of Theta Kappa Rho," she brags.

"Yall hazing them girls?"

"No!" Megan confirms to her audience—the camera lens.

"You better not." Tameka forcefully grips Megan's hair strands, demonstrating how her grip will tighten if she's being lied to.

"Ouch! I'm president of the chapter. I refuse to have my girls hazed," Megan assures, squinching deep into the chair as the pain intensifies.

"Umm-hmm." Tameka softens her grip to part the next section. Megan's phone vibrates on the vanity. Tameka sees the notification of Jeff's heart-emoji response to Megan's last text: ***Bye. Love you.***

~

Members from the Atlanta chapters of ZAPhi had met at the frat house to retrieve items for Tony's funeral service then trailed each other ten vehicles deep to Tony's hometown, Savannah, Georgia. It's customary for the fraternity to perform an acknowledgement service after the funeral ceremony of the deceased, ensuring their membership continues into the afterlife with respects to the work achieved in the brotherhood. The deceased member's chapter president during the deceased's initiation is to lead the ceremony. Taking on the great task, Jeff chose to ride in the backseat in one of the brothers' cars to study the ritual book. He receives this duty as an honor and hopes this responsibility will ease the guilt that's placed a growing knot in his stomach.

President or not, Jeff's never participated in a ceremony like this, but then again, he's never had to bury a ZAPhi brother before either. He's been to plenty of funerals for guys from his neighborhood, but that was expected. It was the norm from where he's from. But this wasn't supposed to happen to someone like Tony. He was one of the good guys, coming from a two-parent home with a full-ride scholarship. An academic scholarship, not some sports scholarship that most of the small number of Black guys on campus had.

The brothers approach the church, parked in spaces reserved for the fraternity. Exiting the car, Jeff tucks his phone away inside his jacket suit pocket after responding to Megan's text with a heart emoji, signaling his arrival to the funeral. The men line up in Zeta Alpha Phi fashion to walk orderly into the brick-laid church, wearing matching black suits with Zeta Alpha Phi ties and black shiny dress shoes. Some of the seasoned brothers balance on their green-and-black candy-striped canes as they somberly file into their reserved seats surrounded by Tony's friends and family.

The service heightens with heavy words from the pastor. Sniffles can be heard throughout the room. A collage of Tony's greatest moments is displayed on an overhead projector while "I'll Be Missing You" softly channels through the speakers. Jeff chokes up seeing a picture of him and Tony, arms around each other's shoulders at Megan's probate show. The picture reminds Jeff of how grateful he is to have an amazing girlfriend. She understood his need to share this moment with his brothers.

STEPPING DOWN

A candid picture of Tony laughing with Toya and Jasmine at the Theta Kappa Rho Rush Week table is highlighted on the screen. A slight sniffle is heard from the far corner of the church. Jeff follows the sound, and Toya is spotted in the back holding her baby with a soggy ripped-up tissue wiping away tears. Jeff is slightly surprised to see Toya in attendance.

At the finish of the remarks, the fraternity is given a nod from the director to prepare their service in the church parlor. The fraternity rises and enters the space provided for their service. Once the items were set up, a member makes the funeral director aware that their service is ready to begin. The crowd comes out into the area, and Jeff stands before all in attendance alongside his brothers. He notices a group of family members walk past, obviously annoyed with their set-up, disapproving mumbles trailing behind them. The guys are posted in a semi-circle around lit candles and their shield. Standing in the center of the semi-circle, Jeff opens the ritual book to the eternal brotherhood ritual and begins reciting the eulogy.

"The eternal brotherhood service is a rite of passage that Zeta Alpha Phi gives its deceased brother. It's fitting that we Zeta Alpha Phi Fraternity pause here for a moment of silence of loving tribute to our brother." Jeff gives the moment of silence about fifteen seconds, which felt like a minute. Then he rushes back into the eulogy. "Brother Tony Grier remained true to his sacred oath of honor. He loved ZAPhi and its principles. He faithfully attempted to practice them in his daily life. He sought to be a loving and compassionate brother. Humble-minded. He lived fully, laughed often. He looked for the best in others and gave the best he had. His life was an inspiration, and his memory will be a blessing."

The brothers clasp hands and recite together:

"Do not stand at my grave and weep.
I'm not there because I'm elsewhere, asleep.
As long as Zeta Alpha Phi numbers multiply
I will live on in the eternal. I will not die.

Do not stand at my grave and cry.
I am not there because my spirit in Zeta Alpha Phi will never die."

The guilt knot in Jeff's stomach dissipates as he recites the last line. He lets out a huge sigh of relief. The guys blow out the candles surrounding the shield. As each candle is blown out, another sniffle is heard from Toya louder than the previous one as Tony's body is rolled out of the sanctuary into the hearse where the rest of his family awaits.

~

"'Bye. Love you?'" Tameka asks, observing Megan's text notification. Before Megan can reach for the phone to hide the evidence of Tony's death, Tameka playfully grabs it and waves it above her head out of Megan's reach. "Y'all in love now?" she sings.

Megan, with struggled success, grabs her phone from Tameka. She plops down into her seat and embarrassingly shrugs her shoulders, slightly blushing. Tameka swivels the chair around, grabbing her sister's face to receive an honest face-to-face answer. "Are. You. In. Love?" she asks again, serious this time.

After a moment of thought, Megan exhales and peace comes over her. With a smile she answers, "Yes. I think I am." Her eyes gleam at the realization that she doesn't think she's in love. She *is* in love.

"Why do you think you are in love, Megan?" Tameka asks, getting down to the root of Megan's new physical display. Tameka discerns Megan's relationship with Jeff—it's different from the relationship explained in their last phone conversation with him being her plus one to Sharon's wedding. Observing the shift in her sister's eyes and body language, Tameka turns the cameras off and asks, "Did you have sex with Jeff?"

Megan, ashamed to verbally confirm the act, turns away looking for her comfort, her keyboard that used to take residence against the wall. Remembering that her comfort is at her Atlanta home, she whispers, "Yes. We did."

"What!" Tameka yells. She takes a moment to calm down. Then, remembering their parents are out making a few errands, she continues yelling, "You had sex, Megan?"

"Yes. I did." Megan confirms, wishing she could disappear in the arms of the salon chair.

"You were supposed to push the button so it can make a noise like a foghorn, Laney!" referencing *She's All That*, where Laney explained a contraption that prevented a sexual encounter. "I haven't had sex with Marcus yet and we're *engaged*. We're waiting until marriage. Like you're supposed to! Did you use protection at least? How many times have you had sex with him?"

Megan's phone rings. Grateful for the interruption she answers, "Hello." Tameka stands with her hands on her hips waiting to resume the conversation.

"May I speak to Megan?" the unknown voice asks.

"This is her," Megan responds.

"I mean Number Four, Blue. May I speak to Blue?" the voice corrects themself.

"This is her," Megan responds.

Tameka studies her sister's face, trying to decipher the situation.

"You are the tail. You crossed fall twenty twenty-two and… and…" The girl begins to stutter.

"Who is this?" Megan asks. "You can tell me. It's fine. Who am I speaking to?"

There's a long pause on the other end of the call, and a silence fills the room as Tameka freezes in position also awaiting information about the caller. Eventually the voice admits, "My name is Shay."

"Why are you calling me, Shay?" Megan softly asks, not to startle the caller.

"Big Sister Legacy told me to call you. I called Big Sister Brace Boldly and Big Sister Soul Glow."

"Are you being hazed?" Megan asks with concern.

Shay hangs up the phone, leaving both Megan and Tameka stunned at the event.

"Girl, you lucky them cameras are off," Tameka reminds her.

✝✝✝

SPRING 2024 — Interest Meeting

"Just how I remember," Patrice happily states as she applies the last strip of tape along the edge of SASU's conference room door adorned with shiny blue wrapping paper. The left-behind nine have arrived an hour early to set up rows of chairs, expecting to fill the room with TKRho potentials. One by one, as tasks are being completed, the girls take their positions along the walls of the room waiting for the spring official interest meeting to begin.

Megan takes her position in the front of the room in preparation for her opening speech as president. "I hope we have a line of forty. Then there's no mistake of hazing," she announces.

April ignores the comment, busying herself at the refreshment table arranging snacks and bottled waters. Megan has expressed her disapproval of hazing to April and how it will not be tolerated as long as she's president of the chapter. Her demands have been ignored. After her encounter with Shay, more girls have been calling all hours of the night reciting her history. She's even noticed a consistent seating arrangement of girls behind April every Sunday at church.

A clueless Sharice interjects, seated in the front row. "The number of initiates will determine who shows up today. If forty girls show up and turn their paperwork in on time, then we'll have forty neos." She turns toward April. "April, did you pass out all those flyers and post them around campus?"

"I sure did," April answers, avoiding eye contact.

Trish approaches the refreshment table, placing a tray of blue cookies beside a glass bowl of blue-wrapped chocolate kisses.

"Let me know who eat those," April requests, pointing to the blue goodies before taking her position along the wall with the rest of the girls.

At exactly 19:10, April opens the door, and four girls walk in. Among the four is Shay—the girl who'd inconspicuously handed April the plate of food on the yard. They're all wearing black business attire, in line according to height. They take their seats, the same seating arrangement Megan observed in church. While waiting for more potentials to arrive, the four visit the refreshment table, avoiding the blue treats, quietly talking amongst themselves. Minutes pass and no other girls walk through the blue door. Sharice, oblivious to the obvious underground pledge behavior, mouths, "That's strange, only four?" She motions for Megan to begin the meeting.

Fully aware of what's taking place, Megan stands at the front of the room and clears her throat, hinting at the start of the meeting. The four quickly take their assigned seats, giving her their undivided attention. Megan goes through the itinerary as planned, discussing the sorority's mission and accomplishments. She concludes her portion of the event by asking, "Are there any questions?" The girls sit quietly. The room is silent. April clears her throat, and Shay raises her hand. Megan gives permission for her to ask her question.

"Hi, I'm Shay. How do you balance sorority life with school?"

That's a deep question, Megan thinks to herself. *I'm still unclear on how to do it.* Megan's hesitation empowers Patrice to answer. "Make sure you prioritize what's important to you and don't let the organization, or anyone for that matter, overwhelm or bully you," she states with a sly look in April's direction.

Sharice adds, "We are very understanding. We pride ourselves on good grades. So, if you're falling behind in schoolwork, we may ask you to sit out of an event. TKRho is forever. School isn't. So yes, like Patrice said, you must prioritize."

"Any more questions?" Megan asks.

The room sits silent. It's apparent April has gotten to these girls. No one's asking uninformed questions like, "Is this a hazing sorority? How long will it take for me to become a member? When will we learn the steps and strolls?" It's obvious these girls have been prepped by Big Sister Legacy.

April releases Megan from her post, introducing herself as Dean of Pledges, which these girls seem to have already known given their lack of surprise. No gasps and whispers amongst them, just undivided attention. April breezes through an explanation of her role and its importance to their initiation. Sharice then releases April, taking her position in front of the room and proudly continuing the meeting with her robotic speech that's verbatim to the one given when the resurrection line filled these seats two years ago. Sharice goes on to add that if the sorority is interested in a potential, the girls will have two weeks to collect all required materials. "A meeting place on campus will be in the letter where you will hand-deliver said items. Then your MIP membership intake process shall begin," Sharice proudly states with a sincere smile.

Yep, it's the same spiel, Megan reminds herself, but this time no one is questioning Sharice's mention of a membership intake process beginning after required materials are turned in. The statement that had Megan squirming in her seat two years ago has no effect on these girls.

"Any questions?" Sharice asks before dismissing the group.

Megan remembers a part of Sharice's speech that was not mentioned. She stands up, taking a bold stance beside Sharice, and adds, "This is not a hazing sorority. If anyone is caught divulging in a pledge process, everyone involved will have to deal with major consequences." The girls uncomfortably squirm in their seats.

Guilty.

CHAPTER 16: THE RITUAL HOUSE

"Don't urge me to leave you, Theta Kappa Rho, or to turn back from you, Theta Kappa Rho," all in attendance recite. "Where you go, I will go, and where you stay, I will stay. Your people will be my people and your god my god. Where you die, I will die, and there I will be buried. May the Theta Kappa Rho deal with me, be it ever so severely, if even death separates you and me."

"Hold hands. Be led," Megan prompts. The blindfolded candidates grab their partner's hand. April guides them through the sorority house, circling a standing wall while the sorority members chant, "Life is a maze, which we must wander all our days." Their seventh circle is complete, and April leads the four to a back room to change into their second degree of initiation: all-white attire.

As president of the chapter, Megan has assumed many responsibilities, but standing at the large wooden altar—abound with the white pledge book and Bible, the sorority's emblem and shield, blue statuette birds, founders' pictures in frames, symbolic sorority paraphernalia, and lit royal and baby blue candles that dominate the front of the initiation room—is the most taxing duty yet. Expectation presses down on her from the candidates and the graduate sorors scattered throughout the room.

Preparation for midterm exams caused Megan to stay up later than usual last night to skim through the ritual book. As far as she knew, all she had to do was follow verbatim the instructions in the book. However, upon entering the sorority house, she was made to feel that more was needed to prepare for the occasion, receiving great pressure from the members to carefully lead the new candidates into the sorority.

"This is a very important ritual. Everything must be followed to the T," they demanded. "I memorized the ritual book when I was president," one member made sure to mention. But now Megan's feeling a heavier demand as she waits for the girls' return. A heavy weight presses on her heart, but she's unsure of its cause.

"Candidates are entering," April announces.

A bead of sweat forms above Megan's right eyebrow as the blindfolded candidates, dressed in their white dresses with interlocked arms, form a semicircle around the altar.

"You may remove your blindfolds and hand them to the Dean of Pledges," Megan commands.

As April collects their blindfolds, Megan tightly grips the ritual book, attempting to steady her shaky hands. She opens it to the designated page and begins reading aloud. The bead of sweat trickles down to the crease of her eye. She takes a deep breath to steady her voice to recite the opening lines.

"Tonight, we gather in the name of our sacred sisterhood..." The sweat tear slides down her cheek, and her heartbeats increase with every word, bringing intense conviction. "...Pledging ourselves to the values and to the spirit of Theta Kappa Rho." Megan's spirit is disturbed with the feeling of putting a curse over herself and the girls. Although she'd skimmed over these lines the night before, her eyes are now opening to the significance of these words. Mesmerized as they pop off the pages, boldly highlighting their meticulously crafted echo to the words of the Bible, she's unable to stop in the middle of her reading to cross-reference with the Bible on the altar due to the intense stares landing on her. So she's taken mental note to do it later.

Sharice tiptoes toward Megan, handing her a folded tissue to wipe the tear from her cheek. "Thank you," Megan mouths, dabbing her face.

"And thou shalt love Theta Kappa Rho with all thine heart, and with all thy soul, and with all thy might." She continues, simultaneously hearing Pastor Jones' sermon along her reading. "And thou shalt love the Lord thy God with all thine heart, and with all thy soul, and with all thy might. Deuteronomy 6:5, KJV." Megan's throat tightens, each phrase creating blurred lines between sacred and secular. She's noticing a consistent pattern. The ritual replaces God's name with Theta Kappa Rho.

Megan flips the page to continue. "Theta has been written upon your hearts and minds. You're now ready to receive the light of Theta. Remember our motto as you light your candles before you on this altar."

The girls receive their unlit candles, patiently waiting for further instruction.

"Recite the motto with me as you light your candles, your new life," Megan reads from the ritual book.

The girls light their candles from the arc of founders and recite the motto in unison. An instant flash of Megan's vision of the altar catching fire at her initiation begins to come into memory. Terrified of the unclear memory and its relevance, she questions, *What should I do—knock over the founders' arc, lighting the tablecloth on fire?*

"To our founders we bow. Blow out your old light, now that you have entered the new," Megan reads from the ritual book instead. April, with wet eyes, collects the unlit candles. "These candles signify the light that burns whenever Theta Kappa Rho are assembled. It guides your footsteps as you work in the name of our sorority," Megan reads as conviction grows.

"You've come to the most serious part of the intake process, the second degree of initiation. Taking the Oath. I caution you to take heed of the words that you will repeat after me. This oath must be your constant guide because, once a Theta, always a Theta."

Trish pulls out the blue pillow from underneath the altar. The candidates are prompted to kneel on it, placing their right hand on their heart and left hand on the Bible, which Megan now holds in hand. "You kneel before thee. Repeat the Theta Kappa Rho oath. Then sign your name in the book of knowledge leading to enlightenment and sisterhood."

Each initiate kneels one by one in front of the altar on the pillow, repeating the oaths recited by Megan, followed by a signature in the white book of knowledge. "I," the candidates say their names, "pledge myself to the spirit of sisterhood, embracing the legacy of Theta Kappa Rho Sorority with unwavering devotion." Each candidate repeats, and Megan's unease grows with every repetition.

The overwhelming thought of TKRho's initiation being demonic causes Megan to disassociate from the room. Moments have gone by, and she finds herself in a closed circle holding hands with the new initiates. She has no recollection of how they've gotten to this point of the ritual. Oblivious to Megan's internal struggles, TKRho continues chanting their oaths. With raised voices, they begin singing the sorority hymn followed by a prayer. Megan's gaze lingers on Shay, wearing a nervous look. Her eyes meet Megan's with a silent plea for reassurance. Megan forces a smile, mustering the confidence she's expected to exude.

The ceremony has reached its conclusion, and Megan's mind is still whirling with the echoes of her pastor's sermons, the contrast of the sorority's rituals, along with her fiery open vision. The neophytes are congratulated with new names and jackets, and candles are extinguished. Megan stands alone by the altar looking at the innocent faces of the new initiates. She wonders if the lines between faith, tradition, and commitment have become dangerous. Did she just lead innocent girls astray?

Megan removes the items from the altar, placing them in their rightful areas and boxes. She makes a silent vow to seek clarity and understanding, to ensure the ritual she has led doesn't send anyone to hell. "I need to check and see what we're reciting," she remembers. With the ritual book in hand, she opens it and retrieves the Bible from the box sitting on the table that was once used as an altar.

"That was intense!" Trish states, rushing past her to join the neos outside taking pictures.

"I saw you up there crying, girl," Donna points out, mistaking Megan's beads of sweat for tears.

"I was crying too. That 'Now bow to the founders' gets me every time," April admits, following the girls outside.

"Group photo!" Sharice yells from the porch of the sorority house. "Where's Megan?"

Megan hears that her presence is needed. She closes the books, placing them in the opened box to access later, and joins the sorors under the white banner with blue Theta Kappa Rho Greek lettering.

"Theta!" they cheese in unison for the camera.

PART 4
PROPHYTE

CHAPTER 17: THE UNEASY GROOVE

The crossover party for the spring '24 line of TKRho is in full swing. The music pulsates throughout the room, vibrating against the walls. The flickering LED lights cast royal and baby blue beams of light across the faces of the partygoers. The ladies of Theta Kappa Rho and neophytes stroll through the crowd, performing new steps, enticing the fraternities while dissing the rival sororities.

Megan leans against the wall watching the unveiling of a new world unfold before her. The first time Megan saw TKRho stroll at the SASU freshman orientation, she felt like she had to be a part of the sisterhood, and now that she's president, she feels like a spectator at her own event. The music is loud, the energy's high, but there still rests an uneasy feeling settled in her stomach.

April, leading the stroll line and stumbling over her steps, has consumed too many Solo cups of Rho juice again. April's intake of alcohol has increased tremendously since pledging Theta Kappa Rho. She consistently dismisses Megan's concerns about her consumption and states that she's stressed and is a social drinker.

But with the number of parties April attends, her social drinking has become habitual.

April, in mid-stroll, spots Megan from across the room. She stumbles over to the bar, getting another cup of Rho juice before approaching Megan. In full TKRho mode, dancing through the crowd, "Megaaaaaan! Why you not daaaaaancing with us?" she slurs over the music.

Megan, adjusting to a more relaxed yet stern position, says, "This is wrong."

"I only had two cups," April lies.

"I'm not talking about your drinking. I'm talking about Greek life. What we are doing, it's wrong," Megan makes clear.

April looks at her in disbelief. "Are you serious?"

An inebriated April pulls Megan outside to discuss the conversation in a quiet environment. April whispers as if she's delivering an incriminating message, "You begged me not to haze those girls. I didn't give them a hell night. You know how I feel about paper. That line should have been made. I'm the Dean of Pledges. I was to make that decision, not you, and now you're saying it's *still* wrong?" she reminds Megan, sipping from her Solo cup.

"It's not just the pledging. It's the rituals. Did you not pay attention to the oaths and hymns?" Megan asks, aware that the process has become a spiritual danger.

"Did you? You *read* them aloud for these girls to repeat!" April snaps back. To avoid a heated back-and-forth, April calms herself and says, "You're overreacting. We pray. We mention God in our rituals, we do community service, and this party is celebrating all of that." April downs her drink, hinting for a refill. Megan's aware that talking to a drunk April is not getting through. She nods in agreement and decides to table this conversation until April is sober enough to comprehend her concerns.

April throws her empty Solo cup in a nearby trash can. She places her hand on Megan's shoulder, attempting to provide comfort while gathering herself. "You're just feeling the weight of being president, Kamala," she states.

With Kamala Harris announcing her run for president after President Biden's drop from the presidential race, April's enthusiasm for a Black female president being a member of BGLO has reached an all-time high. She makes the Megan-Kamala comparison every chance she gets. "Don't let it make you second-guess everything. You just led these girls into the best sisterhood. Celebrate with them," she says, pointing to the girls inside, having the time of their lives.

Megan gives in to the pressure to relax and have a good time. She looks at the lively crowd and agrees, "You're right. Maybe I am overreacting."

"Exactly," April reassures with a smile. "Just take a deep breath, let go of whatever's holding you back, and come stroll with the lovely ladies of TKRho! Chiiiiiirp!" April shouts the call and grabs Megan's hand, pulling her back into the party toward the dance floor to join the sorors. They all respond to the chirp, welcoming Megan into the stroll line.

Megan begins to stroll to the rhythm, letting go of her inner turmoil. The feeling of being an outsider gradually recedes as she loses herself in the rhythm. She steals a glance at April, who's headed over to the bar for another cup of Rho juice.

April yells over the music, "Next party at my place, chiiiirp!"

†††

What's the real meaning of TKRho's shield? Why am I having this conviction about this sorority? Megan wonders. She needs answers.

She places the ritual book, her Bible, and an unused notepad in her backpack for an early morning visit to the library instead of having a sobering conversation with April as intended. April's left at home on the couch with a severe hangover, regretting every sip of Rho juice from the night before.

The library is full of whispers and the rustling of pages. Megan follows the rows of books stretched out in neat lines along wooden shelves leading to the computer stations tucked in the back. She grabs a seat at the last computer, easily concealing evidence of the secret activity her research may reveal. She sits in the chair with worry that her convictions about TKRho are serious, or worse, demonic. If she chooses to share what's revealed, the truths of the sisterhood she's proven worthy of could cause her sorors to despise her.

Megan avoids keywords that could reveal anything negative about the sorority. After minutes of reading about its community service and good works, which is leading her nowhere, she gives in to what no one wants to admit: the dark side of sororities. In order to get this information, she knows she needs to type in keywords that would uncover information she has a hunch exists. But what? *Rip off the bandage, Megan.*

She exhales and slowly types in the search engine, *the evil of sororities*. Her eyes scan the screen in amazement at her findings. The algorithm of the phrase used did not hold back. "How could I have missed this? Secret societies?" she asks, clicking on links and opening several tabs. Her fingers dance over the keyboard with increasing urgency as the information spills in. She pulls out her notepad and TKRho pen to jot down the contents displayed on her screen, a collection of occult texts, articles, ancient manuscripts, and tons of information on Freemasonry. "It's all connected," she whispers.

Megan's filled with revelation as her notepad fills up with notes. "Lord, what have I done?"

"Looks like you're digging into some things you shouldn't. Uncovering the secrets?"

Megan freezes, analyzing the voice over her shoulder. A silhouette is reflected on the computer screen wearing a white jacket with the TKRho shield on the wearer's chest. It's Patrice, rubbing her hands together like a spy with incriminating findings. After a moment of her *Inspector Gadget* private detective act, Patrice adjusts her glasses for a better read of the screen. "Fraternities and sororities have adopted Masonic-style rituals and secret oaths." She reaches over Megan's shoulder to open another website tab on the screen and reads, "Annie Williams, founder of Theta Kappa Rho, was an Eastern Star." Patrice pulls up a chair, making herself comfortable. "April won't appreciate you uncovering this information about her granny. Better be careful," she states, threatening Megan with a sly grin.

Ignoring Patrice's antics, Megan decides to take a chance on Patrice, assuming she's aware of TKRho's secrets. If they've allowed her into the sorority after her blackmail stunt, then maybe she has some leverage on them. Maybe she knows things. Secret things.

"Did you know about this stuff?" Megan asks. Patrice remains calm as she listens. "Did you know we were worshipping a god? Lowercase g," Megan emphasizes, for lack of better phrasing.

Unbothered, Patrice replies, "Lowercase g? I don't know about you, but I'm team Jesus."

"TKRho worships an ancient deity that's linked to bringing the light of day. A goddess called Aurora." A lightbulb goes off. "That's why TKRho chirps. It's the morning sounds of birds chirping."

"Yeah, I know," Patrice admits. "Aurora's on our shield, but I don't worship her."

"That doesn't bother you—that she's on our shield—team Jesus?" Megan responds, pointing to the goddess on Patrice's jacket.

"No, it doesn't." Patrice pulls away from Megan's reach. "I've prayed about it, and I've been forgiven. God knows my heart. He helped me join without being hazed," she sarcastically smiles.

"Patrice, this is more than hazing. We're honoring a god by wearing this stuff. We did a ritual. Did you not see what we did in the initiation process? The altar? The candles? It was witchcraft!" Megan leans in, holding her voice at a whisper. "Did you know that the Greek letter for Theta in ancient Greek is a symbol of death? Why are we pledging to death?"

"Ancient Greek? That means it's ancient news, Megan."

Megan ignores Patrice's rebuttal and opens the tab with the image of the Greek goddess Aurora on the computer screen and reads its description, uncovering new truths. "It says, 'Aurora is a representation of dawn, and the sister of the sun and moon. Every day she races to alert her brother and sister of the breaking of a new day.'" With a new realization she adds, "We talk about a new day in our motto. God is in control of night and day, not this demon!" Megan exclaims, fighting to hold back her anger.

Patrice, with unshaken calm, repeats, "Demon?" Shaking her head, ending the conversation, she picks up Megan's TKRho pen and places it in the fold of her ear. "I guess you won't be needing this anymore. It's demonic." She rises up from the chair to leave and says, "It's not that serious, Blue. Just step, stroll, and chirp. That's what I do. That's why I joined."

Megan turns back to her computer in disbelief, realizing that it's going to be a task convincing the girls of the damage they've done. Resuming her research with no pen to jot down notes, she takes the chance of printing her secret findings on the library printer.

"Whose witchcraft papers are these?" a student at the shared printer yells in the center of the library. They wave the stack of papers in the air as more papers are produced from the whirring machine.

†††

"We've been reciting Ruth in our rituals, Jeff!" Megan exclaims, pacing back and forth in Jeff's living room.

"I shouldn't be hearing this," Jeff calmly responds, relaxed on the couch, casually flipping through sports channels in the living room decorated with ZAPhi memorabilia, *Congratulations Class of*

2023 trinkets, and Tony's obituary framed on the entertainment center. The glass coffee table is covered with printed papers of Megan's findings from the library.

Jeff feels Megan's stare beaming on his profile, pressuring him to say more. With nonchalant interest in the topic, he stops his channel surfing. "Who's Ruth?"

"It's a book in the Bible. Where a girl named Ruth tells her mother-in-law that she will serve her God. But we recited the scripture in our initiation and—"

"People use scripture all the time. Kanye West in 'Jesus Walks,' DMX 'Lord Give Me a Sign.' Do you need more examples?" he asks. Proving his point, he returns to the TV screen.

She continues pacing around the room, sifting through her notepad and printed pages for more information. Remembering her vision, she takes a deep breath to reveal her untold burning altar experience. "I haven't mentioned this to anyone, but I had a vision when crossing. While performing my TKRho initiation process—"

Jeff cuts her off, slightly annoyed with her obsession. "Come on, Megan, you know you're not supposed to talk about your process. You took an oath."

"Oh, so now I can't talk to you about it. I'm just trying to talk to Smooth J, who snuck around with me when I was pledging. But I see now you don't want to talk about it," she says, frustrated with his lack of interest.

"Is any of this hurting you?" he asks, pointing to the pages in her hand. Megan remains silent. "If not, leave this conspiracy theory alone. BGLO is for us. Why can't Black people have something without messing it up? We ain't doing nothing wrong. Black fraternities provide a space for support, community, and exclusion from mainstream Greek life. ZAPhi is an organization that's for leadership development and civil rights advocacy."

"Wow, where'd you get that from? Is that the ZAPhi mission or something?" she states sarcastically. "The Black fraternity started because a Black man was rejected from Freemasonry. He started his own Black Mason group." She flips through the pages to find the name of the organization. "Prince Hall Freemasonry. And your founders mimicked their rituals. Their demonic rituals!" She waves the proof in the air.

"We don't do demonic rituals!" Jeff yells.

"You would say that. You took an oath of secrecy."

He lowers the volume on the TV as Megan begins reading the proof from the pages in her hand. "They teach that ZAPhi men walk through life blind, missing many things in life which should be seen. Whether failures or enjoyment. Weren't you blindfolded during your ritual? I know you was blindfolded while having sex with that girl." She shuffles through the pages with no filter on the words flowing from her. She continues reading, "Oh, and what's this? The ZAPhi candidates kneel and eat the food prepared by the gods of ZAPhi during initiation? What gods? And what food? I only eat the bread and drink the blood of Jesus!"

"Jesus? Where was this Jesus when I was in and out of foster homes? He wasn't around. It was ZAPhi that came and changed me."

"Maybe Jesus used those men to guide you. That doesn't mean you had to join in covenant with them. Receive their help and move on. But I wouldn't expect someone who isn't a Christian to understand." At that moment, she realizes that maybe this is a bigger deal for Christians than non-Christians. However, she believes that all should worship the One and Only True God. Wishing she could take back the insult, she takes a deep breath, ready for his rebuttal.

"You Christians are so judgmental. You over-spiritualize everything and have no idea what you're talking about," Jeff responds, ready to move on from the conversation that's causing his flesh to overheat. "This spiritual awakening you're having is dumb. Leave it alone."

Megan's eyes widen with hurt and anger, with an understanding that her two attempts to change the hearts of the hearers of her discovery have failed. "I didn't even get to tell you about my spiritual awakening. My vision."

Jeff's demeanor hardens with frustration. "You don't have to. I've heard enough about this god Aurora bringing in a new day, Freemasonry, and blood oaths. It's all mythical. It's a rumor. People practice all kinds of weird stuff, and they have for centuries. TKRho, ZAPhi, Mu Alpha Phi Alpha, and all the others are just having fun. Leave it alone."

Megan's face flushes with rage. Her voice rises. "Jeffery, this is serious. They have us out here bowing down, worshipping, and hanging up paraphernalia of demons in our living room." She points to the memorabilia around Jeff's apartment. She then adds, not knowing what the repercussions of her next statement will be, "Tony is dead because of this stuff!"

"You have no right bringing him up in this conversation. You didn't even attend his funeral. Toya was even there to show respect. You know why? Because that's what sisters of ZAPhi do. So don't ever mention Tony's name."

"You told me not to go. You wanted to be with your *bruhs*," she reminds him.

Her correction frustrates Jeff. He stands in anger. "That's enough! I will not let you disrespect my organization and Tony! I told you how I felt in confidence and you're using it against me. You don't know nothing about Tony's death! Get out." He points to the door with tears welling up in his eyes. He turns up the volume on the TV and angrily plops down on the couch.

Megan grabs her backpack from the couch, gathering the remaining papers on the coffee table.

Jeff's voice follows her, spiked with anger, as she heads toward the door. "When you let this nonsense go, you know where to find me. With my bros!"

Before placing her hand on the doorknob to leave, she turns toward him, face covered with tears, and asks, "Do you love them more than me?" She painfully waits for his response, knowing that his answer could hurt more than the betrayal she's received from uncovering the demonic truths of TKRho.

"Please leave," he responds, focused on the screen ahead.

✝✝✝

Megan rushes into her apartment, face wet with tears. She heads toward her room, slamming the front door behind her. April is still lying on the couch cuddling an oversized pillow. "What happened to you? Are you okay?" April asks, sitting up from her healed hangover. Megan, startled by April's concern, gathers herself and walks toward the edge of the couch. She sits down, tossing the printed papers on the table in front of April.

"Jeff and I got into a fight."

April, reaching toward the papers, asks, "Over this?" holding up the stack. "You two never fight. It must be serious," she says, examining the pages.

"We had a disagreement about Greek life," Megan responds, wiping tears from her eyes.

"Greek life? I understand disagreements, but why are you crying?" April mentions with confusion as she begins to focus on the highlighted sentences about TKRho's shield hosting the goddess Aurora.

"I told him what I told you. Something about BGLO doesn't feel right. We are worshipping demons," she states.

April ignores the serious matter Megan reveals and reads the highlighted statements on the paper. "'The chirp call represents a bird call in the morning.' That makes sense," April agrees. "These findings are good, Megan. You are uncovering the secrets of TKRho. This is the information they were telling us at our crossing that went over our heads. We're supposed to know this stuff."

"But it's demonic!" Megan yells.

"I respect how hard you go for God, but there is no way TKRho is demonic. I've been blessed because of it. My mother pays for my tuition. She pays for my rent. And it's all because of TKRho. She loves me more now than she did before I got my letters. She expects me to continue this legacy, and I will. It's who the Williams are."

Megan chimes in, "But it's not who *you* are." With an open door to address April's alcohol consumption, she adds, "You weren't an alcoholic when we were freshman."

"I'm going to let that slide… I told you, I'm not drinking because of TKRho. I drink because senior year is stressful," April lies, slightly ashamed.

"And what about junior year?" Megan murmurs, sifting through the remaining papers on the table. She finds the printout about April's great-great-grandmother. Confident this evidence will wake April up to the demonic culture of TKRho, she reads, "Here it says Annie Williams was a member of the Prince Hall Order of the Eastern Star."

"And?"

"And that it has demonic ties."

"OMG, Megan, calm down. What demonic ties? Let me see." April snatches the paper from Megan and reads from the Eastern Star rituals, "'I will not be present nor assist in giving these degrees to any woman not vouched for as being of a Christian disposition, regardless of race or creed. The common bond among members being a fundamental faith in the Fatherhood of God and the Brotherhood of Man. Also, Eastern Stars' mission is to promote charitable, educational, fraternal, and scientific principles while fostering personal growth, charity, and social enjoyment among its members.'" She hands Megan back the paper. "Demonic where? What's so bad about it? It sounds Christian-like to me."

"April, what I'm trying to tell you and Jeff is that I don't feel good about TKRho anymore. I'm crying, I'm confused, everyone is against me…"

"Everyone is not against you. We're just alarmed at the false information you're bringing us; it's a lot. Don't worry about Jeff; you just caught him off guard. He'll come back around." April leans in to give Megan a comforting hug.

"Maybe you're right. I'm overreacting. Jeff's still dealing with Tony's death, and I carelessly dumped all this on him. And if your great-great-grandmother was an Eastern Star that was founded on Christian principles, then with her being a founder of TKRho…"

"We are founded on Christian principles also," April finishes her sentence.

"Right," Megan agrees, nodding, taking it in.

†††

After hours of repeatedly striking keys on the keyboard, Megan is confident she'll ace tomorrow's musical exam. Locking herself in her room with days of repetitive practice, she's reunited with her first love: music. Its melodic rhythm helps her forget her secret society obsessions—an obsession that had her spiraling down rabbit holes of Freemasonry, Skull and Bones, Knights Templar, and Illuminati truths.

However, the shared common interest of music with Jeff has not permitted her to forget his missed absence. He hasn't called her; she hasn't called him; and he hasn't been attending church. She's worried their argument has caused him to pull away from God and his minute belief in Christianity.

Allowing worry to get the best of her, she gets up from her keyboard station and retrieves her phone from the nightstand. She scans her phone's two-week call log to find Jeff's alias, *My Smooth J*. With the hope of reconciling, she's kept his contact in her phone unchanged. Her thumb hovers over the call icon. Exhaling into being the bigger person, she presses it. Her heartbeat increases as she anxiously ponders what to say if he answers. She hadn't thought that far.

It rings once. The call is forwarded to voicemail.

"Leave a message after the beep," his smooth automated voice announces.

"Hey Jeff. It's me. Megan. I'm probably the last person you want to talk to. So, I understand if you don't call me back. I'm sorry about our last conversation. I overreacted. I said some things I shouldn't have... and... I miss you. Please give me a call so we can talk. I'm sorry."

Ending the call, she plops down on the edge of her bed, laying back, observing the whirling ceiling fan's accumulated dust.

Look up why Christians should not join Order of the Eastern Star, a random thought demands. She ignores it, preferring to wallow in relationship sadness. *Do it now!*

Assuming it's the voice of the Lord, she asks, "Why now?" She receives no answer yet obeys the voice.

She lifts up from her comfortable sadness and retrieves her laptop from the backpack conveniently placed beside her. Ready to uncover more truths, she opens the laptop. She goes to her web browser and types in the commanded statement. And to her surprise, she is bombarded with evidence going against her and April's conclusion of OES—that it's founded on Christian principles.

She reads, "A Mason by the name of Dr. Rob Morris founded the Eastern Stars, creating the largest male and female organization, predominantly female. In order to be an Eastern Star, you had to be related to a Freemason."

I wonder if April knows she has these secret societies running through her bloodline, Megan asks herself.

Continuing the article, she reads, "The phrase 'Eastern Star' has occultic meaning. In some occultic context it refers to a powerful star called Sirius, which is the most significant star in Satanism linked to the god Set. Set is a god in ancient Egyptian mythology associated with chaos and storm."

Set? That's what we call our meeting place and it's full of chaos.

"Members will say the eastern star represents the star over Bethlehem, the star the wise men refer to in Matthew two verse two. However, Jesus Christ's name is not mentioned in the OES rituals. Instead they say, 'We have seen his star in the east and have come to worship him,' referencing an upside-down star."

How can they be founded on Christian principles if Jesus isn't the focus?

Megan spots another article written by Harry A. Gaylord, *Dark Matters in the Eastern Star*, that reads, "Rob Morris, the founder of the organization, decided that there would be five degrees on their emblem, the inverted pointed star. Five degrees for five female figures representing the order. He originally chose five goddesses from ancient paganism but then had second thoughts about bringing paganism to the forefront since most of the U.S. were Christians at the time. So, he gave the goddess Biblical names: Jephthah's daughter, Ruth, Esther, Martha, and Electa."

Megan's interest is piqued when she sees the name Ruth—a noticeable connection to TKRho. She realizes that the impact OES had on Annie Williams influenced her to incorporate the scripture of Ruth into the TKRho rituals. She continues to read that Ruth was originally the goddess Flora, the goddess of springtime and flowers. Every year in spring the Romans held the festival of Floralia, similar to Mardi Gras, where the people participated in drunken orgies.

Wow, that makes perfect sense to why April has been drinking excessively, and why I had the urge to lose my virginity before marriage, Megan realizes.

"The five qualities of women are represented on an upside-down five-pointed star, which is also the symbol of the occult, black magic. They sometimes use the right-side-up star, meaning white magic. All magic representing Satan." She scrolls and reads from another article, "Bowing before the altar of the pentagram, in the center of the star of Baphomet, surrenders you to the gods of Masonry. Doing this will give Satan legal rights into your life because of the oaths taken, no matter how deep of a Christian you may be."

Megan closes her laptop. The uneasy feeling of TKRho and its so-called Christian principles brings her back to square one, creating a deep ball of conviction in the pit of her stomach. Because she's knelt in front of an altar and participated in an oath, she's given Satan legal rights to wreak havoc in her naïve baby Christian life.

There's more work to be done, but don't worry, you'll do fine. You now have two tests to pass, says the Lord.

✝✝✝

An overwhelming sense of relief comes over Megan as she strikes the last key on the piano center stage of the auditorium. All music department heads are in attendance at Megan's final exam before summer break, including Professor Hill. With a nod of approval, he hands her a Post-it note with a handwritten reminder to schedule her senior-year academic counseling session. She places the reminder in a secure compartment in her backpack, acknowledging Professor Hill's nod with a smile of accomplishment.

If only she could call Jeff and give him the news—that she's prepared to have a stress-free graduating semester, and her major courses were complete. But he hasn't returned her call.

With an hour to celebrate before her afternoon shift, she treats herself to brunch at a café not too far from campus. She orders her usual bacon burger with cheese fries and a drink. She places her plastic card holder—which coincidentally reads *order number four*—and her empty cup on the table in eye range of the server. As she shimmies into the booth seat, she spots Toya pushing a pink baby stroller out of the family restroom with no sign of the father. She waves her down to take a seat. Toya cheerfully accepts the invitation, arranging herself and the baby into a comfortable position around the table.

Toya reads the order card holder. "Four? The original tail. Number four. Was that planned?" Toya jokes.

"That is funny, isn't it? I guess I'm the fourth customer of the day," Megan responds, aware of the restaurant's slow morning.

Toya lifts the little one from the stroller in response to small whimpers. She gently places her against her chest, pulling a light blanket over her daughter's head. She performs a rocking motion to alleviate any agitation that may develop.

The interaction becomes awkward as Megan observes the mommy feeding her child. Megan uncomfortably fidgets at the uncomfortable scene. She reaches for her empty cup and excuses herself to fill it with a fountain drink. "I'll be back," she states, getting up from the booth.

Filling her cup with a Sprite, she ponders the conversations this meeting could entail. Would they talk about TKRho? Would they discuss the baby and the father? She heard Toya is in the graduate chapter now—maybe they could talk about that.

Megan shimmies back into her seat, taking a sip of her drink. "She'll be cute in a TKRho onesie," she mentions, breaking the silence. *Great job, Megan. Bring the baby into this TKRho mess*, Megan scolds herself.

"Oh no. I will let her decide on what she wants to do. I see parents prematurely initiating their children all the time. Look at April and her mother. It's like she had to prove her love by joining TKRho or she would disown her. That's crazy. I decided on TKRho because it was the best sorority for me. My aunts are Mu Alpha Phi Alpha women, and they've never pushed it on me. I appreciate that. I would never do that to my baby." She coos playful baby noises, pulling the little one from underneath the cloth and placing her back into the stroller.

Grateful for the segue, Megan adds, "I didn't know who to talk to about this, but April is drinking a lot. Ever since we joined TKRho, she drinks alcohol all the time. Is that normal?"

"Girl, don't you see that's what the undergrad chapter is about—step shows, parties, bringing in new girls, and occasional volunteer services. If you can't control your alcohol intake, you will indulge like any other college student. Graduate chapter is a little different. We focus on volunteering and bettering the community. The connections are a plus. A soror in graduate chapter helped me get a job as a paralegal at her law firm. And thank God, because the chapter dues are expensive."

"Cheese fries and a burger?" a young server asks, gently placing a tray in front of Megan off her acknowledgment.

"Help yourself," Megan invites Toya to a fry.

Steering the conversation into a heavier topic, Megan asks, "Were there moments in the initiation that didn't feel right to you?"

"The rituals were weird and the hazing I don't agree with, but the connections are great." Toya helps herself to a cheese fry. "I admit I lied to get out of some of the sets Jasmine was demanding of you girls. When I found out I was pregnant with my little angel, she became my excuse not to attend. Our big sisters made us experience some horrible things, and Jasmine wanted to keep the Omega Zeta chapter hazing tradition. Some sorors want every member to be made. It's giving the nineties, if you ask me."

"There were times I wish you were there because Jasmine had us do some crazy things."

"I bet." A memory hits Toya, and she recalls, "You know I saw you and Jeff coming back on campus after a holiday break. I made sure not to tell Jasmine because set that night would have been brutal. I thought it was cute though, how he sped off trying to be sneaky." She laughs. "Be grateful you didn't have to experience a Hell Week," Toya adds, grabbing another cheese fry.

"We had a hell night," Megan reveals.

"What?!"

"Jasmine gave us a hell night the night before our initiation. We took wood."

"I'm sorry you had to experience that. We took a week of wood." Toya reminisces, shaking her head in disapproval.

"After that night I knew I couldn't haze the neos. I wanted them to feel like they were joining a sisterhood, not a gang," Megan protests.

"Not hazing those girls was the right thing to do."

"I do feel bad about leading them into those demonic rituals."

Toya bursts into laughter. "They do feel demonic, don't they? But there is no changing that; every lady of Theta Kappa Rho performs the same ritual. If you believe in God, it can't affect you."

Megan argues to herself, *If you believe in God, it can't affect you? If you believe in God and perform rituals to other gods, it's worse! Why don't people understand that? That's why the Israelites were taken captive.*

As Megan compiles a softer way of expressing her thoughts, Toya interrupts, "I guess not all hazing is bad. That's how baby Tonya got here."

A moment of silence.

Then—

"I have to use the bathroom. Can you watch her for me?" Toya asks.

Not letting Toya off the hook that easily, "What do you mean, 'that's how baby Tonya got here'?" Megan asks through her confusion.

"Tony's her dad. I was his 'mystery' girl during his hell week; we had sex for his binding ritual. ZAPhi bros approached me, and not wanting to let them down, I agreed. Silly me, right? The effects of a little alcohol would have you do some daring things. I didn't think it would be a big deal, just some quick mysterious fun. I never mustered the courage to tell him that his initiation into brotherhood also brought him into fatherhood," she reveals with tears in her eyes.

She walks off and enters the restroom. Megan sits at the table, mouth ajar, as Tony's daughter cries for her mother.

CHAPTER 18: CHIRPS IN THE BANK

Megan is over it. She's fed up with all the secret society mysteries. Toya's surprising reveal pulled the last straw. She has got to remove herself from TKRho. Something has to be done about this evil hidden behind the "We do good in the Black community" facade. Does Jeff know Toya's baby is Tony's? Of course he knows. He has to assume so. He and his brothers set up the hell week sexcapade, doing exactly what was done to him during his hell week—blindfolding the candidates, coercing them into sex with unknown girls. And for what? To become a part of the brotherhood? And how could Toya agree to such a shameful act? The confirmation of this hazing ritual coming from a member of TKRho has left Megan disgusted. She's ashamed of calling herself a lady of Theta Kappa Rho. A Theta woman wouldn't dare agree to that.

Hiding her disdain for the facts revealed at the café earlier, Megan buries herself in work, assisting a customer with their bank deposit. The silence of the bank is broken by loud high-pitched, squeaky chirp calls. It's April, accompanied by Lyndsey, the ace of the resurrection line. They ignore the customers waiting for assistance, bombarding their way toward Megan wearing their finest TKRho blue. The repetition of the chirps catches the attention of Sharon, who steps out of her office to observe the disruption. Megan, slightly ashamed and annoyed by the disturbance, apologizes to the customers waiting patiently in line. She gives a nod of apology to Sharon, who's observing the commotion from afar.

"Hey, Blue!" April squeals. "I would have texted you, but we were in the neighborhood and decided to come in instead. You know, check out the vibe," an inebriated April states as Megan finishes her transaction with the client. Lyndsey mimics April's obnoxious demeanor with an air of *we are ladies of TKRho, and no one is going to say anything about it, no matter how loud we get*. Lyndsey stands with her hands crossed over her chest, scanning the bank as if she's April's bodyguard.

"I'm hosting a party at our place tonight," April adds.

"Great," Megan mumbles under her breath, remembering the announcement April made at the initiation crossing party for the spring '24 line. April promised the crowd another party, but this time at their place. Megan is shocked April remembers this intoxicated plan that was decided without her approval.

"I know it's a big ask, but can you pick up vodka for Rho juice? You're the only one of age," April begs behind crossed fingers. Lyndsey bats her false-eyelashed eyes as if the fluttering blinks are the magic trick to get the yes they are feigning for. This is why they really came inside the bank. Checking out the vibe? Yeah right. They assumed if Megan could see April's puppy dog eyes and Lyndsey's Tourette blinks, then when asked to pick up alcohol, she couldn't possibly tell them no. Megan, pressured, embarrassed, and slightly disrespected that the girls would enter her workplace requesting a big ask, waits for the customer to walk away before responding.

"Yes, I can," she answers.

She immediately regrets giving in without a fight. She knows the alternate response would have caused a scene. And with Sharon leaning against her office door panel with an unapproving gaze, Megan knew she had to get them out of there quickly. April gives an exclaimed chirp, startling an elderly couple entering the bank.

"But… I won't be attending. I'll be in my room," Megan adds, hoping the mention of her absence will remind April of her uneasiness about the sorority.

April rolls her eyes. "You're really serious about this, aren't you?" she asks, sobering up. She assumed Megan was going through a phase, like buyer's remorse. She thought the conclusion of the Eastern Stars being built on Christian principles had deadened this conspiracy theory of BGLO being demonic.

"Yes, I am serious. It's wrong," Megan states as she waves for the older couple in line to approach the window.

~

Sharon, standing nearby, clears her throat to get Megan's attention. She motions for Megan to end the conversation with the girls and to attend to the couple slowly shuffling toward her station. Aware of Sharon's presence, the girls pivot toward the exit door. On their way out Lyndsey asks April, "What's she talking about? What's wrong?"

April, in earshot of Sharon, whispers, "She thinks TKRho is demonic. I guess she's trying to get out of it or something," she states, rolling her eyes as they exit the bank.

As Megan finishes the transaction with the feeble couple, Sharon gestures for her to close down her station and come to her office. Overhearing the demonic news, Sharon now questions Megan's dedication to TKRho. What a disappointment. Concern and anger manifest into fire, rising up from the soles of Sharon's feet to the top of her slick top knot bun. She paces back to her desk, exhaling her rage, creating a thick tension in the four walls of her well-lit office. She sits in her seat awaiting the young soror who called her sorority demonic. How could Megan call TKRho demonic? Sharon vouched for her to join the sisterhood. She invited her to bless her wedding by singing the sorority hymn with the other sorors at the reception. Sharon is furious. No one talks about her sorority in this way. Especially some undergraduate soror.

TKRho is Sharon's world. She doesn't have many friends outside of the sorority. Actually, she doesn't have any friends outside of the sorority. Her time is consumed with Southern Atlanta South Bank duties, sorority meetings, sorority community service, and now a husband; and that's a miracle. If not for TKRho, she wouldn't have given her husband the time of day. He approached her at a voter registration drive community service event put on by the graduate chapter. They engaged in flirtatious conversation over a register-to-vote survey clipped to a wooden board secured tightly in his hands. His flirtatious inquisitions about her, not the survey, led to consistent dinner dates and an unexpected proposal, leading to a sudden marriage. "Thanks to TKRho," Sharon would say.

Her mother scolds her about giving TKRho the credit for their union. She argues that it is all God's doing. "If you continue to put TKRho above Him, He will take away all things standing in His place," her mother would say in an unwavering tone.

She hates it when her mother talks about TKRho with contempt. Sharon's been an active member for fifteen years and her mother still hasn't come to accept her involvement in the sorority. Sharon was hurt, yet tried to ignore her mother's abrupt departure when the sorors sang what her mother calls a blasphemous hymn at the wedding reception. With fifty people in attendance, including the groom's family, it's obvious Sharon doesn't have a close relationship with her family. So TKRho is her family, and she's not trading that family for anything in the world. And to hear a newcomer, whom she recommended into her family, call it demonic is a slap in the face. How dare this child spread rumors about her sorority.

Sharon's not a devout, never-miss-a-Sunday churchgoer, but she does believe in Jesus. Calling her sorority demonic is calling her demonic, and she's not standing for it. She's not accepting this from some kid in an undergraduate chapter who has yet to even pay her dues. Literally.

~

Megan closes her station and nervously enters Sharon's office. "Mrs. Sharon, you want to see me?" Megan asks, slowly closing the glass door behind her. She's immediately engulfed in the tension cloud filling the atmosphere.

"Have a seat, Megan," Sharon says coldly, motioning to one of the chairs in front of her desk. "I'm very disappointed in you. First, you know I do not allow disruptive noise and chatter in my bank, let alone sorority calls. I don't care if it is TKRho. This is a place of business. Secondly, I vouched for you when you applied for this job. Our bond as sorority sisters was the reason I put my trust in you." Megan squirms in her seat, unable to meet Sharon's stern gaze. "But now, after what I just heard... it's clear you're having second thoughts about TKRho, believing it's *demonic*? What's the problem?"

Megan, with her position at the bank in jeopardy, responds, "I'm sorry, Mrs. Sharon. I just..." She pauses, thinking carefully how to express her feelings about TKRho. "I can't be a part of something that's... evil. I don't believe TKRho is as Christian as we think."

"What's TKRho's motto?" Sharon demands. The cadence of that question triggers Megan. It's an exact delivery of the soror who challenged her that night on set when the girls were forced to eat bird food. Megan replays the night in her head, reminded of all the embarrassment TKRho has put her through. "What's TKRho's motto?" Sharon repeats.

OMG. That *was* Sharon who challenged her. Heat rises within Megan as she recalls the motto.

Sharon recognized the pledgee instantly when she walked into her office inquiring about a job. She was just as nervous as Megan, hoping she hadn't recognized her as the graduate member who hazed her the night they were forced to kneel before a bowl of bird food. Sharon was also quad of her line, and the way the motto rolled off Megan's tongue under pressure without a hiccup impressed her.

Now, snapping into set mode to recall the motto, Megan recites, "That I use my trained intellect to strengthen the name of

Theta Kappa Rho, to use wisdom, knowledge, and have a sound mind to wherever it leadeth me in the new day."

"So why are you not using your trained intellect to strengthen the name of Theta Kappa Rho?" Sharon's eyes narrow. "Beliefs are fine, but you need to be careful about what you say about Theta Kappa Rho, or your words will have consequences. Calling my sorority demonic is not what a candidate I write recommendations for believes." Sharon rises from her seat, hands firmly placed on her desk. "I vouched for you to join my sorority. I helped your prophytes bring your line in, and this is how you treat my kindness?"

Not waiting for a response, she exits her office, leaving Megan sitting with a threat hanging over her head and fear of losing her job. The rift between her and the sorority is now more than just personal… it's business.

✝✝✝

Megan's bedroom is a refuge from the chaos outside her door. The muffled sounds of the party April promised are full of laughter, music, and the rhythmic stomps of feet stepping in unison. The sound filters through the walls, a constant reminder of a life Megan's detached from. She sits on her bed with an open Bible, in repentance for providing the alcohol for the party. Being reminded of her loner days of being the odd woman out, she felt pressure to provide the party with alcohol—the least she could have done for not attending. The girls were grateful, although it seemed they were able to get bottles of their own because when she brought the vodka home, the girls cheered through tipsy eyes and slurs.

There's a knock on her bedroom door. It's April on the other side, slurring over the music. "Megaaaan, your sisters need their Kamala!"

"She's not even president," Megan mumbles under her breath.

April's in denial of the election results, still believing Kamala has a chance of being president until Trump is sworn in. However, Megan's relieved that a member of the BGLO isn't in office. Kamala becoming president would bring these societies to the forefront, and Megan's desperately trying to get away from them. She can see the headlines now: "Kamala Harris's been seen wearing her sorority colors. Kamala Harris's sorority stands in solidarity of her win. Kamala Harris's sorority advocates for women's rights and abortion. Kamala Harris's sorority stands for LGBTQ+ rights. Kamala Harris's sorority, sorority, sorority."

Megan's not sure if Trump's win is any better, but at least there will be no mention of a sorority member in office highlighting their importance in the community while hiding the witchcraft done to gain membership. However, because of extensive research, Megan is not oblivious to the knowledge that most presidents are members of secret societies.

Giving Megan a few seconds to respond, April rejoins the party with chirps and Rho juice refill demands. Megan ignores the request to join the party and whispers to God a plea for peace and quiet as she clutches her Bible. Despite her efforts to hear a response to her prayer, the party sounds begin to seep deeper into her consciousness as the TKRho theme song starts to play. The old-school song has grown on her. A song that was once a family barbecue staple now belongs to TKRho. The chirp calls and stomps get louder and louder on the other side of the door.

She sits on her bed envisioning the moves, mimicking the shoulder and hip thrust as the beat seeps into her soul. The bass from the song increases and begins to penetrate her heart. Acknowledging her entrapment into the song, she refuses further temptation, deciding to resist the thrusting stroll with her sorors circling the living room. She slams her Bible on the nightstand and heads toward the door with the intent to change the music or turn it down.

STEPPING DOWN

She opens her bedroom door, and the energy of the party envelops her. Every corner is occupied with people holding alcohol-filled Solo cups and a few individuals passed out on the couch. Greeks are stepping and strolling, filling every inch of the apartment. Above the framed poster on the wall that reads, *Let the spirit of TKRho hover over you...* she spots dark, shadowy figures emitting from the ceiling. One is the silhouette of the goddess Aurora. The entities spread amongst the crowd, hovering over the partygoers. She quickly closes her door. Now she's really tripping. What was she seeing?

She goes to steal a second look at the craziness her imagination has conjured up and... she really does see shadowy figures hovering above the crowd. These maniacal, laughing gods and demons are manipulating the partiers' moods with invisible strings attached to their puppets. The goddess Aurora is hovering over the TKRho members strolling to their theme song. She sees Atlas, Minerva, Sphinx, Centaur, Apollo, Shekinah, Pallas Athena, Archon, and many other entities having a spiritual party over their covenant-binding group.

The temperature in the atmosphere rises. Megan breathes shallow breaths as she stumbles back into her room. The walls of her bedroom begin to close in around her as she goes into panic. Minimizing the foreshadowed panic attack, she sinks to her knees as tears begin to stream down her face, praying to God, "Lord, what shall I do? How do I get out of this evil I've put myself into?"

She suddenly gets an urge to go outside and call her sister Tameka. She grabs her phone with trembling hands and rushes through the heated living room, avoiding eye contact with the possessed and their possessors.

"Kamala!" she hears April yelling over the music.

"It's a distraction. Keep going," she tells herself.

Megan steps out into the cool breeze, regaining her breath. Pacing outside the front door, she dials her sister's number. The phone rings endlessly before Tameka's voice comes through the line. "It's one o'clock. Is everything okay?"

Megan's voice cracks as she tries to hold back her sobs. Her emotions pour out in a stream of words. "Meka, I don't know what to do. I feel like I'm losing everything. Questioning TKRho has cost me everything. Friends, Jeff, possibly my job…"

"Breathe. I'm here for you," Tameka assures. "What do you want to do?" she asks, with no helpful options in mind.

Despite the pain and uncertainty, Megan begins to feel a sense of relief, realizing her sister has been her support system all along. She responds, "I want to come home."

CHAPTER 19: UNVEILING THE TRUTH

Megan wasted no time packing a weekend's worth of clothing for a comforting stay with her sister. She would have packed months' worth of clothing if her work schedule allowed. As far as she knew, she still had a job. She hadn't received an email or call telling her otherwise. But her last conversation with Sharon hadn't gone well, and she's nervous about their next encounter. Megan's worried Sharon's awaiting an apology she's not willing to give.

Tina and James questioned Megan's surprise visit. Tameka hadn't mentioned the pop-up arrival, stating this was news for Megan to disclose. Megan hesitantly told them about her involvement in TKRho, leaving out details about Jeff, Tony, and Toya. She figured painting Jeff in a bad light wouldn't be ideal if they were to ever reconnect. Bringing up Tony's death was a definite no. There was no need to add fuel to the fire, especially fuel of an alleged murder.

Surprisingly, when Megan expressed the reason for her visit, James didn't chew her head off. "I'm glad you're separating yourself from them devil steppers," James said through chuckles, taking a break from the television. He told Megan that God always convicts the heart of those who love Him and reminded her of the scripture that says train up a child in the way he should go and when he is old, he will not depart from it. In this case, she was the he. And boy, was she running back like the prodigal son. Tina disclosed already knowing about Megan's involvement and that she was giving her time and space to discuss it when she was ready.

~

Tina constantly prayed about her daughter's safety while away at college, and unbeknownst to her, revelations through dreams were revealed. So, when Megan admitted to her TKRho involvement, all the weird dreams made sense.

One dream felt like a nightmare. She saw women in white standing around Megan in a dark room. Megan was kneeling in front of an altar caught up in flames. The ladies' flesh was melting from the heat, revealing muscle. As the heat intensified, their muscles began to melt away, revealing ancient skeletons. There were items on the altar, but Tina couldn't make out what they were or their meanings. She saw Megan clutching a Bible tightly, and the room went up in smoke like an extinguished fire. That morning Megan called after days of silence. Tina didn't mention the dream to Megan because her excitement about the wedding she was attending and the blue dress she'd wear to it proved she was doing well. She didn't want to disrupt the mood with her concerns. However, with answered prayers, Tina is grateful to witness God leading Megan through these secret truths.

~

Tameka initiates mild conversation topics, like her upcoming wedding, while she applies a new MEKA Haircare product to Megan's two-strand twists before getting into the real reason for Megan's visit. Cameras are on and ring lights are fully lit to capture more MEKA content: MEKA wedding blogs, MEKA haircare, and in this case, MEKA family content. Megan sits in the gifted chair from the paid sponsor with her laptop supported on her lap. She pulls up the information she discovered about secret societies to share with Tameka. Finishing up Megan's hairdo, Tameka makes her way to her bed, leaving the cameras rolling and lights lit in case more wedding or hair care tips are discussed. Tameka begins scrolling through her phone, finding YouTube videos about sorority members leaving their organizations. She comes across a video that reads, *The Demons of TKRho*. Her eyes widen with concern.

"Have you seen these videos? Former members are talking about the spirits linked to your sorority?" she asks.

"I haven't had to watch those videos. God opened my eyes to it firsthand. They were in my house! That party going on in my living room when I called you the other night was full of demonic entities controlling these organizations," Megan exclaims. Her body shivers as she relives what she saw that night.

"I can't believe Jeff told you it's just rumors and mythical creatures. Some people's eyes will never be opened to what's real. It's one thing to not believe in Christ, but it's worse when Christians refuse to see the truth. They want to be a part of something so bad that they refuse to see the evil in it," Tameka states as she continues scrolling through YouTube videos. "Look at this video, a girl mentions how she got out of TKRho. Something called renouncing and denouncing."

"Let me see." Megan waves for Tameka's phone. She hands it to her, getting up to stand over Megan's shoulder as they observe the screen. The girls watch the video as a former member of TKRho, about thirty years of age, speaks.

"Some of the things I've found in TKRho are really disturbing. It's like there's a hidden agenda behind the rituals." Megan leans forward, her curiosity piqued. The girl continues her confident speech. "I thought it was just tradition. But the more I got involved, the more I realized there are forces at play that we don't understand. At first, I began to accelerate in everything: a new job, friends, a boyfriend," the YouTuber states with a big smile. "I had a sense of belonging," she continues. "But I then noticed that my life started to crash because I was drinking more, going to parties that were full of dirty dancing, promiscuity, profanity... But TKRho claims to stand on Christian principles. Right? Everyone joining isn't Christian, and I took an oath to be joined together with them. We read Ruth one verses sixteen through seventeen, binding ourselves with nonbelievers at an altar for another god. Aurora." The YouTuber flips through her Bible and begins to read the scripture, comparing it to the TKRho rituals. "'Don't urge me to leave you.' Here we say TKRho." She points out between the two books. "'Or to turn back from you TKRho. Where you go, I will go, and where you stay, I will stay.'" She closes the books. "And the Bible states to come from amongst them. We signed our names in a book to live and die with Theta Kappa Rho. That includes the atheists in the sorority. Do you really want to be joined with atheists?" the YouTuber asks. "And also, the founder Annie Williams said, 'Let the spirit of TKRho hover over you...'" she adds.

Tameka reaches over Megan to pause the video, her eyes reflecting the same concern Megan feels. "This isn't just about weird practices or traditions. It's about the demons you're exposed to."

Megan's mind races as she wonders what to do next. "What am I supposed to do?" she asks Tameka, looking for a solution.

"Renounce and denounce!" Tameka exclaims, as if she's known about this act for years.

"How?" Megan asks.

Tameka takes the phone from Megan and pulls up a blog. She begins to read. "This site says to publicly declare your wrong and then write a letter to the organization saying you no longer want to be a part of the sorority."

"Publicly declare my wrong?" Megan ponders this action. She wonders how she is to do that. The persecution she will face not only from Theta Kappa Rho but from everyone in the Black Greek Letter Organization haunts her.

"And of course repent to God for taking an oath to another god," Tameka adds with a sense of purpose. "You need to do that first."

The atmosphere begins to shift from fear to determination as Megan sees the support Tameka is giving her to continue this path of escaping TKRho's stronghold.

"So…" Tameka takes a long pause, sitting back on the bed out of camera's view. "Are you denouncing Theta Kappa Rho?"

"Yes," Megan answers unwavering. But is it easier said than done?

A thought of Professor Hill and scheduling her last semester classes comes into memory. She reaches for the letter in her backpack and emails Professor Hill to schedule an appointment to select her graduating electives. As she sends the email, she suddenly remembers Professor Hill saying, "I know I'm your counselor, and an old man, but I was also Greek."

A new revelation has come over Megan; she realizes that Professor Hill was once Greek. God has highlighted that Professor Hill can give her insight on how to get out of TKRho. She wants to pick his brain about Greek life. *How did he get out?*

†††

Pastor Jones walks to the edge of the sanctuary's stage for altar call, raising his hands toward heaven. He prompts those in need of salvation and forgiveness to the front while unscrewing a bottle of anointing oil to anoint the individuals' foreheads. Male ushers, including Tameka's fiancé, Marcus, scatter amongst the church directing newcomers and congregants to follow suit. Claps and shouts are heard from the congregation as each person walks toward the altar. The music bursts into celebration. They line up along the edge of the stage with tears streaming down their faces. Once all who are seeking salvation have approached the altar, Pastor Jones silences the congregation. The musicians soften the music with a tune that compliments the ushering in of the Holy Spirit.

Megan's internal temperature rises, a lump forms in her throat, and beads of sweat appear in the corners of her forehead. She receives a nudge from the Holy Spirit to join those at the altar. She replays Tameka's demand, "Repent to God for taking an oath to another god." She knows the reminder is confirmation, giving voice to the nudge she feels tugging at her.

Megan carefully scoots through the aisle, stepping over her family's feet, avoiding the scuffing of their shoes. The disruption shifts the family's attention from the front of the church to Megan's unexpected movement to join the individuals being anointed with oil. Some members fall to the ground, caught and covered with a white cloth by ushers who are firmly planted behind them. James watches Megan's maneuver in wonder, Tameka rests a huge grin on her face, and Tina follows Megan down the aisle. Witnessing an answered prayer of God going above and beyond what Tina could have imagined, tears of joy begin to run down her cheeks. She grabs Megan's hand as they walk toward the front of the church.

"The angels in heaven are rejoicing," Pastor Jones yells over the congregation as he ushers Megan and Tina to an open space. Once the two are secure in position, he anoints both of their foreheads, reciting a scripture too low for either of them to comprehend. A female usher steps up behind them, placing a hand at the center of their backs in case they are subject to falling out. Pastor Jones steps back onto the stage, positioning himself in front of the microphone stand attached to the podium, and politely asks all those lined up in front of him to repeat a prayer of salvation after him. The musicians lower the music, and the prayer is repeated. Megan silently prays a prayer of her own. "Lord, I need Your help. I'm lost and afraid. Show me what I should do about TKRho. I am here to repent of my wrong and ask for Your forgiveness. I want to do the right thing, but I don't know where to start."

Her first prayer for God's help comes into remembrance. "Lord, please help us make it through this set safely unharmed. If You do, I will do whatever You ask of me." This is the prayer she prayed the night on set after the annual step show when Jasmine was drunk, demanding they learn the step show routine. He answered Megan's prayer then; the girls left that night unharmed. He did His part, now she must do hers. But what must she do? What is He asking, or did He ask of her?

A sense of clarity begins to settle over her. The quiet voice of God speaks to her heart, gentle yet firm. *Speak the truth. Denounce and renounce the sorority in front of the organizations. I AM with you. You proudly reverenced the god of Theta Kappa Rho; now it's time you reverence Me. You are forgiven.*

Receiving her next steps, Megan's eyes fill with tears. Opening them to the sound of "Amens" throughout the church, she takes a breath of relief. Pastor Jones motions for the renewed saints to follow Marcus, who's standing under the exit sign at the side of the sanctuary, to a back room. They are led into Christian counseling to determine their next steps as born-again Christians.

Megan sits in a small office with a deaconess who asks her about her concerns and guides her on how to move forward. Megan mentions her situation, and the deaconess, familiar with Greek life, tells her that now she must remove all items associated with the sorority: jackets, clothing, pendants, cups, etc. She tells her that giving these items away will not do; she must either burn them or rid them in the trash where no one can take hold of them. "You do not want to spread this curse to anyone else," the deaconess emphasizes.

†††

Tina invites Marcus's family to join the Mahns for an after-church meal at the Macon Buffet restaurant, a fellowship to become acquainted with their soon-to-be in-laws. Megan chokes on her water seeing Alicia walk through the restaurant doors with Marcus and his family. She's surprised that no one thought it important to mention that Alicia's mom, whom Tina has prayer meetings with, is Marcus's mom as well. Alicia approaches Megan at the center table of the restaurant and, with an exaggerated hug, confirms the unexpected surprise. Megan is gaining another sister. The girls laugh at the coincidence.

The moms talk about upcoming church events. The dads talk sports. Tameka and Marcus talk about their wedding plans, while Megan and Alicia talk SASU. Megan notices that Alicia is abiding by the sorority's strict diet, painfully picking through a full plate of vegetables. Alicia has made subtle hints not to talk about Gamma Alpha Alpha Phi while her family is present. So Megan does not bring attention to the weird buffet appetite; however, she does prefer McDonald's French-fry-eating Alicia over vegan Alicia because that Alicia spills the sorority tea. And Megan can use more dirt on sororities to confirm and solidify her departure from TKRho.

"What made you go to the altar today?" Tina asks Megan through proud eyes. She awaits a response to gain an understanding of how her prayers have been answered as she eats her spoonful of mashed potatoes. Her prayer partner Janet, Alicia's mom, also anticipates Megan's response.

"I went to the altar because of..." Megan pauses to consider how her truth could open conversation for Alicia to talk about her sorority involvement and the post-pledge starvation she's painfully enduring. "I went to the altar because of TKRho. I needed to repent."

"Amen," Tina exclaims. The moms give each other a nod confirming their answered prayer.

Marcus and his dad, Tom, sit in confusion as Alicia shoves a spoonful of carrots in her mouth to avoid being outed.

"What's TKRho?" Marcus curiously asks.

Megan responds, "TKRho stands for Theta Kappa Rho. A sorority I'm in at SASU." She quickly corrects herself. "A sorority I *was* in." Alicia turns to Megan with a nonverbal question through her squinted eyes. Megan directs her response to Alicia. "I'm trying to figure out how to get out of it. I'll fill you in later," she whispers. Alicia doesn't respond. She quickly returns to picking over her vegetables.

"I've been on her about that Greek stuff, but you know how little sisters are. They don't listen," Tameka jokes, giving Marcus a thigh squeeze as they simultaneously snicker, lost in their infatuation phase.

With no understanding of Greek life, buttoned-up Tom chimes in. "Kids should go to school for an education. Why the added pressure of trying to be a part of some sorority group? Be friends with your classmates."

James, matching his tone, agrees. "I'm with you one hundred and ten percent, Tom."

"It's not that easy," Alicia finally responds, eyes glued to her vegetables.

"You've made plenty of friends without having to join a sorority," Janet reminds. "You've never had issues with friends; it's always been the teachers." The moms join in laughter, hinting to an old issue turned answered prayer turned inside joke. Obligated to explain the duet laughter, Janet continues, "Alicia's college experience is a hot topic in our weekly prayer group. We constantly pray that she will get along with the staff at school and the enemy will no longer hinder her from getting good grades, provoking her with problems that caused her to transfer to SASU." She explains while Alicia squirms in her seat, formulating an exit plan.

All attention is on Alicia for a rebuttal. Fed up with the snowballing Miller family lie and no exit plan coming to mind, Alicia exclaims, "I was pledging in a sorority. I got stressed out. My grades dropped. It wasn't about the teachers."

She lets out a huge sigh of relief, tension released from her shoulders, and she goes back to her vegetables. The tension from her shoulders transfers onto the others as they stiffly sit in silence contemplating a conversational turn. The waiter comes over to refill their empty glasses of water. "Thank yous" and "no thank yous" are mumbled amongst the stiff group. Megan, understanding the heaviness of pledging a sorority and its secrets, carries the transferred tension in her throat. She gulps her water down to lessen the uncomfortable knot formed.

Tameka breaks the tension by stating, "Well, going to SASU allowed you to start over. Right? I guess you both have had your fair share of sorority life," bringing Megan back into the heat.

"I rejoined," Alicia admits.

"What?" her father questions, nearly choking on his buttered roll. "What does that mean?"

"When did that happen?" Janet asks.

"When I transferred. I pledged again at SASU, but this time I got in." Alicia reveals, with a slight smile. No smiles are reciprocated from the table. Megan feels bad for her. The knot in Megan's throat slowly reforms. She takes another sip of her water.

"Well, that's not good," James mumbles, stuffing his cheeks with a drumstick.

Tina nudges him and corrects his comment. "What James means to say is we will be praying for you, Alicia," Tina restates.

"Do you want to stay in it?" Marcus asks.

Without waiting for an answer, Tom, wiping the corner of his mouth with his napkin, suggests, "Maybe Megan can help you get out of it. If it's something she had to repent for, then maybe…"

Alicia cuts him off. "I'm fine in it. I don't want to get out. It's great for networking and sisterhood. It's not stressful like it was at the other school." She abruptly gets up from the table, leaving her plate of vegetables. "I'm going for seconds."

Tom grips his napkin tightly as if choking Alicia's neck. Janet grabs his shaking hand, lowering it beneath the table. The others attend to their meals, pretending to ignore the action.

Good thing Alicia left when she did. Tom's about to perform an exorcism, Megan thinks to herself, observing the green vein protruding in the center of his forehead. Taking in small pieces of string beans, Megan remembers the conversation the girls had about how stressful Gamma Alpha Alpha Phi has been to Alicia, but not wanting to burst Alicia's bubble, Megan thinks it's best to text Alicia about it later.

†††

Megan lays on an air mattress inflated in the center of Tina's workroom. She tosses and turns, attempting to adjust her pillow into a comfortable position, and spots the military time 23:23 on the sewing machine's digital clock. She contemplates sending Alicia an "are you alive" text, but with it being so late, she can only assume Alicia's sound asleep. After observing the anger Tom expressed choking the dinner napkin, Megan wouldn't be surprised if Alicia was knocked out unconscious. Alicia's safety baffles Megan's wandering mind, and if there's any hope for sleep tonight, she must send Alicia a text message *now*. She reaches for her phone plugged into a nearby outlet and texts, **Hey Alicia. How are you feeling? I know it was hard revealing Gamma AAPhi to your family today. I'm here if you want to talk.** Send.

Megan lays back on her pillow, eyes staring at the ceiling as a sense of calm comes over her. She closes her eyes in an attempt to take a well-needed snooze. Her phone lights up and the message notification chimes on her phone simultaneously. It's a response from Alicia: **Thank you for checking on me. My family has no clue about Greek life. The less they know, the better.**

Megan's short-lived peace for a restful night is disturbed by Alicia's immediate response that shoots a jolt of excitement through her spine and fear that the house may have heard her phone chime. She lowers its sound, ready to engage in the sorority talk that was forbidden while at the table with their joint family. Megan responds, **You can talk to me about Greek life anytime. Sister-in-law. LOL.** A strike of conviction hits Megan after sending the message. No LOLs. This conversation needs to be serious.

How do I persuade Alicia to leave Gamma AAPhi? Megan contemplates. She practices different wordings and phrases to not sound so extreme, but she must deliver the message with urgency. She begins to type, *I'm getting out of TKRho because...* Megan sees that Alicia is also typing. She stops formulating her sentence to wait on Alicia's message to come through.

Why are you leaving TKRho? Alicia asks.

Bingo. We're on the same page. Megan begins typing. Her thumbs peck one hundred miles per hour to explain everything she found out about TKRho, Greek life, and secret societies. She holds nothing back. A voice message would have been easier, but if Tom is within earshot of the conversation and hears a third of what's being disclosed, the exorcism would begin. She rereads her essay of a message, correcting the misspellings and adding punctuation where it seems fit, in hopes that it's read how she would have verbally delivered it. She makes sure to capitalize words like DEMONIC, ALTARS, and any other word that could put fear in someone she's trying to bring to the light. If this was a school assignment, she would receive an A-plus for her attention to detail.

She finally sends the message, proud of her verbiage. She waits for Alicia's response, which feels like a decade. She gives Alicia grace with trying to understand all the spiritual talk and demonic god-worship revelations Megan's thrown her way.

Alicia finally responds. *How do you know all this? *Why* do you know all this?*

Research, she quickly answers.

Megan realizes she's left no room for Alicia to respond and would not be satisfied if the conversation ended on her saying, "Research." So she asks, *What Greek god or goddess is attached to Gamma?* to keep the conversation going.

Alicia replies, *I'm not sure. I would need to look it up.*

Well, I'm sure that's who you all... Megan immediately erases her response and thinks of another question she's been dying to know in case Alicia has had enough of this sorority-exposure talk. **Did you perform any rituals with candles or recite any mystical phrases during initiation?** Send.

There's a moment of stillness, then Megan sees Alicia typing. The phone lights up notifying her that a message has arrived. It reads, *We did.* Followed by a shocked emoji face.

Well, when you find the goddess Gamma represents, I'm sure that's the deity you pledged to.

Why would this be allowed? Why hasn't anyone come forth or called it out if it is so bad? Alicia responds.

Megan knows from her response that she's not fully sold on the dangers of the activity they've both participated in. She must find a way to awaken Alicia and open her eyes to the abomination that was done before the Lord.

Megan responds out of urgency, **Everyone isn't Christian and don't care about how this makes God feel. Bowing down to another god and pledging an allegiance to it. Christmas don't seem to care, and it hurts God that we did this.** Send. She rereads her message and shakes her head at the typo. She hopes Alicia understands what she means. She sees that the message is read by Alicia, but there is no response or sign of typing. Megan gives her time to ponder the message, maybe she's trying to figure out what Christmas has to do with anything.

The wait builds up an anxiety, so Megan sends another message. Her last text of the night, to end the conversation on a good note: **Goodnight Alicia. I'm here if you need to talk. I was just making sure you were still alive LOL. Sister.**

She lays back on her pillow. She's back to square one, tossing and turning, wondering if she could have delivered the message better. Her phone lights up again with another text notification. She lifts her phone to view a message from Trish in the group chat of the OG line that reads, *What's up girl? Haven't seen or heard from you since the party. You good?*

Megan plugs her phone into the charger, placing it on the carpeted floor, leaving the group on read.

CHAPTER 20: DO IT NOW!

"Professor Hill, do you have a moment?" Megan lightly taps Professor Hill's ajar office door and patiently waits for him to invite her in. He sits at his desk, enjoying a breather before diving into his last-minute paper sorting that's stacked under a stapler.

"Sure, come in," he commands, snapping his fingers. "Oh yeah, we need to schedule your electives," he remembers, shifting from his relaxed position to attend to the computer in front of him. He pulls up her records and motions for her to take a seat while glancing at the time. "You're early. Our meeting isn't until three. But you've been on my mind, Ms. Mahn. How's everything going?" he asks with genuine concern, scanning his screen.

Megan's phone chimes from a text notification. She takes a quick look to see Donna's message to the group: *Megan, why are you ignoring us?* Megan doesn't respond to the text. Instead, she silences the notification and takes a seat at the professor's desk. She pulls out the familiar chair and places the phone face-up on her lap. Another text comes through from April: *Because of TKRho.*

Why would she ignore us because of TKRho? Trish asks the group as if Megan isn't receiving the messages.

The girls haven't seen Megan since she's been back to Atlanta. April was sound asleep when Megan arrived at the apartment late last night, and she left before April could wake to have an early meeting with Professor Hill. The girls can see that Megan is reading the messages, so they're confused as to why she's choosing not to respond. April, on the other hand, knows why Megan is silent. Her concern is whether Megan will pay her portion of the rent on time.

Demonic? TKRho is not DEMONIC! a text reads from Donna.

Megan's anxiety heightens as the text notifications flow through one after another. Megan places her fingers in the visible indentation marks of the armrest that once endured her intense grips. The pressure gets the best of her, and she blurts out, intensifying her grip on the armrest, "I'm leaving TKRho! It's demonic and no one believes me…"

"Slow down!" Professor Hill orders, looking up from his computer.

She attempts to slow her breathing. If only those words were transcribed into the group chat. Relief begins to come over her as she takes in the room's atmosphere. Its musical décor calms her—the same décor that was of no help to her freshman year when she needed its calming effect. She steadies her breath and waits for the professor to break the silent staring contest.

"Sounds like you took a deep dive into Greek organizations and their history. Don't like what you've found?" He waits for an answer, then concludes that Megan perceived the question as rhetorical. He continues, "I've been there. I know it's tough when no one believes you. But I do, because I was a member of Zeta Alpha Phi."

"How did you separate yourself from it? I'm afraid that once I let Theta Kappa Rho go completely, I'll lose who I've become. I like who I've become. I have a confidence I've never had before."

Another text comes through that reads, **Who do you think you are?** A message from Donna, as if she's in the room joining the conversation.

Megan's had enough. She puts her phone in her pocket to hide the conversation on the tiny screen. She continues, slightly ashamed of her next revelation. "I don't know who I am outside of TKRho." She holds back tears to avoid a crying session. She inhales deeply, observing the popcorn ceiling, then exhales toward the framed photo of a smiling Ray Charles sitting at a piano. *How was he so focused while pursuing his dream?* she wonders.

Professor Hill observes Megan's vulnerability and responds carefully. "What did you do before the sorority?" A familiar question he's asked many college students when they've gone off course.

"Music," Megan responds, pointing to the Ray Charles picture. "Piano. That's all I did growing up. My family moved us to Macon a few years ago…"

"Ah, Little Richard and Otis Redding. You've moved to the birthplace of Southern rock," he interrupts, getting up from his desk and walking toward a bookshelf full of books organized by color, separated by music-note bookends. He pulls out two thick books with a quick scan, contemplating if they're the solution to Megan's problem. "Here's one about the history of music throughout the 1900s, and this one's for motivation to help you focus on the main reason you're here at SASU. Focus on your music. You're young. There's a lot more ahead for you."

Megan takes the books, glancing them over. She cradles them in her arms—the support she needs to defeat her enemy, the phone vibrating in her pocket with group chat banter.

"Have you renounced and denounced?" Professor Hill asks as he takes his seat. She shakes her head no. "Send an email to Theta

Kappa Rho's headquarters stating you want to resign as a member. They may ask you why. State your reason. Maybe it will plant a seed in the receiver of your email. Then denounce." Off Megan's silence he explains, "That means to make a public declaration."

Aware of what denounce means, she asks, "Why does it have to be public?"

"Well, you proudly announced that you were a member of TKRho, so it's only right to publicly denounce the organization."

"That makes sense of why, but how?" She grips the books, voicing her real concern. The thought of having to confront Donna, Trish, and April in the group chat has already skyrocketed her blood pressure. Standing in front of a crowd to denounce would cause her to go into cardiac arrest.

"You kids have it good. You have social media. Do a post," he suggests with a smile. "I didn't have it that easy. I stood in front of my fraternity at a chapter meeting and denounced. I felt their heated stares. They were like flaming darts shooting in my back as I walked out the building." He laughs. "No matter the hate you receive from TKRho or other organizations, just know you're making the only audience member that matters the proudest, and that's God. I'll be proud also," he assures, pleased to assist a lost sheep's return. "Honestly, you denouncing doesn't have to be some grand gesture. It's just stating that you are no longer a member. You can tell this to your chapter members like I did. The most important thing is to detach from the organization—not necessarily the people because we are to love one another—but detach from the Greek idol worship."

Professor Hill's mention of God being proud of her gives Megan the motivation to move forward. She rises from the seat and says, "Thanks, Professor Hill. You've helped me more than you know."

"I can't wait to hear what song comes from this new season of your life." He winks as she closes the door behind her.

"Megan!" he yells at the closed door. "We need to schedule your electives."

But Megan is already gone, with a new air of confidence, crossing the Jordan River into her promised land. Now it's time to defeat her enemies, starting with the group chat that has silenced. She pulls her phone out of her pocket to open the group text and begins to type: **Ladies, we need to talk. Meet me at the café in thirty minutes.** She sends the message, unsure how it will be received or if they will even show up since she's ghosted them over the last few days. If they don't show up, no worries—but she only wants to explain her reasons for leaving TKRho once, with hopes of continuing their friendship afterward.

†††

It's a few days before spring semester begins, so only a handful of students scatter amongst an empty cafeteria. Megan nervously waits at a circular table tucked in the corner of the café for her guests to arrive. She figures this location would be good for them to meet just in case things go south. She's not worried about Trish's reaction because she'll do whatever April and Donna do—and *they* could fly off the handle at the drop of a dime. But whether to end their friendship or not? That is the question.

What will I say? How do I start? How will they take it? These questions run over and over nonstop in her mind. She looks around the café to see if anyone's aware of her anxiety. Do they see her heart pumping out of her chest and hear its beats? She spots a digital clock hanging above a banner that reads *Welcome Back Lions!* The time is 12:01. The invitation to meet was sent about twenty-five minutes ago. The girls should be walking in at any moment. Megan looks toward the café entrance and, as predicted, she sees April turning the corner. April scans the room for Megan and they hold eye contact.

Megan nervously waves, but the action is not returned. Instead, April returns a look of disappointment as she approaches the table.

"I know what this is about, so you can save me the details," April dismisses, taking her seat across from Megan with her back toward the entrance. "I just want to know if you have your part of the rent."

"I have it."

April gives a nod of approval and the two sit in silence. Megan doesn't dare utter a word until the others have arrived. Once is hard enough, so she doesn't want to repeat herself multiple times. She also doesn't want to upset April further. Megan's hoping the others show up quickly because April's cold stares are piercing through her overly worked heart. She's sure the café workers can hear it pounding in the back of the kitchen.

"Oh, thank God," Megan whispers. They turn to Donna and Trish walking their way.

"Chirp!" Donna lets out a squeal that startles the other students in the space, filling the cafeteria with TKRho presence. They are both wearing TKRho paraphernalia, looking not at all worried about the reason for their meeting. They seem happy, but Megan knows it's normal for a Theta to put on the persona of having a good day. However, Megan knows that once the girls hear the truth of their meeting, it could go south. She does a short inner dialogue prayer: *Don't let it go south. Don't let it go south*, she prays.

April stands up proudly, returning the call. Trish and Donna skip over to the table. The three embrace in hugs as if they haven't seen each other in years. Megan watches uncomfortably, unsure if she should stand and join the hugs—but seeing how April didn't hint a motion toward her that warranted one, she decides it's best to sit and watch the unapologetic Theta love on display. She has to admit she's going to miss those hugs. The longer the scene goes on, the feeling that this act is intentional makes her feel a certain way—and it's working. It's awkward and painful to watch.

Maybe I'm overreacting, Megan convinces herself. *But why would they embrace me in the same way? I've been ignoring their calls and texts*, she reasons.

After the long, drawn-out embrace and chirps, the girls join lonely Megan at the table.

Donna mocks, "Oh, so it's true you do have beef with us. No chirp back? No hug?"

Here we go, Megan exhales to herself. *It's going south.*

Then she says to Donna, "I don't have beef with you. I'm leaving TKRho." She hadn't expected it to come out like that—no explanation, straight to the point. She scans the girls' expressions to determine her next move.

"We are TKRho!" Trish abruptly exclaims, flipping her long, straightened hair over her shoulders to place her hands on her hips. Megan is taken aback by Trish's response. She's surprised that Trish is the first to fly off the handle with attitude. Megan doesn't like seeing the girls mad at her, especially Trish—the innocent, soft-spoken one, "Soul Glow." She's for sure glowing now. TKRho has given these girls a confidence that's undeniable.

I can't lose their friendship. I would be back to square one—the loner loser. No friends. No boyfriend. Just the Macon girl in love with her keyboard, Megan thinks to herself.

This is not going how she'd hoped. She envisioned explaining herself to the girls, that they would understand her revelation of truth and be happy for her, ending their meetup with hugs and laughter. Instead, she's met with angry stares, waiting for an explanation.

She exhales deeply and lets it all out—her findings, her convictions, her vision at the sorority house and at the apartment party. She even explains how God convicted her and has forgiven her. That was the hardest part of her explanation. It sounded like it was all God's fault as to why she was losing their friendship and sisterhood. A few huffs and puffs were heard when she mentioned Him and her faith.

The girls take it all in, and Trish softly asks with concern, "Do you believe that we are demonic?"

"No, you're not demonic. The process to get in TKRho, the rituals we performed, and oaths we took—those are. It does not honor God. And I'm about honoring Him," Megan states, hoping that's enough to justify her stance.

"I hear you want to be this holy Christian, but that ain't my ministry. I'm a Theta until I die," Donna states, holding the TKRho symbol, waiting for the others to join. April proudly throws up the symbol. They look at Trish, and she joins in as well.

"I see. I just wanted to let you know how I feel about it. I'm going to let Sharice know, and I'm sending a notice to headquarters. I can't be a part of it anymore. I love you all like sisters and I hope we can still be friends… best friends." Megan begins to tear up. This breakup hurts more than being ghosted by Jeff.

The four sit in silence as teary-eyed Megan struggles to inhale the thick, intense cloud exhaled by the three. April breaks the silence by asking, "Are you going to pay this month's rent on time?"

Megan's shocked by the repeated question. She wipes her tears and responds, "*Yes*. I *told* you it's covered."

"Well then, you still have a best friend, sister," April smiles, getting up from her seat to embrace Megan with a hug. Megan's eyes swell up again with tears. The others join in the embrace. Donna lets out one last chirp.

Trish shushes her.

"What? I'm still a Theta," Donna retorts. "I was hazing her out. Making sure she didn't chirp back."

They all laugh.

"You're still our sister, and we love you," Donna adds.

"But I better not catch you chirping," a bold Trish jokes.

They fill the corner with laughter again and embrace in a familiar hug.

†††

Months have passed and Megan still hasn't sent her renouncement email to headquarters. Sharice's approval of an unofficial suspension that prohibits her from TKRho activities and meetings has helped further the procrastination. But now's the perfect time to send that email. She leans back against her wooden headboard, hesitantly opening her laptop. She hears the members of TKRho practicing their synchronized stomps outside her bedroom. With two hours left before the annual step show, the performers flush out last-minute kinks before moving on to hair and makeup. She reminisces on the fun times stepping with the girls, a skill she's found to be surprisingly good at, but she knows her current assignment is greater than performing in a Greek step show.

She opens her email and sees a revised work schedule from Sharon. Her request off to attend Tameka's small, intimate wedding of a few friends and family next weekend has been approved. Megan thanks God, because Tameka has expressed many times, over wedding-planning phone calls, the words she would have with Sharon if her sister, maid of honor, and only bridesmaid could not attend the wedding.

Sharon has been surprisingly nice to Megan. After their one-and-done conversation expressing disappointment with Megan leaving the sorority, she's been professional—keeping business business, no sorority talk. Jeff, on the other hand, still has not called or texted. Megan discovered through one of her social media stalkings on Jeff's page that he's going on the road as a traveling producer with an up-and-coming independent artist. A job he got through a ZAPhi connection, or so it seems. The post consisted of a picture of him standing alongside the artist and an older frat who appeared to be the artist's manager. She often thinks about Jeff and the moment they shared. She wonders if it's possible for one to move on as quickly as he has. If so, she prays to learn to as well.

Tying up loose ends and distractions from starting her renouncement email, Megan sends a reply confirming her work schedule and opens a new tab to start an email to TKRho headquarters. She nervously begins to type.

Subject: *Theta Kappa Rho Release — Megan Mahn*
To Whom it may concern,

She pauses to look at the time. It's 5:07. She needs to set her alarm for seven o'clock. This will allow time to write the email, take a quick nap, and shower before the show. She struggled with the idea of going, but after days of prayer, she believes it's best to make a public statement at the show. Everyone who's Greek will be there.

She sets her alarm for 7:00 and continues typing:

I am stepping down from my position as President of the Omega Zeta chapter of Theta Kappa Rho and being a member of Theta Kappa Rho Incorporated. Due to my beliefs this organization no longer serves me.
Thanks,
Megan Mahn

She proofreads and rereads and proofreads the email over and over to make sure it's clear enough for the organization to understand her withdrawal. Her heart pounds against her chest as she doubts her wording. *Do I need to explain more? What if they want to know what my beliefs are? Should I explain my beliefs now?* she contemplates. She reads over the letter again and again, knowing that once the email is sent, it's confirmed and affirmed that she is serious about her exit. No more unofficial suspension; she will be deactivated, terminated, and disaffiliated from the sorority officially.

"Chirp, chirp, chirp!" The chirps of departure startle her. The members are headed to the auditorium. She was so zoned out and focused on the email that she forgot the girls were in the apartment. Her fingers slightly tremble as she clicks the send button. A sense of relief comes over her. She looks at the time. With all the proofreading and rewriting, it's taken her longer than expected. She has no time to take a nap and barely enough time to get dressed and manage her nerves before her big show—the denouncement.

†††

Megan swiftly maneuvers backstage through the performers stretching; some are gathered holding hands in prayer, preparing to prove they're the best of the best. She spots the ladies of TKRho marking their steps in unison, preventing those around them from seeing their performance full out. As they end the routine, Megan positions herself close to the original four in solidarity—not approving of their involvement but being a supportive friend. She desperately wants to tell them she's an official former member of TKRho, but she decides against it. She doesn't want to put a damper on their excitement.

"Would you like to lead the prayer before we go on, Ms. Christian?" April asks Megan with a wink as she takes a sip of water. Megan's flattered, being asked to pray for the girls, but her prayer will not be the prayer they'd want to hear before a TKRho performance.

"No. I'll let you have it," Megan responds.

She begins a silent prayer of her own. *How am I supposed to denounce the sorority in front of this crowd?* Megan asks as she peeks out the left wing of the stage to see the SASU auditorium packed with students and alumni full of energy and excitement. Their cheers and hollers amplify with each change of tune the DJ plays through the speakers. Colorful lights flash across the stage representing each Greek organization in attendance. The Greeks are divided amongst themselves. Thetas are seated together with Jasmine leading chirp calls, and Toya's holding baby Tonya, who's surprisingly wearing a *future Theta* T-shirt. Across from the Thetas are ZAPhi. She spots Jeff amongst them, preoccupied on his phone. Looks like he's brought business with him to the show. *I guess the artist released him from the tour to attend,* Megan thinks to herself. Unwanted familiar feelings come over her seeing him in attendance. Their last conversation ended in a breakup due to her views on Greek life, and now he's about to see her denounce, telling everyone how bad Greek life is. If there was ever a chance of them speaking again, she knows there's no chance after today.

April gathers the TKRho performers together. She looks in Megan's direction, inviting her to join. Megan politely declines and stands within earshot to hear what April's prayer entails.

"God, help us to have a great performance. Let us shine like never before. Let us show them who's the best sorority alive. And help Trish with that one-two step with the hop turn. Amen," April prays. The group laughs. Trish sucks her teeth jokingly.

Megan begins to override April's prayer with a silent prayer of her own. *Please forgive them, Lord, for they know not what they do.*

"Amen!" the girls repeat in unison, followed by chirps.

The stage lights dim, and a loud siren blares through the speakers. A slow melodic song follows, and a very serious member of ZAPhi solemnly walks toward the center of the stage. He yells, "Moment of silence!" with a militant shout.

The step show attendees halt to a silence, and a clothed backdrop of Tony wearing his paraphernalia drapes over the upstage wall. Gasps and whistles are heard amongst the auditorium. Dean Jackson quickly approaches the mic stand and repeats, "A moment of silence, please." The crowd follows suit.

Do it now. Megan hears a voice. She looks around to see where it's coming from. *Do it now. The crowd is silent*, the small voice repeats.

She whispers to the invisible voice, "I don't want to be rude. It's a moment of silence for Tony."

But she agrees—the voice is right. Once the memorial is over, nothing but stomps, yells, and chants will fill the space. She must do it now while everyone is quiet. To Megan's right, Zeta Alpha Phi lines up in show formation to go on stage. They wait anxiously for the DJ to deliver their music cue. Megan looks toward the DJ, who's scrolling through his laptop to play their coming-out song.

Do it NOW!

With no hesitation, Megan rushes to the mic stand. The crowd watches, thinking it's part of TKRho's performance. She locks eyes with Jeff and releases the mic from the stand. Her hands tremble as she grasps the mic with both hands, holding it up to her mouth, concealing the sweat forming above her lips. The Greeks backstage murmur amongst each other, "What is she doing? TKRho's not up first." Megan takes a deep breath and releases her gaze from Jeff, who is emotionless. She scans the faces of her former sorority sisters and the audience, then—

"Excuse me, everyone." The speakers squeak. She shifts her position slightly away from them and continues, "I have something important to say."

If you tell these organizations they're demonic, they will cancel you. The voice of Jeff echoes in her ear.

You need to be careful about what you say about Theta Kappa Rho, or your words will have consequences. Sharon's voice reminds her.

Megan wipes her sweaty palms down the side of her pants one by one. She begins to have doubts as the stares intensify.

A shout is heard from the audience. "Do something or get off the stage!" The crowd roars with laughter.

You proudly announced that you were a member of TKRho, so it's only right to publicly denounce the organization. Professor Hill's voice overrides the roars.

Do it now. Speak the truth. Denounce and renounce the sorority in front of the organizations. I AM with you. You proudly reverenced the god of Theta Kappa Rho; now it's time you reverence Me, God's voice demands.

Filled with words, Megan says, "I am no longer a part of Theta Kappa Rho Incorporated. I've made the decision to distance myself from the practices and rituals that I understand to be wrong."

Boos shoot at her like arrows from the crowd with shouts of "traitor" and "liar." She scans the crowd and locks eyes with Jeff, whose piercing gaze penetrates through her soul. He shakes his head in disdain. It hurts, but she continues, catching eyes with Shay and the neos standing backstage—the spring '24 line.

"I'm truly sorry to the members who came in under me. I realize now that I misled you and didn't see the full truth. For that, I am deeply sorry."

The OG line stands embarrassed. April is stiff, wide-eyed with her mouth dropped, unsure of how to save Megan in this moment.

The dean approaches Megan, snatching the mic from her intense grip. "Everyone, I will handle this matter. Continue with the show." He prompts the DJ. "Give it up for Zeta Alpha Phi!" The cued music begins. The guys come out strongly, overcompensating with steps and chants to uplift the mood. They saturate the stage, nearly knocking Megan over.

The dean, wearing his ZAPhi jacket, sternly whispers in Megan's ear, "This is not the time nor place to stand your ground. Now go!" He points toward the side door with a steady breath. The crowd erupts in cheers as ZAPhi puts on their show-stopping performance.

Megan finds her way to the side door, taking one last glimpse of the crowd. She spots Professor Hill in the back of the auditorium giving her a slight smile and nod of approval. Then he exits through the double doors at the entrance of the auditorium.

Megan's startled by her phone's text-notification vibration. The chime intensifies. It's a text from Tameka that reads, *Did you go to the show?*

Megan looks at the time that reads 8:43 p.m. "Oh no, I overslept!" Checking her alarm, she sees it was set for seven a.m. instead of seven p.m. "Lord, please give me grace. I overslept."

It was all a dream. She hadn't denounced. Did she even send the email?

She quickly opens her laptop and sees the email to headquarters unsent in her drafts. She had fallen asleep before sending it. She sits up on her bed, well rested, to give it another try. Send. "Lord, please give me grace," she pleads again, with guilt.

CHAPTER 21: A DAY TO REMEMBER

Tameka reveals her wedding gown in the full-length mirror hanging on the back of Tina's office door. She stands in awe, admiring her long white laced fitted gown draped over her shoulders. Megan adjusts the back of the oversized train, evenly spreading it out for a photo.

"Say 'Tameka Mahn-Miller,'" Alicia cheeses the command, smiling on the other end of her camera lens. She snaps a quick flash photo and shimmies over to the table of gifts, taking scenery snapshots and footage for Tameka's social media channel. Her latest venture—*The Stylish Bride*. Tameka made sure to do everyone's hair and makeup to ensure her skills are imprinted on every photo captured in hopes of gaining bride-to-be followers and wedding beauty partnerships.

"Make sure to get photos of Megan when she's completely dressed in her last look," Tameka demands. "Megan, get dressed! I need a photo of you," she shouts, observing Megan, who's wearing her chicken-stained SASU Lion T-shirt and ripped jeans. Because it's

STEPPING DOWN

Tameka's wedding day, Megan doesn't give a sarcastic response. She follows orders, stepping into the lavender dress Tina patterned.

Tina enters the room, stepping over Tameka's train that's blocking the entranceway.

"Don't put the dress on the floor, Megan!" Tina shouts. She runs toward Megan to help with the dress zipper caught on a piece of string. Alicia snaps a shot of the mishap. "You can delete that one," Tina states, frustrated with the commotion she's entered into.

A light knock is at the door. In walks April.

"Hey, hey, hey," she sings, handing Tameka a white bridal bouquet as she tiptoes around the train. "I was going to buy blue flowers but…"

Tameka cuts April an eye. "Thanks for not," Tameka states sarcastically, practicing how she will hold the bouquet walking down the aisle.

"Okay ladies, let's say a quick prayer," Tina suggests, pulling out her anointing oil from a hidden pocket in her dress. She approaches Tameka with an oily finger.

"Ma, no! Just say the prayer. You're going to mess up my makeup!"

"Mrs. Mahn, do you carry that oil everywhere you go?" April asks, remembering her first encounter with the spiritual weapon.

"Oh yeah. I still owe you one." Tina playfully waves her oiled finger in April's direction.

Giving in to Tameka's request, Tina begins to pray. "Bow your heads. Dear Heavenly Father, we come saying thank You. Thank You for delivering us. Saving us. Loving us. Bringing families together that love You and worship You. I pray this union fulfills its purpose—Your purpose. I pray it's full of love and joy. May You touch and heal everyone standing under the sound of my voice." She pauses, looking over at April, giving her a wink. April gives a chuckle in return. "Lord, we love You. Let Your will be done. In Jesus' Name, Amen."

"Amen," the girls repeat in unison.

Janet, draped in a silk lavender pantsuit—another Tina original—peeks her head through the room door. "You look beautiful, Tameka. Are you ready?"

"Yes. I'm ready," Tameka responds.

"She better be ready. I've been waiting to walk her down the aisle for the past twenty-four years," James complains outside the door, ready to walk his daughter down the aisle. Janet smiles, shaking her head and closing the door behind her.

"Well, that's my cue. An impatient man is on the other side of the door," Tina jokes. She gives Tameka an emotional hug. "I love you, Meka," she states, eyes watered. She clears her throat and positions herself into drill-sergeant mode. "Alright, ten minutes—be in position," she says, looking at her watch.

"Five minutes!" James yells from outside the door. "I need to catch the evening game."

"James, you not going to miss the game. The ceremony is in our backyard. You can see the game from the yard," Tina nags, walking out the door.

"They're so funny," Alicia states.

"And annoying," Megan adds.

"Real quick, before we go out there, Megan…" Alicia places her hand on Megan's shoulder as if the placement would help Megan hear her clearer. "I know we haven't talked since our last conversation that night after the restaurant, but I want to let you know that I've been doing some research about my sorority, and you might be on to something. But I don't know if I'm as bold as you with leaving. Pray for me."

"I have been," Megan assures her with a smile, placing her hand on top of Alicia's. Megan's relieved to hear that her boldness has helped at least one person. She looks over at April. "One down, another to go," she halfway jokes.

"Don't even try it. I'm a Theta until I die," April smiles, knowingly getting under Megan's skin.

"No sorority talk. It's my day. Me Phi Meka," Tameka whines. "How do I look?" She gives one last glance in the mirror before exiting the room to become Mrs. Miller.

"Beautiful," the girls agree in unison.

The adoration is interrupted by continuous dings from Tameka's phone. "Thank God that's happening now. I need to put this phone on silent." Tameka lifts her train, scurrying to her phone on the gift table to observe the disturbance.

"What in the world!" she exclaims, looking at the phone's contents. "Megan, you've gone viral!"

"What? How?" Megan exclaims, rushing over to see the unbelievable evidence. The girls circle around Tameka to look at the phone that displays Megan in Tameka's salon chair during her visit home after experiencing the open vision of evil spirits in her living room.

"I uploaded the conversation we had that day and put together a video on *Salon Confessions*—a platform where I do hair in the salon chair and people come to Christ—called 'Stepping Down.' It's been up for months. It's finally getting traction!" Tameka jumps for joy. "OMG this is the best day of my life. I'm getting married. My platform's about to be monetized. I'm about to lose my virginity to my husband. Life is good!"

"You better not!" James yells from the door. "Come on out here, girl!"

"Okay, Daddy, I'm coming," Tameka bashfully responds. She shoves the phone in Megan's hands to silence it.

Alicia and April follow her out the door. Megan stands in the empty room, amazed with the video's performance.

"Are you denouncing Theta Kappa Rho?" Tameka asks off-camera on the tiny screen.

An unwavering Megan in the well-lit ring-light studio answers, "Yes."

Megan stands in amazement, in awe of the views and number of likes she's received. "Wow, this is my denouncement."

She lets out a huge breath of relief, no longer alone in her decision. The comments confirm that she's not the only one. Many agree these organizations are damaging to the soul. She tears up, knowing that she has a community of former Greeks who've made the same decision, but most importantly, she's made the only audience member that matters proud of her.

She hears a small voice in her spirit say, *Well done, My child.*

Satisfied with the completion of her mission, she's now ready to transform into bridesmaid mode.

Before placing the phone on the gift table, it chimes, reminding her that she'd forgotten to silence it. In the top corner of the phone, Megan sees there's a comment under the viral video from @TheSmoothJZAPhi that reads:

"Interesting."

She stands there reading Jeff's message over and over again, then takes a deep breath, silences the phone, turns it face down, and walks out to join her sister for her ceremony.

2 Timothy 4:3-4 NIV

For the time will come when people will not put up with sound doctrine. Instead, to suit their own desires, they will gather around them a great number of teachers to say what their itching ears want to hear. They will turn their ears away from the truth and turn aside to myths.

A NOTE FROM THE AUTHOR

This book is for anyone who wants to belong so badly that you ignore the quiet tug in your spirit that says, "This is not who you are or where you need to be."

This book is for those who have been torn between approval in the world and Truth.

This book is for those who wrestle with their faith in spaces where it feels unwelcomed.

'Stepping Down' is a fictional story, however the emotions underneath it are real.

As you walk with Megan through her journey, my hope is that you feel seen and reminded that conviction is not weakness. Stepping away from something that doesn't honor your faith belief is not failure—**it is strength.**

I pray this book brings clarity, comfort, and courage. If you are reading it simply as a lover of stories, I pray the Holy Spirit that moved me to write this novel moves you all the same.

To every reader who has made it thus far - Thank you!

Thank you for letting this novel be part of your journey. Thank you for supporting the movement.

ACKNOWLEDGEMENTS

First, I would like to acknowledge my readers. Thank you for opening your heart to this story. Your willingness to step into these pages with an opened mind, to feel, and journey with Megan, means more than I can express. I'm sure the Lord placed this story upon my heart for you. You are the reason this book exists beyond my imagination.

To my husband, thank you for loving me with patience through the moments when my vision was unclear. Thank you for giving me freedom to create without judgment. For believing in my voice long before it made its way onto the page. Thank you for supporting my dream so deeply that you retired me from everything that drained my creativity, so I could create from a place of peace.

To my mother, thank you for nurturing creativity in me before I even understood what it was. For allowing imagination to take root in my childhood and for creating a home where stories, ideas, and expression were welcomed.

To my family, your encouragement, prayers, and steady support- some from afar- have been a constant blessing. Thank you for celebrating every spark of creativity in me and reminding me that my gift is not accidental.

To my supporters Daron Council, Karen Johnson and Anna Adams thank you! You've made finishing this project possible. I don't take your contribution for granted.

To my editor, Felice Laverne, thank you for taking this story beyond the limits I thought it had. Your insight, your skill, and your dedication elevated this book into something fuller and sharper than I imagined. I am deeply grateful for your partnership in this journey.

To everyone who had a hand-large or small, in bringing *Stepping Down* to life, Thank you. To former members of these organizations, that boldly expressed their denouncement and pledging process in which I was able to research, apart from my own experience, thank you.

To LaTarica, for bringing together an amazing group of women to fast and pray with me to receive the motivation needed to finish this book, thank you. The Lord has heard our prayers.

And lastly, the most important, to the One whom all things flow from. God. I thank You every day for the gifts, the words, the divine connections, the plans and purpose, even when I don't understand its meanings. I thank You for choosing me to deliver this important time sensitive message. Thank You for Your trust and love to carry me through this challenging yet fulfilling journey. Thank YOU!

DISCUSSION QUESTIONS

1. Megan enters college longing for friendship, confidence, and a place to belong.
   What moments in your own life reflect this same longing for acceptance?

2. In what ways can identity become entangled with groups, titles, or approval?
   Where do you think true identity should come from?

3. Megan believes sorority life will give her community and sisterhood.
   What did she gain from Theta Kappa Rho?
   What did she lose?

4. Have you ever received pressure from a group, even subtly?
   How did you respond?

5. Hidden behaviors and rituals gradually appear in the story. Why do you think Megan ignored the warning signs at first?

6. Have you ever felt your beliefs challenged by a space you wanted to be part of?
   How did you navigate it?

7. The sorority's traditions rely on secrecy and silence.
   Why is secrecy so powerful in controlling people?

8. What is the difference between discipline, bonding, and manipulation?
   Where is the line crossed?

9. Leaving a group, especially one tied to identity, can feel like a loss.
   What do you think Megan grieves the most?

10. What does healing look like for Megan after stepping down?
    What might healing look like for someone in real life?

11. Which character did you connect with or understand the most? Why?

12. What moment in the novel stayed with you after reading? What did it reveal to you?

13. How has this story challenged or encouraged your faith, choices, or sense of identity?
    a. **Scripture Connection:** Share a verse that reflects courage, discernment, or identity.
       Discuss how it relates to the story.
    b. **Character Debate:**
       1. Should Megan have stayed and tried to change the system?
       2. Was stepping down the only way to preserve herself?

ABOUT THE AUTHOR

Dani Guevarez is a former member of Alpha Kappa Alpha Sorority, Incorporated, whose personal journey through Greek life and her decision to later renounce membership, informs the depth, honesty, and tension in her writing of Stepping Down.

Her 15-plus years of storytelling experience in entertainment have helped her create a vivid novel that explores faith, identity, and the pressure to belong.

Visit her website at daniguevarez.com

www.ingramcontent.com/pod-product-compliance
Lightning Source LLC
LaVergne TN
LVHW091717070526
838199LV00050B/2430